The
Sleep-Over
Artist

Thomas Beller

W. W. Norton & Company

New York · London

Grateful acknowledgment is made to the periodicals in which portions of this book
appeared, often in different form:

"Falling Water" in the *New York Times Magazine*; "Great Jews in Sports" in
Southwest Review; "Stay" in *The St. Ann's Review*; "Caller ID" in *Writer's Harvest 3*; "Personal
Style" in *Time Out New York*; "Say It with Furs" in *Elle*; episodes of "Seconds of Pleasure"
in *Harper's Bazaar* and *Reportage*.

For information about permission to reproduce selections from this book, write to
Permissions, W. W. Norton & Company, Inc.,
500 Fifth Avenue, New York, NY 10110

The text of this book is composed in Weiss with the display set in Elspeth.
Composition by Gina Webster. Manufacturing by Quebecor, Fairfield.

Library of Congress Cataloging-in-Publication Data

Beller, Thomas.
The sleep-over artist / Thomas Beller.
p. cm.
ISBN 0-393-04925-6
1. Motion picture producers and directors—Fiction.
2. Young men—Fiction. I. Title.
PS3552.E53364 S55 2000
813'.54—dc21   00-026111

W. W. Norton & Company, Inc., 500 Fifth Avenue, New York, N.Y. 10110
www.wwnorton.com

W. W. Norton & Company Ltd., 10 Coptic Street, London WC1A 1PU

1 2 3 4 5 6 7 8 9 0

For my father

The truth is not a crystal that can be slipped into one's pocket, but an endless current into which one falls headlong.
—Robert Musil

Contents

The
Sleep-Over
Artist

Falling Water

ALEX FADER GREW UP IN AN APARTMENT ON THE FOURTEENTH floor of a large prewar building that took up an entire block of Riverside Drive. From his bedroom window, which looked north, he could see a broad patch of sky, the tops of buildings, a multitude of wooden water towers, and off to the left, visible only if he pressed his cheek to the windowpane, the Hudson River. The view that most fascinated him, however, was the one to be had by looking directly down.

Once when he was six, he suddenly rose from his bath, opened the narrow bathroom window above it, and leaned out. He balanced on his wet stomach, arms and legs outstretched like Superman, contemplating what it would be like to take the plunge and if his life so far had contained enough satisfaction so that it could now reasonably come to a close. He stayed teetering on the windowsill, looking at the distant pavement below, trying to imagine what it would feel like to land there and what he would be thinking during those thrilling seconds of flight.

Half his body felt the moist familiarity of the bathroom, and the other half, wet and gleaming like a dolphin, hung in the cold air of the unknown. Then a faint curiosity as to what would happen after his fall—the ensuing hours and days—asserted itself. He pictured himself in a steaming heap on the concrete below, and a few minutes later his parents would be staring confusedly at the bathtub, full of murky water, but empty of him. He teetered for a while longer. The image of his parents trying to make sense of the empty bath was amusing at first, but then became unpleasant. With the same entranced conviction with which he had got up on the ledge, he got down, closed the window, and resumed his bath.

Having decided that he would not throw his body out the window, he began throwing smaller, less valuable objects.

First a cracker: it went spinning out the window and out of sight, and its absence seemed profound. Next were water balloons, whose wobbly downward trajectory he always monitored until they hit the ground, after which the small figure of the doorman would appear hustling onto the wet pavement, looking up. Alex loved the sight of this tiny figure, so formidable in real life, appearing on the sidewalk, but in watching from above, he was usually spotted from below.

Things were different at his friend Walker's apartment. Walker lived a few blocks south of Alex on Riverside Drive, also on the fourteenth floor. They were ten, and new best friends, and Walker was constantly surprising him with new and interesting ways to express malice. With regard to throwing things out the window, it was Walker who introduced the idea of a human target. They would stand perched at Walker's kitchen window, both holding on to a pot full of water balanced on the ledge, waiting for a suitable victim.

The windows of Walker's apartment all looked out over the Hudson River, and directly below was a broad lonely patch of sidewalk onto which people arrived like actors walking onto a stage.

They once observed an attractive young woman walking briskly with a bouquet of flowers in her hands towards a man who was standing with several suitcases around him, as though waiting for a taxi, right beneath their window. He was a perfect victim. They were about to douse the man with water, but it looked like something incredibly romantic was about to occur, some long-awaited reunion, and Alex and Walker instinctively held back and watched.

The woman had a strapless top on, and even from the distance of fourteen floors Alex could make out the subtle jump of her shoulder muscles and the tremulous softness of her breasts as they bounced up and down with each step. The flowers had delicate pink petals. The man with the suitcases stared at her as she approached with bold strides. His body was still and unmoving. His gaze fixed. He was oblivious to everything else in the world but her. She walked right up to him and bashed him in the face with the bouquet, a violent forehand smash. The petals scattered like confetti. Then, without missing a beat, she turned on her heel and stomped back in the direction she had come, still clutching the considerably less flowery bouquet. The man just stood there.

Alex and Walker were so transfixed by this scene that they forgot to pour water on him.

Other people were less fortunate. Alex and Walker would

stand guard at the kitchen window until someone appeared on Riverside Drive. There would be time to size up the target—gait, posture, clothes. At a certain ideal moment the water would fall forward from their pot in one solid translucent mass, and then split in half, and then in half again and again, so that what started as a single glob on the fourteenth floor ended as a thousand pellets of water on the ground. The pale pavement darkened and the victim became completely still. This momentary freeze was, for some reason, the most delicious part.

There was one set of victims who stayed in Alex's mind for a long time afterwards. A little girl wearing a pink coat, white stockings, and shiny black shoes ambled down the sunny street, a half step behind her mother. She looked as if she was on her way either to or from a party. She walked with unsteady steps, and her mother walked beside her, looking down and talking, but also giving the girl her independence. They were two small objects alone on the sidewalk. The water hit the ground in a great hissing mass and they froze like everyone else.

But in the several seconds between the pour and the splatter, as Alex watched the water fragment and descend, a tremendous pang of regret leapt up in his stomach instead of the more familiar thrill. As he watched the jerky awkward expressiveness of the little girl walking beneath the water's widening net, he understood that there was a small corrupting moment about to take place— one kid introducing another to the random world of fate and bad luck.

Natural Selection

ONE AFTERNOON IN MAY, WHEN SPRING WAS IN FULL bloom and the school year almost over, the entire fifth grade was assembled for a special announcement regarding Becky Salatan. They were gathered in the science section of the huge, loftlike space in which the fifth grade spent their days. For the traditionalist Wave Hill School ("Educating Young Boys Since 1907" had once been its motto, until it also started educating young girls), this open-plan arrangement was a departure.

The special announcement was that Becky Salatan's father had died the previous day, and everyone should be considerate of her when she returned to school tomorrow.

Mr. Gold, the science and social studies teacher, delivered the news. The science section, with its miniature zoo, was Mr. Gold's domain. Located next to the room's entrance, it was a maze of desks and chairs and numerous clear glass aquariums within which fish and rabbits and guinea pigs and turtles and a garden snake writhed and twitched and nibbled and slept and shat.

Alex Fader thought that perhaps the real purpose of these glass boxes was to make him and his fellow students appreciate the amount of space they could roam in, while other species, and even other humans (like sixth-graders), had to occupy limited and constrained spaces and generally live much less free lives.

Now they all sat quietly amidst the animals and listened to the news. Mr. Gold looked solemnly at the assembled class before speaking. His forehead, made huge by a receding hairline, was a bit like a lightbulb, and tended to color whenever he felt any strong emotion. His mouth was exceedingly broad and expressive, like a clown's, and in repose possessed a clownlike sadness. His ability to provoke emotion on the part of his students was always just exceeded by his ability to provoke contempt.

"There is nothing you can really do for Becky, except be considerate," he told the class. "Be nice to her, give her some space, try and respect the gravity of what has happened."

Several people groaned. Mr. Gold's solemn face seemed to empathize with his students' pain. But the groans were in response to his use of the word "gravity." The uncensored version of this story had already made the rounds at lunchtime, when word got out that Becky Salatan's dad had jumped out the window and Becky had been the first person to wander into the room, just home from school, and find the window wide open with the sounds of shrieks and screams emanating from the sidewalk twenty-two stories below.

Alex had thoughtfully chewed his microwaved pizza upon hearing this and tried to remember what Becky had been like before, so he could better gauge how this event might change her. His own father had died exactly a year minus one day earlier. He had died of natural causes (to the extent that cancer, compared to jumping out a window, was a natural cause), but he didn't think he would want to be the subject of an announcement like the one made for Becky. He was of the opinion that disaster ought to be respected with silence, the better to acknowledge that nothing can be done to reverse it.

Tomorrow afternoon he and his mother were supposed to drive up to the cemetery and visit the grave.

"Later this week it's going to be one year since Papa died," his mother had said a few days earlier. "We'll bring flowers and good things and have a visit."

"We can't visit him," said Alex. "He's dead."

"We're going to visit the grave," she said.

"We're going to have a picnic on his grave?" said Alex.

"Not on it, exactly," she said. "Next to it. We'll spend some time and try and make it nice."

His mother was always, as far as Alex could tell, trying to make things nice. It was tiring.

"What about school?" he had said. On the day of the funeral he had missed school.

"I'll pick you up after school and we'll drive up."

"You don't have a car," said Alex.

"I'll rent a car," said his mother.

"What if we're not allowed to sit on the grass?" he had said.

————————

HIS MOTHER WAS a dancer. This meant that she could be found on certain afternoons on the second floor of a building on Eighty-ninth Street and Broadway, standing barefoot and in a leotard on a vast wooden floor, often in some strange position. His father had taken him a couple of times to the empty room with an upright piano in the corner. Together they walked up a long narrow flight of dimly lit stairs, at the top of which was a large sunlit space. Sweating men and woman in leotards were either jumping around or standing and watching some other person jump around. Their leotards gave them the quality of something encased, like M&M's. His mother always stood in their midst, panting.

She was also a *choreographer*. Alex understood this word to mean that she could tell people what to do, and they would listen. Once, when she told him he had to take a bath, he responded, "You're not my choreographer," which had the desired effect of shocking her into a kind of marveling silence and therefore post-poning, if only for another ten minutes, the bath.

She was a *modern* dancer. This distinction confused him. He asked his father about it.

"It means she's not a member of the Rockettes," he said.

One day, when he was seven, she told him that she would soon be having a concert.

"What's a concert?" he said.

"It's when I perform in front of many people with my com-pany."

"What does your company make?" he said.

"It's a dance company," she said. "We make dance."

"Can people buy dance?" he asked. At the age of seven he was demonstrating certain capitalist proclivities that had the effect of making his parents look at him with concern, as though he might be coming down with a fever.

"They can buy tickets," she said.

She seemed to take some odd pleasure in his questions. He was trying to deal in facts and work things out logically, but she was always able to attach an invisible meaning to the facts which made her smile.

As the concert approached, she rehearsed more and more frequently, and certain routines were interrupted. Alex often found himself alone in the apartment with his father. One day his father cooked dinner for just the two of them while she was at rehearsal.

"What's for dinner, Papa?" he had asked.

"Wiener schnitzel," said his father. He said it in that slightly emphatic but questioning tone teachers use when they are calling attendance and someone does not respond, and they then repeat the name a second time as if perhaps the person (in this case, Schnitzel) had just been nodding off, though they are also posing the question: What happened to Schnitzel?

On the occasion of being chef, his father took off his jacket and went so far as to loosen his tie, but that was all. It was as though he was determined not to let his wife's rehearsal schedule impinge on the normal rhythms of the household, though the very fact he was making dinner was unusual.

Alex was very pleased with the whole situation and particularly liked the way his dad pronounced that night's meal. So he kept asking, "Papa, what's for dinner?"

"Wiener schnitzel," came the matter-of-fact reply each time.

The seriousness with which he said it—"Veeena Schnitzel"—combined with the fact he said it with a slightly German accent, and the additional fact that the words themselves had a strange relationship to each other, as if they were a comedy team (Laurel and Hardy, Abbott and Costello, Wiener and Schnitzel) made Alex burst into laughter every time.

His father's accent was a normal American accent beneath

which bubbled a vast cauldron of linguistic weirdness called "German," which sometimes splashed out in an odd-sounding phrase or word. When his father actually spoke the language, Alex went into hysterics. German, as his father spoke it, was the language of a person bitterly complaining that someone has opened his box of chocolates and taken a bite out of *each and every one.*

Alex once heard his father have a screaming fight on the telephone in German, with his sister, while in his underwear. Alex thought it was the funniest thing he had ever seen until his father shouted at him to go to his room. This shut him up, because his father rarely raised his voice. From that point on, though, German was the language of someone being really angry while in their underwear.

Sometimes his mother laughed with him, though she had her own strange linguistic cauldron, something called Hebrew, which was, measured purely on the quantity of strange sounds, an even more comic language, but which had a much less amusing effect on Alex. There was something in his mother's voice when she spoke it—melodic, hopeful, wary—that made him feel disorientingly sad.

His father concentrated while he cooked. Alex liked his dad's face when it was concentrating. Once, when his father had been staring at the crossword puzzle for a long time—the clean lines of his eyebrows furrowed, his forehead crinkly with ridges which disappeared only when he laughed—he had sighed and looked up and said, to no one in particular, "What I don't know could fill a textbook."

Alex had found it a fascinating concept: the book of things his father didn't know.

His father spent a lot of time preparing each piece of meat in flour and bread crumbs, and then he lowered each piece rather lovingly into the frying pan to the accompaniment of a fierce sizzle. Then he stared at the pieces with a concerned look on his face, poking them occasionally with a fork. His father was a doctor, which Alex grasped, and also a psychoanalyst, which he didn't grasp at all, but which he intuited to mean he treated patients in a manner similar to the way he was currently treating the Wiener schnitzel. Alex loved the look of concern of his father's face.

The Wiener schnitzel was good. They ate in silence, sitting across the table from each other. Then his father, without any warning, threw his balled-up napkin at Alex.

"Papa!" he yelled with wide, delighted eyes.

This was one of their favorite games, a rare treat. One of them would launch a sneak attack, and his mother would always cry out in mock displeasure at this breach of civility. Order would be restored, the meal would continue, and the other would bide his time, waiting to retaliate with his own napkin attack. It would give the whole meal a suspenseful air. Now Alex bided his time. But without his mother's protest it wasn't the same.

HIS MOTHER BROUGHT home a poster advertising her concert. It was a picture of her spotlit against darkness in a flowing white dress, her head tossed back, arms raised over her head, and one knee raised. Her hair fell straight back, like a horse's tail. The raised leg had a vaguely military quality.

"Mom, you look like a horse," he said.

"Thank you," she said, laughing.

She looked disturbingly weightless, as if she were an angel floating in the night, being recalled to heaven for minor repairs. She hung the poster in the kitchen.

As the concert drew near, dinner was composed of one meal that she cooked for him and his father, and another special meal she cooked for herself, her training diet, as she put it, which was invariably boiled chicken and which, he informed her with no effort to be diplomatic, was disgusting. Once she had bit into a chicken leg and some blood squirted out. This confirmed his suspicion that his mother was an animal.

The night of the concert had been full of anxiety for Alex, even though all he had to do was sit there in the dark and watch. He sat with his father, in the front row. They were in an auditorium somewhere inside the looming Gothic structure of the Riverside Church. The place was full of people. That poster on his kitchen wall was everywhere; his mother floating through the night. There were three dances. In the first two the stage was filled with dancers flinging themselves around the stage and arriving at strange positions. He observed a peculiar something in the way his mother danced—she danced with abandon. The last dance she did by herself. At a certain point she stood very still and her knees trembled. Alex sat still amidst the crowd in the dark theater, next to his father, who had also been very still throughout, and wondered if her knees were trembling because she was nervous, or if it was part of the dance and her knees were supposed to tremble. At the end someone took his hand and pulled him from his seat while everyone was clapping. They rushed him backstage, where they shoved a bouquet of red roses into his arms (they were about the size of his torso) and gently pushed him onto the stage. He tottered out and presented her with the roses. People were clapping. The applause came down like sheets of rain. The lights were bright, white, and cruel. He held the roses up to her and for some reason felt worried that they would be too heavy for him to lift. He would collapse under their weight in front of the whole auditorium. She took them from him, smiling wildly, a frightening look on her face. He could see her makeup, thickly applied, theatrical, and the little beads of sweat that pressed out from beneath it. The applause was a crashing wave. Her smile was so wild. She kissed him and then in front of the whole theater wiped the lipstick from his cheek with her thumb.

Later, when the storm of applause was long past and the auditorium an empty shell, all the dancers and his mother took down the set. A bare lightbulb illuminated the scene. He sat beside his father and watched, appalled that so much effort should be in service to such a fleeting thing. His father sat with him in the front row, holding his chin in his hand as if he were tolerating something. In the end they went home without her.

AFTER MR. GOLD'S announcement, Alex made a pit stop in front of his cubby before heading over to English at the far end of the room. He liked visiting his cubby. The very word made him happy. *Cubby.* Standing in front of his, seemingly so alike in size and shape to all the other cubbies yet so distinctly his own, he muttered the word in long sustained hummed sighs: "cubby cubby cubby cubby." This sound was similar to the humming sound he made when he was particularly enjoying some food he was eating, about which his mother had scolded him on a number of occasions as being impolite and unseemly, even though it was just the two of them at the dinner table and he had pointed out that by humming a little he was indicating that he was enjoying the food and therefore paying her a compliment.

Alex stared into his cubby, about to extract his English book, and then glanced at some of the surrounding cubbies. Though identical in shape and similar in content, they all possessed a certain glamour his did not. They also possessed something else his did not—a pencil case. These pencil cases were made of denim and had little pockets, or made of industrial rubber, or done in colors like canary yellow or mint green. And they all bulged with hidden contents.

He reached his hand into one of the other cubbies, took a pencil case—a denim one, the most popular model—and put it in his own cubby. He had been relieving his classmates of their pencil cases for weeks.

This transaction complete, he headed across the room as though it were prairie and he an adventurer setting off for new territory, but not before casting an urgent glance in the direction of Mr. Gold, to make sure he hadn't seen anything.

A peculiar pang of sadness sprang up within him when Mr. Gold smiled at him as he walked by.

Mr. Gold had some sort of minor speech impediment. Little bits of spittle often flew from his wide mouth as he spoke, and when he found himself stammering his forehead would change color. Something about his mouth and forehead communicated feelings, and this made Mr. Gold somewhat pathetic. He was always going on about the theory of evolution, origin of the species, natural selection, and other rules that governed the world of animals and humans alike. "Survival is the fundamental most basic activity of every species," he had said. "These animals have learned to survive over thousands of years."

He seemed very intent on communicating his love for science and for nature. But what he best communicated was that if you loved little animals, and the theory of evolution, and spat a little when you talked, and had feelings, then you would be a science teacher whose best friends were gerbils.

The English section was the most comfortable part of the room. There were huge pillows on which you could loll and huge wooden blocks of various colors on which you could sit. Its most exciting feature, however, was the teacher, a young British woman named Stacey, whose brown hair bounced and shimmered whenever she turned her head.

Stacey's breasts, like the pillows and the blocks, were oversized. She usually wore faded blue denim, often in combination with a light blue kerchief around her neck, and eye shadow that was pale blue. Sometimes she wore a blue dress. Sometimes she wore light blue silk shirts with the top two buttons undone. The combination of her sleekness, her pale blueness, and her breasts made it seem as though she might at any moment lift off and float away, and she so entranced the male population of the fifth grade that her English classes were markedly more hysterical, emotive, and unruly than any other class.

Alex was obsessed with Stacey. She was the faculty supervisor on his school bus, and so he saw her every morning and afternoon. He felt a special bond with her. She lived near him, on Eighty-third Street and Broadway, and he often entertained fantasies of breaking into her building and knocking on her back door at some unlikely hour, and of her opening it in just a sheer bluish nightgown which would hang over her body like a thin transparent veil. She would invite him in.

During English class Alex administered a neck and shoulder massage with one hand to the grade's most popular boy, Arnold Gerstein. Arnold looked like a doll. He had blue eyes and clear skin and buttony features, and his brown hair sat atop his head like a helmet.

One day Alex had sat next to Arnold in English and said, "Do you want a massage?"

He had recently seen a gangster movie on television in which the head gangster was given a massage by one of his assistants. The head gangster tended to his business while his neck and shoulders got a rubdown. Alex calculated that the role of massage administrator to head gangster was as high as he was likely to get in the complex hierarchy of the fifth grade.

Arnold and Alex were friends, though this didn't prevent Arnold calling him fathead and lardface and so forth with a casual thoughtless cruelty that nevertheless had the effect of making Arnold the object of a certain kind of obsession and almost love

for Alex, whose reflex for obsessing about (and almost worship-
ing) his tormentors was sadly well developed.

He often went to Arnold's house after school. Arnold lived on
Fifth Avenue in a modern building not far from the Metropolitan
Museum. Like the museum, Arnold's house had a uniformed
guard. Her name was Mary. She was a black woman and wore a
white uniform that made her look like a nurse. Her job, as far as
Alex could tell, was to keep the house clean, to do the dirty work
of incessantly reminding Arnold and his older siblings to behave,
and, Alex could vaguely sense, to absorb all the random hostility
that Arnold might otherwise vent on his parents.

There was a stretch of fifth grade when Alex essentially became
an honorary member of the Gerstein family, coming over for many
afternoons, and often spending the night on weekends. He was
often present for the strange scenario of Mr. Gerstein coming
home from work. Mr. Gerstein owned a company that manufac-
tured pet food, and seemed to want nothing more out of life than to
come home from work and be allowed to submerge, without harass-
ment or interruption, into his easy chair with the *New York Post* sports
pages, an act which was always accompanied by a momentous
groan that never ceased to amaze and fascinate and repulse Alex. It
sounded as though Mr. Gerstein were lowering himself into a bath
that was much too hot but which he was nevertheless committed to
entering. It was at precisely this near-orgasmic moment that Mrs.
Gerstein, with the timing of a predator intimate with its prey, would
present the day's troubles to Mr. Gerstein.

One day Mr. Gerstein walked in the door, and she began to
complain bitterly that Arnold's older sister, Gabby, was spending
too much time with Eve Blum, who was a bad influence. It was an
acknowledged fact among the Gerstein family that Gabby was, as
Mrs. Gerstein once put it, "fragile." Whenever she had an exam
she barricaded herself in her room and the whole house was put

on silent alert, as though Gabby were spinning an incredibly delicate web between herself and a good college that a single raised voice could tear to shreds.

The idea that there were bad influences—and therefore a group of people who were bad, and another group who were influenced—captured Alex's imagination, though it should be said that almost everything about Arnold Gerstein and his family captured Alex's imagination, held it down like a prisoner, and tortured it. But that is another matter.

ONE DAY, WITHOUT any warning, Alex's father went to the hospital. And then ten days later he returned from the hospital. It was an April day near the end of fourth grade. The bus dropped Alex off in the usual spot and he ambled the two blocks to his building, and then up the elevator, and when he entered the front door he encountered a suitcase in the foyer. Voices emanated down the long hallway from the master bedroom. One of them was excruciatingly familiar, a woman's voice, his mother's; the other was also familiar, and he felt its deeper reverberations somewhere in his chest.

He ran down the hall and discovered his father in bed, propped up on some pillows and wearing his blue seersucker robe. He sat there looking very much like himself, his thick black hair in a state of mild rebellion, the newspaper spread out to his side. The television was on low, a nature documentary of some kind. He was clean-shaven. When Alex hugged him and kissed him he felt the reassuring sandpaper of his cheek.

The very sight of him in that bedroom, unadorned by tubes in his arms, a white smock, a plastic wrist band, filled Alex with relief, though it was mitigated by a strange instinctive caution. Prior to his father's stay in the hospital there had been no such thing as normal—there had been his mother and father and himself, all tumbling through life as though swept forward by an infinitely cascading wave, its sound and light and shape changing and evolving but never with an end in sight. His father's departure to the hospital was like that moment when the wave crashes onto the beach and then, spread thinly over the sand, hissingly retreats into silence.

The documentary on television was about these wild, cowlike animals called wildebeests. They spent a lot of time grazing on the vast plains of Kenya.

His mother fussed over the two of them. Her mood was festive. It was like a holiday, a weekend, and someone being sick all rolled into one event. His father sipped black coffee in bed and peered at the stock market pages with the same mildly perturbed and mystified expression that Alex always enjoyed spying on. That vast array of tiny symbols was obviously part of the book of things about which his father didn't know.

They turned the volume up a little, and his father alternated between watching the wildebeests and perusing the newspaper, and when he absentmindedly reached up and ran his hand through his thick black hair, Alex shuddered for some reason.

Apparently, the wildebeests were migrating.

"I want you to know that certain things are going to change now," said his father.

"Like what?"

His father proceeded to dole out dispensations like a king. Allowance was to increase. Sporting events would be attended. And from now on he was going to start calling him Alex, as opposed to Alexander, a silent wish Alex had expressed only to himself. That his father knew about it filled him with awe, gratitude, and suspicion.

The wildebeests staggered in a huge horde amidst a cloud of

red dust from watering hole to watering hole, trying to elude the many perils of their migration. Sometimes they were relaxed and grazed calmly; other times they ran in a panic. Alex sat with his father, who seemed in high spirits, and contemplated the new regime of his life now that his father was back from the hospital.

"And I'm going to quit smoking," said his father.

They turned to look at each other. Alex's great passion was finding and stealing his father's cigarettes. These packets of Marlboro Reds, or sometimes Dunhills, were like treasure. He would steal them, hide them, and wait for his father to erupt in rage upon discovering their absence. Then he either would or would not break down and tell him where they were, depending. It was a test of wills.

He absorbed this news with a tinge of regret. He had been looking forward to stealing the cigarettes again.

"Are you sure?" he asked.

His father nodded.

"Then what are those?" said Alex, nodding at an unopened pack.

"Those are for show," said his father.

They turned back to the television.

There were so many wildebeests! There was something soothing about their sheer volume. They grazed peacefully, but when frightened they bunched up and ran so close together it was as though they were a single undulating being; they looked like the surface of a brown ocean. At one point a whole horde of them fell over a shallow cliff. Plumes of red dust rose in the air as they struggled to clamber back up.

Their brown bodies were sympathetic and interesting. Their mooing was emotive. Their necks were less graceful than a horse's, but more elegant than a cow's. Their shoulders were bony and anxious, as though they worried too much. But then they had a lot to worry about: drought, disease, predators everywhere. When they ate and drank they seemed truly happy, and when they got scared they really did seem scared. Even on television, the atmosphere of panic when a lion came close was palpable, a deep animal fear. They made fearful sounds that struck a chord in some placeless part of Alex's body; their desperation reverberated from the top of his head to his toes, a feeling similar to a roller coaster's first rickety plunge.

Six days later his father went back to the hospital. His mother spent a lot of time there, and left Alex with the upstairs neighbors, the Diamonds, whose son, Jerry, was an old friend of Alex's from back when they were three. The Diamonds had an enormous state-of-the-art television. One evening, when the Muhammad Ali–George Foreman fight was about to come on, he received a call from his mother summoning him to the hospital. He wanted to watch the fight. There was a tense discussion. In the end Mr. Diamond took him in a taxi. Nothing much happened when he got there. His father lay asleep, unshaven, tubes in his arms.

His mother had purchased an electric razor for his father, but it sat unopened in its box, and Alex took it out and plugged it in and preoccupied himself with the razor and its three vibrating coils.

There was one last urgent late-night visit, a few days later, during which Alex had been effusive and cheerful.

"Hi, Pop!" he said with real exuberance when he walked in. He had never before called his father "Pop." But as his father had instituted the Alexander/Alex change, he thought he would go out on a limb and retire "Papa" in favor of "Pop." His father was groggy and never surfaced from his sleep, though he briefly became restless.

That night he slept over at the Diamonds again. The next day there was a Mets game on, and he and Jerry munched from a big bowl of sour-cream-and-onion potato chips that sat on the coffee table and watched the game. His mother came over towards the end of the game and looked very ashen and asked him to come downstairs, but he wouldn't come. He refused. Then Rusty Staub struck out and he went home and was told the news at the kitchen table.

"What does 'passed away' mean?" he said.

When she explained, he said, "Oh, but I prayed!" and slammed his fist on the table and broke into tears. He and his mother cried together. But the strange thing was that as he cried he wondered if he had just told a lie. Because he hadn't really prayed. He had thought about praying. But he hadn't actually done it, or he hadn't done it wholeheartedly. He had tried to engage God in a discussion as to whether or not He existed. God had not been forthcoming on the matter.

After a while he composed himself, sat up, and looked at his mother. "What's going to happen to me?" he said.

EVEN AT AGE ten, Alex vigilantly guarded his father's death from the threat of interpretation. If throwing yourself out a window could escape interpretation, then dying of cancer should be left alone as well. He felt that to hold his father's death up as a cause and draw a line to some effect diminished the event and missed the point. It was like saying that hairstyles changed drastically after the earth lost its gravitational pull.

He took every stolen pen and hid it carefully in the depths of one of the apartment's closets. The house was generally stuffed with writing implements left over from his father. You couldn't open a drawer without finding some. It was as though Alex were hoarding these extras in anticipation of the day they would all run out.

After school Alex smuggled the pencil case onto the bus. Whenever Alex boarded the bus, Stacey gave him a warm but also knowing and somewhat forbidding smile, meant to remind him to behave so that she wouldn't have to walk to the back of the bus to scold him. Alex cherished these looks, just as he cherished her scoldings, which always seemed to involve Stacey coming very close to him and speaking in precise, clipped tones while her breasts hovered in front of his face. He wondered, in these moments, when her breasts were so close, if she was doing it on purpose, giving him a hint, an invitation. He would stare back at her with wide eyes, as though by the sheer power of his expression he might provoke her to lean forward and whisper, "Yes, visit me." Now, as he boarded the bus with his stolen goods under his shirt, he had to close himself off, and her eyebrow twitched in recognition of his new demeanor. But nothing was said. He went and sat in the back seat and, with a pounding heart, opened the pencil case to examine his loot.

The bus ride took forty minutes. Every day in the morning Alex would sit with his forehead pressed to the window and stare at the passing scenery which unfurled before him in triptych form. On one end was West End Avenue, that long parade of heavy-lidded buildings from whose lobbies emerged old European ladies and gentleman in elegant clothes, peering up and down the avenue as though they had somewhere to go.

The other end of the triptych began with the Stella D'oro cookie factory in the Bronx, in whose vicinity there was always a sticky sweet smell. This was followed by the slightly dilapidated area of the Bronx over which loomed the subway tracks, which in turn gave way to the opulence and cleanliness and order of Wave Hill, where the Wave Hill School was located.

In the center of the triptych was Harlem. In the morning it was a quiet, shuttered place, with few people on the sidewalks, a place where the burned-out buildings mingled with buildings that had that same heavy-lidded dignity of the ones on West End, with various grandeur-inducing embellishments illuminated by the bright morning sun. The stores were all shuttered and gated and covered with illegible graffiti, except for the ones with murals advertising the store and providing a faintly uplifting message in the process. Mango Records had a mural featuring a disc jockey with a funny hat and an unbuttoned shirt holding a gleaming vinyl record over a turntable and smiling a toothy grin and giving them a thumbs-up; the name "Chico" was proudly written out in the corner. The store was a landmark of sorts that Alex passed every morning and enjoyed a great deal, as he seemed to be getting a personal vote of confidence from the Mango Records disc jockey. This same Chico had also done a mural on the grocery store, which featured a series of break-dancing vegetables with happy faces: mushroom, broccoli, carrot, and one other vegetable that Alex, in his morning-addled state, could never identify (maybe it was a turnip, but he didn't really know what a turnip was), whose mystery slowly came to obsess him on his morning ride, a tiny tremor of frustration presaging the earthquakes of the day ahead.

The afternoon was altogether different. Alex was awake, buzzing from a hit of after-school candy, and Harlem was awake, too. It was alive and full of people, all of whom, to a uniform degree that never ceased to amaze him, were black. The bus moved fast enough so that few individual faces had a chance to take hold. It was a montage of faces and strange clothes, and cars, some dilapidated and others well-looked-after. A few were so dismantled that they resembled the carcass of a huge, long-dead animal, and others, extravagantly ornamented in chrome and with shiny tires and strange fuzzy dice hanging down from the mirror, were attended to by one or even two or three people carefully polishing it with wax.

Now he peered out the windows at the effusion of life and activity, viewed at high speed, riding through Harlem in the silver bus. At times like this it seemed as though Harlem were another of Mr. Gold's glass boxes. And at still other times he felt as if the bus itself were the box, and he a specimen.

The bus stopped at a red light, and Alex found himself staring at a group of young boys not that much older than himself. Something about the bus caught their attention. Alex, forehead pressed to the window, stared with interest as their body language changed and all their attention became focused on the bus. If he had been in a different state of mind he might have noticed that their attention was not just focused on the bus, it was focused on *him*, but he wasn't thinking of himself as a distinct entity. He could not have pictured himself. He was just a perceiver. And so he watched without so much as a twitch as one of the boys reached down to pick something off the street and started running towards him. The bus had started to move again, and his ears were filled the roar of the engine as it struggled to thrust the vehicle into motion. The boy ran towards him, his face contorted with anger or, to look at it another way, possessed of the pitcher's concentrated glare as he is about to release the ball towards home plate. Alex watched as the boy reached back from a distance of about five feet and threw something. He didn't see what it was. He just saw the contortion of pain and spite on the boy's face as he released it, and felt a calm impassive wonder at what it could be, and what was going to happen next.

The sound was shockingly loud—a popping, shattering sound, followed by shrieks from all the passengers, who, being between the ages of seven and seventeen, were not generally reluctant to scream for whatever reason. The rock hit the window with a huge crash, somewhere a little below where his chin was. The window cracked but did not shatter. The bus roared forward.

Alex had moved his forehead an inch off the glass just before impact, and after the sudden blink that the impact provoked, he kept staring at that face that he had been staring at a moment

before, which was strangely, almost miraculously, transformed—
anger had become laughter. Stacey came quickly down the aisle
to see what had happened, and Alex kept staring at this suddenly
happy black kid as he turned towards his friends.

Only at the last moment did he realize that he was clutching
the pens and pencils in his hand. When Stacey leaned her fragrant body over him, and asked what had happened in a concerned, almost angry voice, and then asked if he was all right in a
softer voice when she realized he hadn't done anything wrong,
the image that stuck in his mind was that transformation from
anger to happiness on the boy's face, and also the transition from
the clear transparent veil of glass to something fractured and
blurred. And he couldn't help noticing, as he frantically tried to
stuff the bouquet of pens and pencils into his pocket, that it was
the clear pane of glass that had delivered the anger, and the shat-
tered one that transmitted the happiness.

"HOW WAS SCHOOL?" his mother said when he got home.

"It was good. Everyone signed everyone's yearbooks and someone threw a rock at me," he said.

"What?"

"I mean at the bus. It was no big deal."

"I see. Tomorrow I'll pick you up after school and we'll go make
our visit."

Alex looked down glumly. The grave, he remembered, was on
top of a steep hill with a majestic view of trees and rolling hills
and far off in the distance something that resembled a castle. The
whole cemetery was built on a hill, and at the top was a patch of
unused land. Theirs was the first grave up there. Everywhere on
that hill there was a neat carpeting of green grass, exquisitely ripe
and soft, except for the raw unruly spot where they had dug a

hole. Alex had been embarrassed by that hole. People threw flowers into it after the coffin was lowered, stepping with their black shoes on the reddish soil at the hole's edge, and Alex felt the flowers were some kind of apology to the earth for having so violently interrupted its surface. He couldn't imagine a picnic next to that gash in the earth.

After the flower-throwing and some general snuffling and outright weeping from people he had never seen before, everybody began to move down the steep hill, leaving his mother alone up near the hole. He had wanted to go and get her, but there was some kind of respectful distance being kept, and his mother was kneeling next to the hole and had her hand pressed against her forehead. From behind, even at a distance, he could see her back move with her breathing. Or was it crying? She seemed to be pressing her hand very hard against her forehead. She had high heels, and after a couple of minutes one of his father's friends went up and got her and helped her down the hill, and Alex wondered if the high heels were digging into the soft grass and giving her extra traction.

"I've brought you something nice," she said now, and went to refrigerator, returning with a plate of three small delicate-looking pastries she had brought home from Eclair, on Seventy-second Street, where she always went for occasions she considered special. But what was the special occasion? It was just another day at school. One of the pastries was a small pink tower with a cherry on top. If someone made a chess set out of pastries, this would be the castle. It was his favorite sweet. He felt a pang of exasperation with her, an enormous wave of anger at her incomprehension of the facts of life as he was experiencing them. She had no idea about pencil cases and cubbies; she didn't know about the way he ran his fingers over Arnold's back; she had never seen the jittery steps of a kid freeze under a net of descending cold water. She didn't know about Stacey and his planned midnight visits. She didn't understand about the pleasures of rock throwing. And here she was putting out treats the day before they were supposed to go to a cemetery and have a nice picnic. Yet he also felt a strange kind of gratitude.

His anger lasted all the way until dinner. That night she made Wiener schnitzel. Halfway through he balled up his napkin and threw it at her.

"Alexander!" she said, and looked at him with surprised, wide eyes.

He took another bite as if nothing had happened. He waited for a few minutes and then gave up hope, at which point from across the table came flying a balled-up napkin that hit him on the head.

Great Jews in Sports

IT WAS FRIDAY NIGHT AND ALEX LAY ON HIS MOTHER'S BED, watching television with glassy eyes while his mother sat in the kitchen reading, or talking on the phone, or doing whatever it was she did in the kitchen while he watched television. He secretly suspected that what she was doing was giving him the privacy to watch television alone, which made the use he put this privacy to even more unsettling. As eleven-thirty approached, his pulse began to quicken. When it arrived he turned down the volume and changed the channel.

It was at the age of thirteen, when cable television was

installed in his home and Bar Mitzvah season commenced, that Alex was hit by the twin lightning bolts of sex and religion, two previously unrelated subjects that came crashing into his life simultaneously, as though holding hands.

Eleven-thirty on Friday night was when a program called *Ugly George* aired for half an hour on Channel J. *Ugly George* was a television show about the adventures of a man named Ugly George. The plot was very simple and yet never lost its suspense from one show to the next. The opening scene would invariably be a shot of a busy street somewhere in the city. The camera was mounted on Ugly George's shoulder as he strolled along, pointing his camera this way and that while he described the scene for his viewers in the singsong voice one might use to read a bedtime story. This introductory segment was equivalent to a magician's showing the audience that the top hat was empty, before reaching in and producing a rabbit. Ugly George was showing his viewers that this was the real world, the same sort of crowded street they might have walked down the other day, looking at faces, making tiny judgments about people, having fleeting moments of lust, and proceeding on without anything eventful happening. Ugly George, on the other hand, possessed the ability to make things happen.

Alex did not. He had experimented with petty forms of vandalism and theft, as well as belligerent wisecracks at school that left him stunned and amazed at his own audacity moments after he made them, as though he had been momentarily possessed by some strange demon. Yet everyday circumstances continued to sweep him along, diverting his plans and wishes, impervious to his efforts to change his own life. He had been planning to do something about his crush on Tania Vincent, for example, and yet had hardly been able to meet her eyes. He felt like a captain who drew up elaborate navigational plans for his ship, only to discover anew that the wind and waves would dictate his path, and nothing else.

For Ugly George, the sailing was not smooth, but the direction was clear. If a young woman walked by, Ugly George would point his camera at her and begin talking. He was cordial and polite, but he got to the point fairly quickly. The point was: would the woman care to duck into an alley, or a rest room, or some nook and cranny of the city which Ugly George was always able to find, and show him, and his camera, and a large portion of the subscribers to Manhattan Cable, her breasts.

Ugly George was an anthology of rejection. The styles were as varied as the women. But every now and then a woman said yes. The amateurism of the footage and the awkwardness with which the whole thing progressed added to its intensity and its immediacy. There was no airbrushing here, no poses and props as in dirty magazines, just this strange voluntary gesture of a woman exposing herself to a man with a camera, usually after considerable coaxing.

Alex watched *Ugly George* in a state of extreme excitement and agitation, because all this visual delight had to be experienced with his mother sitting in the kitchen at the end of the hallway, in her slippers and robe. His Friday-night bedtime was midnight. The floor of the hallway was carpeted. And though Alex had developed a hypersensitive device in his ear to detect his mother's footsteps in the hall, all the erotic stimulation of *Ugly George* had to coexist with an intense vigilance for her arrival.

He watched now crouched in the small space between the television and the foot of her bed, arm outstretched, with his hand on the cable-box dial, ready to spin to another channel at the first sound of her steps. This was the position he maintained for the entire half-hour duration of the show.

Ugly George had gone to the auto show to see what he could

find. He found the latest cars from Detroit and Japan, as well as hot rods, and drag racers, and men demonstrating incredibly sharp kitchen knives that would stay sharp no matter what you did to them. Scantily clad women stood on platforms next to the cars like gigantic live hood ornaments. Ugly George approached one after the other.

"Excuse me!" he called out pathetically. "Excuse me, ma'am, can I talk to you a moment?" He was ignored. Or he was told, "I'm busy." Or "Go away." Men in suits approached him. Representatives of Ford, Chrysler, and General Motors told Ugly George to get lost. There had never been an entirely fruitless *Ugly George* program, but it was now eleven-fifty, ten minutes until his bedtime, and things were looking bleak. Then an attractive woman standing next to a car with a lot of chrome started paying attention to what Ugly George had to say. She listened to him with a serious expression.

"I'll talk to you on my break," she said.

Suddenly she was standing on a dark staircase and talking about her modeling career. The bright light on top of the camera gave her face a pale washed-out quality. Ugly George told her that many women had had their careers launched on his show. While she spoke, a hand appeared in the lower corner of the screen and tugged gently at her spandex top. "Could you pull this down a little?" he asked.

She pulled it down, showing more cleavage, and said, "Is this good?" She was quite young and looked a little confused by the bright light.

"Yes, that's great," said Ugly George. "Great." Then the hand reappeared at the bottom of the screen. Ugly George was persistent. His hand was like a pale moth that kept flitting back to the bright light of her breast. "You know what would be ideal?" he said.

Her face responded coolly to the suggestion. "You want me to take it *all* the way off?" The hand reached out and gave a gentle tug. She cooperated. Two breasts popped out. Alex and half the adolescent male population of Manhattan let out a silent, heart-thumping cheer. Unfortunately the palpitations of his heart were echoed by his mother's footsteps thudding gently in the hall. He spun the television dial and threw himself back onto her bed. The spin was as arbitrary as roulette.

Alex's mother often walked in on her son watching strange programs. Cooking shows. News specials. And now she found a preacher extolling his congregation on the merits of God and the perils of sin. He made exaggerated gestures with his arms and punctuated his sentences with long meaningful stares into the camera. Alex stared at him with the same blank rapt expression he always had when he watched television. She watched this for a while, standing next to the bed. Finally she turned to him and asked, "Does this interest you?"

"Sort of," he mumbled. "It was just on."

This exchange depressed him far more than abandoning the beautiful woman and her breasts. The real business of his life was, more and more, conducted on a subterranean level, out of his mother's sight, and he felt a pang of sadness and pity for her now, as she puzzled over this strange new fragment like an archaeologist who has found yet another incongruous item on her dig.

"This is a mistake," he wanted to explain. "This guy talking about Jesus is a fluke. It doesn't accurately reflect my interests and you shouldn't draw any conclusions from it." But this explanation would have to lead to other, impossible explanations, and so he just kept quiet, and suffered through five minutes of the preacher vehemently insisting that Jesus Christ loves you, and that if you love Jesus He will save you, but only if you let Him into your heart. Then it was time for bed.

THE NEXT MORNING Alex stood still while his mother helped him with his tie. She tugged at the knot, tightening it, and he pretended to be having an out-of-body experience, so as to not be so close to her face. His father had not lived long enough to teach Alex how to knot a tie, and his mother wasn't too good at it either, so they made it a perennial joint enterprise, a shared task of pulling and tugging until they got it right. Alex felt he could do it on his own at this point, but wasn't quite ready to deprive his mother of the task.

He was on his way to Phil Singer's Bar Mitzvah. It was a cold blustery day in April, and Singer's Bar Mitzvah was the grand finale of a year-long circuit of Bar Mitzvahs. Under his arm was a gift-wrapped copy of *Great Jews in Sports*. In a rare moment of foresight last fall, Alex had fished ten copies of this book out of a discount bin and had them gift-wrapped, thereby resolving the Bar Mitzvah gift problem. They sat in an ever-shrinking stack in his room.

"It's cold," his mother said as he headed for the door. "Let me get your scarf." He stood in the doorway while she went and got his scarf. He could picture all her movements through the apartment by the sounds of her footsteps, receding and then approaching again, hurried and purposeful. She handed him the scarf. "Have a wonderful time," she said.

He glared at her because of the word "wonderful," which was a typical word for his mother. It was impractical and romantic and strange. Furthermore it was too dignified. There was something barbaric about these Bar Mitzvahs. Without the context of either school or home, whatever humanity existed within each individual eighth-grader was submerged, and they became one pulsating headless group of stimulation seekers, constantly seeking out new life forms to devour. Bar Mitzvahs were like petri dishes in which the germs that composed his class were allowed to commingle and multiply.

Today's Bar Mitzvah boy, Phil Singer, was the coolest person in the grade and, amazingly, someone Alex felt close to, but he did not think "wonderful" was the word for what lay in store.

"I'm not going to have a wonderful time," said Alex stoically. "I may have a good time. And that's a maybe."

"All right," she said. "Then have a good time. Have whatever time you want to have."

He stood in the small vestibule outside their apartment, and she stood in the doorway while the elevator came.

"You look very handsome," she said, smiling, as though she knew she should refrain from this sort of comment, but couldn't resist.

There she goes again, he thought. *Handsome.* What kind of word was that? When a girl at school liked another boy, she called him *cute.* But then did he want his mother to call him cute? The thought was disturbing. He was rescued by the elevator.

"Goodbye," he said. The elevator door closed. There was a small window in the elevator door through which they could see each other for one last second. It was only at this moment, as his mother stood framed by that little window, smiling at him and meeting his gaze, that his feelings of contempt and disgust for her abated, and were replaced by a wrenching and overwhelming sensation of love. Then the elevator dropped, the picture disappeared, and he was descending in what he had come to feel was the world's slowest elevator, a tiny decompression chamber between his home and the real world.

HE TOOK A taxi to the Park Avenue Synagogue, which in spite of its name was located on Madison Avenue. There was a group of boys on the sidewalk standing around talking in their gray three-piece suits. Gerstein, Conroy, Fluss, Edelman, and Cohen. They sounded like a law firm, and all except for Gerstein would eventually graduate from law school. Gerstein was a cynical and manipulative creep who had been popular and attractive ever since he stood up in the sandbox. These waning months of eighth grade would be the last uncomplicated and happy months of his life; soon the world would get complicated, and he would be unable to get complicated with it.

Someone racing up Madison in a taxi might have mistaken this group for a bunch of brash young executives, but Alex recognized them as a bunch of leering and belligerent adolescents, spoiled brats, and, he had to admit, the sorry group of humans he spent a lot of his time with. Alex had by now witnessed rabbis of all shapes and sizes explain that the Bar Mitzvah was the ceremony that celebrated a boy's passage to manhood. Gerstein, Edelman, and Fluss had already had theirs. The transformation was not evident.

Alex joined the group.

"Nice jacket, Fader," said Gerstein, his good friend. "Do you wear the same underwear to every Bar Mitzvah too?"

"Nice face," Alex replied, and immediately marveled at his inability to say anything insulting to anyone else, while, on the other hand, every insult directed at him was like a radioactive thorn which leaked poison into his system for hours if not weeks after it was inserted. Already he felt a tiny vibration of hatred towards his mother for having bought him this stupid blue blazer and gray slacks. At least, he reflected, Gerstein had not called him fat. He was not even that fat anymore, but he had been when he first arrived at the school in fourth grade, and had continued to be for several years, and now he was like a character actor who is not allowed to change his character—Fat.

"Today is going to be good," said Cohen. "The Plaza."

"Singer is a maniac," said Fluss.

"I hope we get a good gift," said Gerstein.

"I hope it's better than a little cup that says 'Arnold's Bar Mitzvah' on it," said Fluss, referring to Gerstein's Bar Mitzvah gift a month earlier.

"I wonder if Singer will be wasted when he reads from the Torah," said Cohen.

"Scott would be so pissed if Singer messed up," said Fluss. Scott was Phil Singer's father.

"Scott!" said Edelman.

"Scott!" replied Fluss, as though responding to mating call. "Scott Scott Scott Scott!" he continued. All the boys started bleating the name "Scott." They sounded like honking geese. Alex joined in meekly. It was the strange custom of all of Alex's classmates to refer to their own and everyone else's father by their first names. The mention of one of these names sent all his friends into peals of ecstatic laughter, as though it were the most ridiculous thing they had ever heard. Were his father still alive, Alex could not imagine taking any pleasure in referring to him as Sol and to chanting his name derisively with them.

When the chanting subsided, the boys turned to go inside. The Park Avenue Synagogue, at Eighty-eighth and Madison, was just three blocks south of Alex's barber shop, Michael's, and Alex suddenly thought of it. Michael's specialized in children. It had been founded sometime during the Kennedy administration, and its interior design had not been revised since. The walls were covered with pictures of the Kennedy kids sporting a haircut called the John-John. The chairs were large imperial contraptions made of white porcelain and red leather that went up and down, and some of them had little toy cars, orange and green, built around them, for the youngest children, which gave the place a carnival atmosphere. Every kid got a Tootsie pop while his hair was cut. There was a small room in the back where particularly distressed children were taken, so their screams and wails would not disturb everyone else. Alex had been a frequent visitor to this back room when he was very young. He remembered the cooing sounds of the barber, his mother's hand caressing him, and the shrill snip snip of the scissors next to his ear. Above all, as he entered the cool interior of the Park Avenue Synagogue, he remembered his own screams. A bloody corpse would not have provoked more hysterical cries of distress.

Why had he screamed like that? Now, at age thirteen, it was a mystery to him. Already a small pool of his own humanity had slipped forever beyond his reach, locked under a pane of glass through which he could only peer, as though he were looking at an exhibit at a museum. He no longer cried in Michael's barbershop. But then, it occurred to him, he rarely went. His hair was long and unruly. There had been a palace coup on the subject of hairstyles a couple of years ago, and the John-John had been deposed. He took his seat amidst the pre-service hum of conversation and took out a Bible from the rack in front of him, not to read, just to hold, like an amulet. He too, in his own small way, had taken steps away from being a boy and towards being a man, although there had been no ceremony to commemorate it. He wasn't even sure it was an event worth celebrating.

THE IDEA OF a Bar Mitzvah had never been discussed between Alex and his mother, and he had never given it any thought until the beginning of the eighth-grade school year, when the invitations began to arrive. He remembered the first one, which he and his mother had puzzled over with the unabashed awe of primitives who have found a functioning matchbook. It was a large square envelope, cream-colored and made of a paper stock less flexible than certain kinds of wood. The type on the enclosed invitation was thick enough to read by touch. There were copious amounts of gauzy tissue paper in there as well, and other envelopes, already stamped, with RSVP cards asking for commitments to far-off dates. The slightly askance stamp was the only evidence that a human being had had anything to do with this assemblage of objects.

"What I don't understand," said Alex at the time, "is that I don't think Richard Edelman even likes me. Why is he inviting me to his Bar Mitzvah?"

"Maybe he does like you," his mother, ever the optimist, had replied.

"No, that's not an issue, okay? That's not possible. Maybe he just invited the whole grade." He was making a joke.

Edelman had in fact invited the whole grade. Six weeks after the invitation arrived, Alex had been stuffed into a jacket and tie and sent off to attend a service in which Edelman, a nervous boy who, at the age of thirteen, had a body that suggested that not one single pubic hair had yet sprouted on it, stood robed in strange garments and read Hebrew for an interminably long period of time. Alex sat there in the synagogue along with the rest of his class. The boys sat in one section and the girls in another. Afterwards there was a bus that took everyone down to the World Trade Center. The invitation had said: "Reception at Windows on the World."

Windows on the World was a restaurant on the top floor of one of the World Trade Center towers. Therefore it had a view. Everyone was very excited about the view, and for the first ten minutes the whole class flocked to the windows and pressed their faces against it, peering out at New Jersey or the Atlantic Ocean, depending on which way they were facing. Windows on the World was a distinguished restaurant which served very good food at exorbitant prices, and the presence of fifty screaming kids would have depressed and angered many of the lunch patrons, had they been there. But no one was there, because, for a fee equal to about two years' school tuition for their son, the Edelmans had rented the place out.

Alex was one of those whose face was pressed eagerly to the glass one hundred and one stories above the ground. But in a short while he unstuck his nose and began walking around the tables, looking at the name cards that were written out in neat script and sat on every plate.

He lingered among the tables, feeling intimidated by the array of silverware and the fancy lettering on the name cards. He had sat through that lunch with a stiff posture, had spoken hardly at all, and had made a point of keeping his elbows off the table. For some reason he was under the impression that his mother was going to be judged by his behavior here, and he wanted to make a good showing.

His classmates did not feel the same compulsion. Specifically, the gang of boys, led by Phil Singer, who more or less ran the grade, and to whom Alex had tangentially attached himself, discovered that Mr. Edward Edelman, who was presiding over this celebration of his son's Bar Mitzvah with evident pride, smoked a pipe. To correspond with his son having invited his whole eighth-grade class, Edward Edelman had invited the entire executive staff of the electronics firm of which he was vice-president, and was busy greeting them and making jokes and spotting small intrigues of conversation and affiliation that were bubbling around the room. So he was very surprised when a rumor welled up among the younger generation that the stuff in his pipe was not tobacco, but marijuana. He reassured himself that no one actually believed he was smoking pot, but Edward Edelman was, on some deep and partially buried level, a nice man, and furthermore he was genuinely moved by his son's Bar Mitzvah, and proud of the event he was putting on, and all these genuine human emotions made him vulnerable. Alex's classmates had a desire to attack vulnerability that was as natural and innate as their ability to detect its presence.

And so from the depths of the party came the chant "Eddie is stoned! Eddie is stoned!" And soon kids were running around laughing hysterically and screaming, "Crazy Eddie! He's in-*sane!*"

Soon Mr. Edelman's expression became strained. One of his colleagues sidled up to him and said, "What's up, Crazy Eddie?" Mr. Edelman had the nauseating premonition that it was a name that would stick around the office for years. The sight of a gang of thirteen-year-olds running around calling him Eddie was not part of the fantasy he had long nurtured for how this day would unfold. He put his pipe away. He stopped milling around the party and hung back in a corner, looking a bit tired and aggrieved. Eventually he was discarded as the favored object of scorn because the troublesome group of boys were distracted by a more interesting target. They began harassing a group of girls. One girl in particular seemed to be the object of their scorn and desire. From across the room he could see that she looked genuinely frightened by the group of boys that encircled her. An hour earlier Mr. Edleman would have intervened, but he had been mauled into submission and simply turned his gaze elsewhere, back to the real world of adults and serious business.

WHAT CRAZY EDWARD Edelman had looked away from was a heated discussion between a group of girls and a group of boys. Greg Neuman, who did double duty as class clown and class pervert, had tried to grab Marcy Goldblum's breast. Marcy—who was still two years away from the nose job she already fantasized about, who was popular, and who didn't have much of a breast to grab—knocked his hands away with an aristocratic slap. A conversation, or rather an inarticulate screaming match, followed, in which the girls more or less tried to explain that the boys couldn't just grab, they had to at least try and talk to them. After a minute of this, Greg, who was crashing from the initial sugar rush of euphoria he experienced whenever he touched a girl, walked over to Tania Vincent and grabbed her breast.

Tania had wavy golden hair, pale skin, and a pretty nose. Her claim to fame in the eighth grade was that she had breasts. Her breasts made it impossible for most of the boys in the grade to interact with her in a civilized manner.

Now, everyone watched Greg's knotty little fingers sink into Tania's right breast. She screamed. The girls shrieked and the boys let out a yell as though someone had just hit a home run, and in one short instant the essential architecture of Bar Mitzvah socializing for the remainder of the year had been established. It was a peculiar form of flirtation that mixed elements of tag and rape. There was a weird element of status involved as well, since only the more popular boys did the grabbing, and only the more popular girls had to run around with their hands over their breasts.

In the midst of all the screaming, Alex looked across the room and was amazed to see Mr. Edelman off in the distance, watching the proceedings, but standing immobile. He had been beaten into submission by the eighth grade. Years later Alex would still think about the Bar Mitzvahs of that year and wonder that such behavior was allowed by the adults. But by then Alex would know that adults were full of their own fears and anxieties, and were as mortal and prone to error as any eighth-grader, if not more so.

EDELMAN'S BAR MITZVAH was just the beginning. A few months later, Alex was a veteran of Windows on the World, which seemed to be the destination of choice for Bar Mitzvah parties, although there were other opulent destinations as well. He had seen adults get drunk, and had stolen half-finished drinks off the adult tables to drink himself. He had watched classmates anxiously sing Hebrew words, be praised by rabbis, and later receive envelope after envelope from friends and relatives, each containing a check of biblical proportions.

He had been barraged by clowns and magicians and enthusiastic disc jockeys who played "Ring My Bell" and "Push Push in the Bush" when they wanted to get people dancing, and who then played the soundtrack to *Saturday Night Fever* once they were. He possessed, along with a closetful of stupid door prizes, the more abstract but lasting memory of himself jumping around spastically on the dance floor in a rare moment of inhibition, while simultaneously puzzling over whether what the Bee Gees said about the *New York Times*'s effect on man was true.

And now it was spring. The stack of *Great Jews in Sports* was down to one, and it made sense that Phil Singer should get the last book. Phil was good at sports, the fastest kid in the grade, but the connection went beyond that; he had the special grace of great athletes, a kind of magic that infuses their every gesture with possibility. He would change things. He already had, in the small scale of the eighth grade. He was the grade's leading mystic and delinquent. And he was Alex's friend.

Singer's Bar Mitzvah promised to be different from all the others, and at first glance it was—it was even fancier. After Phil had done his duties at the Park Avenue Synagogue, they were all loaded onto a pair of waiting buses and shipped down Fifth Avenue to the Plaza Hotel ballroom. Bouquets of flowers sat on each table, above which hung clusters of white helium balloons. Already Alex could sense a weird panic in the eyes of his friends. There had been such a buildup to this Bar Mitzvah that something had to happen. A big brass band played quietly, though ominously, as though they were just limbering up, and would start to seriously swing once people had had a chance to digest.

The boys wore their suits and exulted in the discovery that the bartenders scattered around the Plaza ballroom were willing to serve them drinks. The Singer myth expanded another notch. The girls, meanwhile, continued to refine their adultlike behavior. They wore dresses and elegant suits, they had had their hair done, they wore makeup and jewelry, and they carried it all off with a kind of ease, as though they dressed this way all the time.

Alex was seated at the same table as Tania. She looked assured and womanly as she engaged in conversation with Marcy Goldblum.

"And then she got up to go to the bathroom and missed the backseat scene," Tania was saying now, "and when I told her about it later she was so pissed."

"That was the most intense scene of the movie," replied Marcy.

"What backseat scene?" said John Goldman, who was sitting next to Alex. "Why is it that I never understand what the hell anyone is talking about?"

"They're talking about a dirty scene in a movie," said Alex.

"We're talking about *Saturday Night Fever*," said Marcy from across the table, in a loud aggressive voice that seemed to scold the two boys for trying to have a conversation of their own.

Tania didn't even look over. She just tossed her hair a little. She nodded knowingly as she spoke and elegantly brought her fork to her mouth. She was quite womanly, Alex thought. She was wearing a pretty dress with lace frills around the collar and sleeves; a provocative pink ribbon tied together the two pieces of fabric holding her breasts, as though it were a shoe lace. Alex stared intently at her hands as she used her silverware, as though for tips, and occasionally he stared at the space between her breasts, covered but not entirely obscured by the ribbon. He imagined Ugly George's hand reaching out and gently tugging at that ribbon until it came apart.

"I didn't see *Saturday Night Fever*," said John. "My mother wouldn't let me."

Alex stared at him incredulously, torn between hating him passionately for being a geek and admiring him for having the audacity to say the truth, which, as it happened, was the same truth that applied to Alex. He would have seen the movie anyway had it not been for the fact that the *Jaws 2* experience still lurked, with accompanying soundtrack, in the back of his mind. He had been forbidden from seeing *Jaws 2* but had snuck in on his own one afternoon a few days before leaving for sailing camp. He returned from sailing camp with awards in riflery, archery, and tennis, but the only water that had touched his skin either came out of a shower or was heavily chlorinated, and every time someone touched his leg in the pool he became hysterical.

Something about the way Tania moved, the way she talked, the way she brought her fork to her mouth, made her seem much too good for the bacterial fungus that composed eighth-grade society. Alex was intent on interacting with her in a civilized manner, but could not seem to manage it. She liked art, and spent time after school in the art studio painting, and once Alex had seen her all by herself after school, walking with a canvas wrapped up under her arm. He was by himself as well. This was the perfect opportunity for him to express his admiration for her, to show he was interested in art, and to generally distance himself from the baboonlike behavior of his classmates. Practically hyperventilating with effort, he had made himself call out to her as she walked by.

"Let me see it!" he said.

He was referring to the canvas, but Tania hurried past without looking up. He stood there amazed at this misunderstanding, but unable to correct it.

Now he tried to glance at her surreptitiously, but his glances kept devolving into stares, which would be broken only when her eyes raked briefly across his face and he immediately looked down. Unwilling and also unable to muster the grabby aggressive prerogative of his classmates, or Ugly George for that matter, he had no strategy except to be so passive and pathetic and conspicuously inept that she would be forced to take pity on him, approach him, talk to him, get to know him really well, and then, on her own volition, for no real reason—and here Alex's thoughts became vague and possessed of the illogic of dreams—she would take off her shirt, and let him see, just because she felt like it.

He understood that this was an unrealistic scenario, but was at a loss for anything to replace it.

Eventually the party became wild and dispersed. The grown-ups got drunk and danced. The kids got drunk and danced. The usual ritual of boys grabbing girls was played out. The swing band was replaced by a disc jockey. Phil Singer made out very publicly with Audrey Stevens, and then they both disappeared, and a joke made the rounds that they had rented a room. Then Audrey reappeared and said Phil had passed out on the one of the couches outside.

Gradually all the kids came out to view the body. He lay there looking very peaceful, with envelopes bulging out of all his pockets. The only thing askance was his feet, which were not really in a comfortable position, but turned in towards each other.

"Oh jeez, Phil becomes a man," said Mrs. Singer when she saw her son. She stroked his face and put a pillow under his head and then went and got a shoe box and put all the envelopes in it. An older lady came out and looked down at Phil and then at the assembled youth who were standing around.

"Who did this?" she demanded of the crowd, as though some-one had forced Phil to get drunk, or had perhaps hit him over the head and robbed him. "Who did this to Philly?"

She was, Alex surmised from the "Philly," the grandmother. He wanted very much to explain to this woman that no one had done anything to Phil Singer, quite the contrary, this was yet another small bit of philanthropy that Phil had doled out to the rest of the class in a moment of generosity—he wanted to explain that her grandson was a great guy because he had single-handedly changed the definition of cool in the eighth grade—he had written the word TULL on the back of his down jacket, instantly catapulting Jethro Tull into the front rank of popular bands in the grade, and had then, once this happened, drawn a single canceling line through the word. This in a class where the most popular boys had previously been neat fastidious creeps like Arnold Gerstein who didn't even want his down jacket to get *wet*. Phil did bong hits before the morning bus and once brought a bottle of vodka into school, which he shared with a large group of boys during lunch, leading to Allen Fluss's infamous vomit in geometry episode. Phil was a rebel who understood that things were fucked up and was willing to do something about it. If what he was willing to do was pass out at his own Bar Mitzvah, then so be it!

All this raced through Alex's mind, which the woman seemed to read like a ticker tape, for she turned towards him and said, with a quivering accusatory finger raised in his direction, "You! What have you done to Philly?"

"Me?" said Alex, more a croak than a statement.

"You! The ringleader!"

This was perhaps the least accurate description of himself that Alex had ever heard. He couldn't face this hysterical woman, and he suddenly couldn't face the mirth of the Bar Mitzvah party. He saw that a number of people were drifting off into an adjoining room, and he followed them.

He walked into the cream-and-candy-colored sitting area which was adjacent to the ladies' room. Couches and easy chairs and throw pillows were placed elegantly here and there, and the beige carpet gave the strange piece of theater unfolding before his eyes a hushed, unreal quality.

Greg Neuman and Jack Gold were struggling with Tania Vincent, who was strangely quiet while she tried to get them off. After occupying the huge cathedral of the ballroom for so long, this small, pretty, enclosed space seemed illicit and private. The room was filling up with kids, as though some accident had just occurred, and they were gathering around to rubberneck. Except the accident was in progress.

"Stop it!" Tania finally gasped. "Stop it!" She kept saying that over and over again. What was so strange was that rather than performing a hit-and-run attack, which was the normal mode of operation, Greg Neuman and Jack Gold were struggling with Tania as though she were a running back in football whom they were trying to tackle. Then there was a ripping sound. Jack Gold had managed to get his hand into that space where the pink ribbon was, and had torn the dress, and just then Arnold Gerstein came running over and grabbed both of Tania's arms and held them behind her back, and for one split second Tania's dress was pulled all the way down to her waist and her breasts fell forward, completely exposed, jiggling and awkward. Every person in the room screamed. The girls screamed in horror and the boys screamed as though they were at a sporting event and the home team had just scored. Alex started laughing with hysterical glee, and within his own laughter he heard hoarse yelps of panic and fear. Everyone was yelling and running around, and he just stood there watching it unfold, amazed at the momentum of events.

Tania was crying now, her hands cupping her breasts, while several pairs of hands tried to pry them off or squeeze the parts that were not covered. Her friends came to the rescue. There were shrieks and screams. Ellen Levine was pounding Jack Gold in the face, and Tania broke away and ran for the ladies' room.

Every boy in the room followed in hot pursuit. There was no context to their actions, just wild giddiness, the chase, the yelling, the brief glimpse of that which had been imagined for so long. Alex, swept up in the momentum of what was happening, ran with them.

Tania pushed through the door to the ladies' room, and it had hardly closed before eight more boys were clamoring to get through the same door. The cream-colored hues of the sitting room had given way to the harsh reality of the fluorescent light. Tania ran into one of the stalls, slammed the door shut, and locked it. The boys leapt over its sides like braying animals. Tania shrank back in tears. Alex was among the first to leap onto that flimsy metal partition. He looked down at Tania. The first thing he saw was her braces. Tania didn't have the kind of mouth that showed her teeth, but now her mouth was configured in the figure eight of sobs, and they gleamed in the light. She clutched her torn dress to herself.

She was crying real sobs. Under the bright fluorescent lights, all that womanliness was gone. Alex could see the thin blue veins on her chest and neck and face; her whole body seemed pale and bluish in that light, except for her flushed cheeks; her tears streaked mascara and her hair was a mess.

For one brief moment, as he vaulted up onto the edge of the bathroom stall, Alex had felt ecstatic. For the first time he felt part of his group, part of his class, and his world. Then, when he saw Tania, the feeling abated. He hung there, feet dangling, eyes bulging from the strain of the thin metal wall pressing into his stomach, looking down at her. He wanted very much to say something. He wanted to apologize. But this was not a good time for apologies. His pride at finally having done something vied with his shame at what he had done.

Eventually he was herded into the group of boys that the Plaza Hotel security staff, who had burst onto the scene in their uniforms, walkie-talkies cackling, identified as the criminal element. The criminal element stood there unworried.

Phil Singer's grandmother appeared on the scene and again became hysterical at the sight of Alex. "It's him!" she cried. Alex was amazed to note that he felt flattered by this misunderstanding.

"What are you going to do?" Gerstein said to one of the men with walkie-talkies. "You're just security guards. We pay you guys." They were kept in the room just long enough for the truth of this statement to dissipate a little. Tania, for her part, had rearranged her dress and seemed amazingly composed. She walked out without saying a word, her chin held high, flanked by all her friends, who called the boys assholes over their shoulders.

Soon afterwards the party began to disperse. Alex walked through the Plaza's glittering lobby, his knees loose and bouncy with nervous energy, the plush springy carpet making him feel as though he might float up towards the ceiling. None of the guests in the lobby knew of the events that had just occurred in the ladies' room, yet it seemed as though they could fathom them, understand their context, grasp the dreamlike quality of their sequence, and perhaps forgive them with a knowing wink.

The same could not be said for the world beyond the Plaza's heavy front door, the real world. He pushed through it and was greeted by a slap of cold moist air. It was dusk, and cloudy, and the city looked a bit blue, as though it weren't getting enough oxygen. He had moved through the ballroom, and that small warmly lit sitting room, and the bright fluorescent bathroom, like a Super Ball racing through the air for longer than seemed natural. But now gravity reasserted itself, and time returned to its normal pace.

He walked up Central Park South to Sixth Avenue, shivering a little in the cold air. He took his scarf out of his pocket and tied it tightly around his neck. He had cab fare but decided, as some kind of penance, to take the Number 5 bus. He waited for the Number 5 until the sky was black and his teeth were chattering, and then decided to come up with some other form of penance and took a cab.

When he got into his apartment he felt its warmth envelop him as though a blanket had been thrown over his shoulders. His mother was sitting at the kitchen table, reading. He fled past her to his room.

"Did you have a nice time?" his mother called after him.

"Yes!" he said, more a yelp than a comment. He stepped into his room, and pulled the door shut.

The Harmonie Club

ARNOLD GERSTEIN OFTEN TOOK FRIENDS TO HIS FATHER'S club, the Harmonie, on Sixty-first just off Fifth Avenue, where they could "use the facilities" (as Arnold's father put it) for free. They would shoot hoops on the small basketball court, whose wooden floor had taken on a yellow-orange patina from years of use. Then they would smash a squash ball around in one of the bright cubelike squash courts, and when they got tired of that, spend some time heaving barbells in the weight room. From there they hit the sauna and then, after showers, went downstairs to the dining room for lunch, which Arnold signed for on his father's account. (Arnold usually had turkey with mayo, on white.)

Arnold had been going to the Harmonie Club on and off all his life, at first with his father and later with friends. There was some sort of formality about checking in that his father never observed; instead he just nodded to the men at the front desk, a curt but friendly nod accompanied by an equally curt and slightly face-tious salute. It was an acknowledgment that these men at the front desk existed, that they were manning the ship, keeping at bay the hordes that thronged through Fifth Avenue and Central Park. Arnold absorbed this gesture thoughtlessly; everything he absorbed was as though through osmosis, so that the things he was good at, such as math, or wearing an expression that com-bined elements of sweetness and hostility in such a way as to make everyone around him seem beholden to him, he understood intuitively, without any sense of struggle up from a base of igno-rance towards a peak of understanding, and those things he did not understand intuitively, such as English, or having any kind of emotion that was motivated by something other than greed, he did not absorb. "English," for Arnold, was just a subject in school, but his inability to understand it was symbolic of his inability to understand or have any natural affinity for such things as memory, feeling, camaraderie, compassion, curiosity, and even love, all of which were out of sight, shrouded in a fog bank of ignorance, and therefore didn't bother him.

When Arnold entered the Harmonie Club he gave the men at the front desk the same vague nod as his father, and walked by without giving it any thought.

ALEX FADER, WHO accompanied Arnold on some of these visits to the Harmonie Club, gave it some thought. That nod was like a secret password that no one had told him about; it was a key that, by his witnessing it, had accidentally fallen into his possession. He pocketed it coolly, knowing that he would one day put it to use.

He put it to use one Tuesday during spring break of his freshman year in high school, when, having confirmed that Arnold was absolutely definitely not going to be at the Harmonie Club—he was on a family vacation in the Bahamas—Alex paid a visit on his own.

There was a small blue awning above a discreet door. The only thing notable about the whole building was the large American flag that hung from a pole, echoing the flags out in front of the Plaza Hotel a couple of blocks away. Across the street was the grand empire of the Metropolitan Club, which, even at a glance, suggested power and prestige and, with its forbidding black gates and arched doorway, exclusivity. Alex didn't know that the Harmonie had been founded over a hundred years earlier by a group of German Jews whose chances of gaining membership to a place like the Metropolitan were approximately zero; it didn't occur to him that the sober limestone facade of the Harmonie was a gesture of discretion, something low-key. For Alex it was just a different kind of opulence from the one across the street. It was a place where you could swim, play squash, shoot hoops, sweat, sign for sandwiches (Alex usually had a BLT on toasted whole wheat), that had an elevator and thick carpets and a huge empty ballroom through which Arnold and Alex had once wandered, stoned. (It was Alex's pot, he was the instigator, it is true, but he was not Arnold's corrupter to the extent that Abigail Gerstein, Arnold's mother, later contended. Once the shortcomings of her blue-eyed youngest son began to manifest themselves in his deteriorating relations to the rest of the world, Mrs. Gerstein became obsessed with the idea that everything that went wrong with Arnold was all Alex's fault, so that by the end of eleventh grade she was to become so obsessed with Alex Fader's satanically negative influ-

ence on her innocent son that while watching a television documentary on voodoo she gave serious thought to buying a small
doll in Alex's likeness and sticking pins in it.) For Alex, the Harmonie wasn't a place to be occupied so much as infiltrated. It was
the inside towards which he felt compelled, with a peculiarly
reflexive intensity, to burrow.

Alex often used the city's semipublic property for his own private use. He frequently took the elevator of the Plaza Hotel to
the top floor, walked up another flight of stairs, wound his way
through a storage room of beds and bedding, and up through a
trapdoor that led to the roof. He used the roof of the Plaza Hotel
as a sort of personal clubhouse, and had twice done the same at
the Essex House up the block, whose towering sign ("Essex
House") was visible from almost everywhere in Central Park. But
the Plaza and the Essex House were large institutions whose staff
were used to strange faces sauntering into the lobby as though
they owned the place. Their lobbies were teeming with anonymous faces, while the Harmonie Club's lobby was funereally
sparse. It was an institution whose entire point, as far as Alex
could tell, was to provide a small number of people the opportunity to see nothing and no one they hadn't seen before.

Alex arrived at the front door to the club and marched up the
few steps and then into the lobby. It was a cold, rainy, and for the
most part gloomy day, and the trees on Fifth Avenue were all still
barren. The doorman let him in with a tiny but perceptible bow,
the same one he offered everyone. Alex walked straight to the
elevator. At a certain point he turned his head in the direction of
the front desk and offered a slight nod. The men nodded back.
He hit the elevator button—the small, black, upward-pointing
arrow became illuminated by an orange glow—and waited to
ascend to the locker room. He felt their eyes on his back. When
the door closed behind him he breathed a huge sigh of relief.

The locker room was empty. He undressed, balling his clothes up in the corner, since he didn't have a locker. He had shorts on beneath his pants, and he wore his T-shirt, so it was just his coat and pants in the corner.

He went to the basketball court and shot around for a while. Usually, when shooting around alone, he drifted into an elaborate fantasy about a tense game, dramatic buzzer-beating scenarios, and so forth, but today the place seemed too barren and empty and he couldn't relax. The old leather ball was brown with age and bounced funny. From the squash courts he could hear the distant thwacking of the little black ball bouncing against the white walls. The basketball got louder with each bounce. Alex was seized by paranoid feelings. He headed for the weight room but then decided to go straight to the sauna.

The sauna had made a strong impression on him during his previous visits. It was populated by nude men, sometimes rather old ones, all perched like walruses on the reddish wood, reading the paper or sitting, head bowed and still, while fat drops of sweat dropped to the wooden floor one at a time and began to evaporate. Alex and Arnold had been hairless, thin, and insubstantial presences amidst these hulking mounds of prosperity, worry, fat, and back hair.

He arrived in the sauna equipped, as was the custom as far as he could tell, with absolutely nothing save a copy of the newspaper. The room was occupied by two men sitting at opposite ends, on the upper benches. Alex took a seat between them, on one of the lower benches. One of the men was muscular and hairy in that peculiar way that involves nose hair, ear hair, chest hair, back hair, but nothing on the top of the head. He sat with his elbows on his knees, his torso almost entirely obscured by the *Wall Street Journal*. The other man read the *Times*. Alex had with him the *Times* business section, and he began to read it. But he couldn't concentrate, because the man reading the *Wall Street Journal* had an enormous penis. It hung down from the bottom of the page like a thick heavy rope, and it was as though the *Wall Street Journal* had an enormous penis. Alex stared at it blankly. Then he stared at his own forearm and saw tiny beads of sweat appearing there. He did not sweat in the same way as the men, who secreted moisture in fat drops. Alex secreted moisture as though it were being pushed through a very fine sieve. After a minute, the *Wall Street Journal* was abruptly folded, and it and its penis exited the sauna.

The sauna was now occupied by two people reading the business section of the *New York Times* and a big wet spot on the opposite bench, delineating two cheeks and a lump of flesh in between. It was evaporating quickly.

After a few minutes of scrutinizing the paper, which included a feature on an up-and-coming steel excutive, Alex turned to the man and said, "What do make of the steel guy?"

The man was middle-aged and had a bit of paunch, but was self-contained and prim; he had none of the spilling-over qualities of the departed *Wall Street Journal* man. This man, the *Times* man, had salt-and-pepper hair cut short, side-parted, and very white skin with relatively little hair.

The man looked over with a friendly and slightly incredulous smile.

"You follow the steel business?" he said.

"Not very closely," said Alex. "But I keep my eye on it."

"Tough business," said the man. He said it in a tone of voice that suggested that further conversation, while not likely, was nevertheless possible.

"Why?" said Alex. "Why is that?"

"Steel? In America?" He chortled inwardly, as though appreciating his own joke. "It's not what it used to be, I'll tell you that. A different ball game now. If you're in steel," and here he cast Alex a confiding glance, as if this were just a secret for the two of them, "get out. That's my call."

The man's body was covered with fine hairs and a very thin layer of sweat. The hairless body and the white skin and the oily moisture made him seem a bit like a newborn baby. His fat was innocent fat. His fingernails were carefully trimmed. He was younger than the fathers of Alex's classmates, and yet he had the glow of prosperous male adulthood about him. He was energized, distracted, slightly irascible. He gazed at Alex over his paper, or rather he let his paper fall moistly onto the leg that was crossed over his knee, and turned his head to regard the young newcomer more carefully. Alex looked back. He saw the man's fingers (he wore a ring), his stomach, his hair, yet there was an odd disconnected aspect to their exchanged stare. It was as though the two naked men were looking at each other without actually seeing anything.

"What do you do?" Alex said.

"I'm in the insurance industry," said the man. "How about you?"

"I'm in high school," said Alex.

"Then why aren't you there?" said the man. It wasn't a hostile question. He smiled a little as he said it, as though he were sympathetic in advance to whatever explanation Alex would provide. He smiled the smile of a potential co-conspirator.

"I'm taking the day off," he said. It was a perverse lie, considering it made him sound as if he were playing hooky when he could just have explained that it was spring break, but Alex was finely tuned to the needs of whoever was asking him questions, and this man seemed to need him to be a little bit out of bounds.

"Wanted to make a visit to the Harmonie Club for therapeutic purposes. I understand. I'm doing something a bit like that myself. Is your father a member here?"

Alex stared at him blankly as if he had just spoken a foreign language. A wave of fatigue came over him; he could feel, for a few beats, his own pulse. The man looked at him curiously, but with a slight penetrating edge to his stare.

"I just had the day off and wanted to come by," Alex said.

"You a member?" the man said.

"My father is a member," said Alex.

Alex didn't think his father would have been a member of the Harmonie Club. There was, within the deep grooves of his father's pensive forehead, a certain refinement that would have been ignored here, and that would in turn have found distasteful the whole acquiring ethos that pervaded the place like cheap perfume.

But he also fantasized, vaguely, about his father's being a member of this club, and many other such institutions through which he could cruise without having to feign prerogative; it would be the real thing.

Alex was adept at a particular bit of emotional gymnastics in which he would enshrine his father in that sanctifying halo of nostalgia reserved for the dead; once this reverent shrine was sufficiently beatific, he would trash it with all the vigor and bile to be expected of any fourteen-year-old dead set on proving that everything his parents stand for should be thrown in the gutter.

So he was his father's chief guardian and chief assaulter, a double duty that didn't trouble him except in moments like this, when he saw his desire to both protect and attack his father for what it was: his inability to do either.

The man smiled at him, as though he knew Alex was telling a lie, and in that sweaty little instant his civilized and pleasant aura fell away and something more primitive and vicious peeked out. It leered at Alex for a split second, a smug gleeful acknowledgment of its own power and prerogative, and in that split second Alex's spirit collapsed, and he wanted to call time out and restart the day, the week, the year, his whole damn life all over again, so that it could wind its way down a different path and leave him somewhere other than where he was right then, naked and sweating in the presence of an authority figure who was devolving predictably into dickishness. For some reason he shot a glance over to where the *Wall Street Journal* had been sitting. The wet spot had completely evaporated.

"What's your name?" said the man.

"Alex," said Alex.

"Alex what?" said the man.

"Alex Fader," said Alex. He felt helpless and terrified, and half imagined he was about to be marched, in his moist nudity, back down to the very front desk he had sauntered past a hour ago.

"Well, take care of yourself, Alex." With this the man stood, folded his paper, raked Alex with one last leering glance, and departed the sauna.

Alex sat in there for a long time afterwards in the hopes he wouldn't have to see the guy again in the locker room. When he couldn't take it anymore he emerged and found himself standing by the pool, dazed, watching an old man swim laps. The old man swam very slowly. He was doing the crawl. His palms slapped the water, and each time he lifted his head for air he gasped terribly, as though this breath would be his last.

What Ever Happened
to the Yippies?

IT WAS A BRIGHT WINTER DAY FRANTIC WITH HOLIDAY shoppers, the sun so high and sharp and fierce it was hard to grasp that in just a few hours a brutally purple dusk would envelop the city, and Alex was walking down a particularly barren stretch of Crosby Street, desolate but for himself and a woman walking in his direction, being led by her dog.

He had just left the mayhem of Soho and was heading towards the mayhem of Canal Street, where he was hoping to find some unusual presents among the industrial stores. It had taken a while, but he had finally reached the moment of grown-upness when gifts were as fun to give as to get. He was twenty-four.

Unfortunately you could only give a gift once you actually *had* one, which usually required purchasing something. The streets were filled with people for whom the pleasant post-Thanksgiving episode of whimsical thoughts about just what to give whom had morphed into an anxiety-ridden dash for any suitable present. Alex was walking around town and peering into every store window he passed with a wild and slightly ravenous expression, like someone who has lost their keys and irrationally scans the sidewalk everywhere he goes in the hope of spotting them lying on the ground. To one shopkeeper after another he said, "No thanks, just looking," when what he wanted to say was "No, you cannot help me!"

He was shopping for his girlfriend and his mother. This made things more complicated than was necessary. He looked at blouses and sweaters and little handbags and big shoulder bags and hats and cameo brooches, and his uncertain sense of aesthetics was greatly confused by who, exactly, would be wearing the thing. No sooner did he decide *I am shopping for my mother* than he saw something that might suit his girlfriend. It worked the other way, too.

The lady with the dog brought him out of his reverie.

She was a thin, pale woman in a navy-blue peacoat, and she was struggling to control her feisty Doberman pinscher. The dog pulled her forward, faster than she wanted to go. She leaned back against the leash, like a sailor hiking out on a boat, and her shoes clapped flatly against the pavement as she lurched forward. "Billy!" she gasped. "No!"

This image—the dog straining forward, the woman leaning back, and the taut line of the leash connecting them—stirred something within him. The dog's ears were wrapped in white tape, and he tried to remember the reason that Doberman's ears were sometimes wrapped up like that. Then, from out of the depths, sprang a memory: yippies.

IT HAD BEEN a day of business and infiltration, a freezing cold Saturday of empty streets which, given the nature of his errand, made Alex uneasy.

Alex, at fourteen, had already made up his mind about crowds—they offered a feast of solitude and anonymity. In a crowd he felt like a spy; in public he felt private. And he liked the strange flashes of empathy with strangers that invariably occurred: an exchanged look, a nod, a few words of commiseration, a door held open, a bus seat relinquished; these moments were like the sea parting so that the ocean floor, and all its mysterious treasure, was briefly laid bare for a glimpse. Then it closed back up, and he was safe in the anonymous street.

He took the subway down to Bleecker Street and walked east. Bleecker Street was empty, and he felt exposed. On Mott Street he stopped at a pay phone, removed the piece of paper, and dialed the number.

"Research," said a voice. It was a surreptitious and preoccupied voice, a small nervous voice.

"This is Alex Fader. I'm just down the block. I'm a friend of Walker Eggfield's. He took me to your place about a month ago and you said I could come by if I called ahead."

"You alone?" said the voice.

"Yes," said Alex.

"Friend of Eggfield?"

"Yes," said Alex.

"Hold on."

Alex held on.

"You wearing a green army jacket?"

"Yes," said Alex, and looked down the block, towards where Bleecker met the Bowery, expecting to see a head sticking out a window, looking at him. He didn't see it.

"Come on by," said the voice.

Alex walked the last short block until he came to a red doorway with a small black sign on it that read "Research Laboratories."

He rang the bell. Across the street was a ramshackle storefront above which was a wooden sign, painted in swirls of loopy colors, that said "Yippies." He remembered leaving the building with Walker a month earlier, nearly floating out the front door, and Walker exclaiming, "That's where the yippies live."

He had been too stoned to ask what a yippie was.

The yippies sign was painted in the psychedelic style, with colorful letters, but the colors were faded and the sign looked beat-up. A metal gate was pulled across the front window, which had been covered from the inside with paper so no one could see inside. It seemed a bit like a fortress, a conspicuous outpost of rebels and holdouts against . . . something. But it was a futile fortress. The yippies had clearly been overrun. Or maybe whatever they were holding out against was no longer there.

The door at Research buzzed. He entered a small space that resembled a prison holding cell; a bare lightbulb hung from the ceiling, and there was a steel door in front of him to go along with the steel door that had just clicked shut behind him. The black eye of a video monitor peered down at him, a wire threading up out of it like a raised eyebrow. He had a moment of fear and apprehension; then the second door buzzed and he pushed it open. A long creaky flight of unlit wooden stairs rose before him. After three steps a dog appeared at the top of the stairs and started barking. It was a Doberman pinscher. Its skin was sleek and brown. Its ears had been taped up with white tape. Its teeth were also white. There were a lot of teeth and a lot of barking.

"Arnie! Get over here!" came a woman's voice. The dog kept barking at an amazing volume. "Jesus fucking Christ," said the woman, and her white arms appeared around the dog's brown neck and wrestled him away.

When Alex got to the top of the stairs he was standing in a rough loft space. Light streamed in through the windows at the far end, but their bottom half was painted black, so the room felt dim. Two men sat at a table down towards the windows, and beside them a woman was bent over the dog, stroking it and whispering in its taped ear. Alex marched apprehensively in their direction. When he arrived, the woman walked past him without saying anything, leaving the dog, and disappeared in back.

"Have a seat," said the man behind the desk. He had thinning curly hair and small eyes hidden behind wire-rim glasses. "I'm Roy. Have you seen the menu?"

He handed Alex a menu.

Alex sat in one of the chairs. On top of the table was a scale and a pile of pot, a huge fortune of marijuana. Roy pushed his glasses back up his nose again and again even when they hadn't slid down. It was like people who spend all their time flicking the cigarette between their fingers even when there is absolutely no ash.

"What's your name again?"

"Alex."

"Alex, Alex, Alex," he muttered. He didn't look at Alex directly. His lips were wet and red. There was something a little shriveled and prunelike about him, but also he radiated a certain odd warmth. "So how's Eggfield?" he said suddenly, looking at Alex.

"He's all right," said Alex.

"Eggfield's crazy, isn't he?" said Roy to no one in particular. He said it to the table, as if he were talking to the pot. "He's a good kid. But crazy. I can tell."

"He's always seemed pretty together to me," said Alex.

"Huh?" said Roy. He looked at Alex very hard, nearly squinting, as though just noticing for the first time he was there. "What can I do for you? Have you seen the menu? Have a look at the menu. Levi, this is . . . kid, what's your name?"

"Alex."

"Hi," said Levi, and they shook hands.

Levi wore an army jacket and faded jeans and combat boots and a yarmulke. He had a beard. His face was heavily lined but he also looked young. He sat with an unlit joint between his fingers, which were nubby and nail-bitten. He looked like a badly lapsed rabbi.

"So anyway," said Levi. "Dylan was there, and we were all wondering when the next bus was coming, and there was the whole question . . ."

"Of who was going to get on the bus," said Roy.

"Exactly," said Levi. "We were all committed to very specific projects, so one of us was going to have to drop everything . . ."

"And follow the motherfucker," said Roy.

"Exactly," said Levi. He reached over to the table for a lighter, flicked it, and lit up the joint. After he took a long drag he held it out to Roy, who then held it out to Alex.

Alex looked up from the menu. It was like a menu at a restaurant except instead of food the menu listed different kinds of pot—Acapulco, Colombian, Panama Red, and Thai Stick—along with an assortment of mushrooms and acid. The last time he had been here with Walker they had bought some Thai and it had gotten them and quite a few of their friends incredibly stoned.

Alex had subsequently, and with Walker's permission, called all his friends and taken orders for more, collecting the money in advance, and was now holding a fairly large sum of cash in preparation for a major score. Part of him thought he should be straight so he could figure things out and be clear about what was what, especially since the whole business involved fractions—each of his friends had signed on for an eighth—and he was terrible at math. The other part of him wanted to get stoned.

He took a hit of the joint and held his breath. The two men kept talking in the fairly paranoid, abstract, and unintelligible way they had been, while Alex tried to concentrate and figure out how much of what he wanted to buy.

"Kid," said Roy. "You know the rules, right?"

"I think so," said Alex.

"The rules are you never come without calling first, you never bring anyone without telling me first, and you don't smoke anything near this building. And you don't tell people where you got it. Okay?"

"Okay."

The phone rang.

"Research," said Roy. "I'm not going to talk to you about Nixon," he said into the phone. Alex watched him chew his lips. He was very anxious. What Nixon had to do with pot he couldn't imagine. He listened some more. "It's all going into the book. You can read about it when I'm finished." He put the phone down. "Fucking parasites," he said.

As soon as he put the phone down it rang again.

"Research," he said. "You alone?" he said. "Hold on."

He stood up and went to the window, opened it, stuck his head out very quickly for a peek down the block, then came back to the phone. "Come on over," he said.

Then he turned to Alex.

"So," he said. "What can I do for you?"

———

NOTHING MUCH WAS different after having smoked. But it was.
He became more aware of the dog sitting quietly at Roy's feet.
The long emptiness of the loft became theatrical and fraught with
possibilities. The air had an earthy, dank smell, the smell of things
rotting and growing. His thoughts began to burn and tingle; he
felt like the edge of a piece of paper that was catching fire. The
thoughts and sensations rushed faster and faster. It was as if his
thoughts were asteroids appearing from the future, smashing
against the hot protective atmosphere of reality and exploding in
balls of fire. The point where the future turned into the past was
right in front of his nose and everything kept rushing marvelously
past him and then it was gone.

There was no hurry, apparently. Alex watched another customer, a wiry man with a baseball cap and a mellow demeanor,
come and go, making a quick order for a half ounce of Panama
Red. Then a fat man in a suit with a head of dense curly hair,
much denser and thicker than Roy's, came in with another guy in
a long trench coat. They asked for an ounce in accents that were
so heavily inflected with mobsterese that Alex thought it was a
joke. Then they proceeded to tell—or rather the fat guy told,
while the other guy stood silently behind him listening and nodding—about how he was recently in a shootout and had been
shot in the leg. "I had no choice but to go into a roll," he said. "So
I got hit in the leg instead of the stomach, which was good,
because the stomach *burns*, let me tell ya." Then he lifted his
pants leg and there was a white gauze bandage and he lifted that
off and there was a round bloody hole scabbing over. It was about
the most thrillingly gross thing Alex had ever seen.

"So then I take out my piece and get off like five shots." At this
he reached under his jacket and removed a handgun, pointed it at
some imaginary enemy at the wall, and went, "Pow pow pow pow!"

"Whoa, man! Hey! Hey! Put that away! Jesus," said Roy.

"That was only four shots," said Levi.

"Whateva," said the mobster, and put the gun back. "That's how it went, right?" His accent no longer seemed like a joke.

The man in the trench coat nodded.

What followed was a long session of misunderstanding between the mobster and Roy, who by comparison was a sweet innocent guy, hardly a criminal at all, more like a neighborly hot dog vendor.

Roy said, "The ounce is on the house," and tossed a plastic baggie of pot across at the mobster, who put his money down, which required Roy to clarify that the pot was for free, to which the mobster replied that he wanted to pay for an ounce, to which Roy said, "No, I insist, really."

Finally what became apparent was that if Roy was giving an ounce away, then the mobster would take a second ounce too, and pay for that one; just from looking at him his general ethos seemed to be the more the better. It took a long time to work out, because everyone was either very stoned or stupid or both.

When the mobster left, Roy sighed and went to the back and returned with a drink. "It's a lime rickey," he said to Alex and Levi. "You guys want one? It keeps the blood sugar up."

Alex and Levi both declined. Alex took a look at Levi sitting there in his army jacket, then looked down at his own. An army jacket was about being really pissed off at some unnamable corruption in the world. It was Alex's prize possession.

The thing about it he so liked was the multitude of pockets inside and outside, of different shapes and sizes, into which he stuffed money, or tissues, or gum, or whatever.

He liked it so much he had worn it all through the previous sweltering summer, in the middle of which he had been mugged. Two boys threw him into an alley and pressed him against the wall. They frisked him while one of them put his wide palm on Alex's mouth so he wouldn't scream. He didn't intend to scream but meanwhile he couldn't breathe. The two kids were wearing tank tops. One of them had a big afro. They had tan skin, very pale, and were very lean. They pushed their fingers into the army jacket's myriad pockets. This went on for about five minutes. Alex stood there trying to breathe through this kid's palm. Eventually he was getting very short of breath and just pointed to the pocket within which was about four dollars. At the time he felt vaguely proud of his jacket for its powers of concealment. He brushed himself off and watched as they ran down the street with the long loping strides of happy antelopes. He thought they were beautiful, and right away he knew there was something strange about this thought.

Later, when he got upstairs, he went to take a pee, and while he was standing there in the soft bathroom sunlight, with the warm summer air on his skin, watching the pee go into the toilet bowl, he was suddenly convulsed with tears. It was weird how it happened that way.

Finally Roy turned to Alex and asked, "What can I do for you?"

He had told Roy how much he wanted (three-quarters of an ounce, all in eighths) and had put his money on the table when a young girl emerged from a back room somewhere and ambled up to the table with a leash in hand. She had dirty-blond hair and freckles and very wide and, Alex thought, experienced eyes. She looked very mature for a kid, like one of those extremely precocious children who have to wait around through most of their youth until they're old enough to have experiences they have for a long time been ready to have.

"Here, pookie," she said. She nudged the dog with her foot. It growled. "Come on, kiddo. Time for a walk."

The dog scumbled spastically to its feet. She put the leash on.

"Do you need anything from the store?" she said to Roy.

He asked for a Coke.

Alex walked out with her. The cold afternoon air braced his red cheeks. Everything was spinning, and there, again, across the street, was the swirly yippies sign, sitting mysteriously above the ramshackle storefront that looked already like something discovered on an archaeological dig far off in the future. The girl yanked the dog in one direction and the dog yanked her in the other. Alex, stoned as hell, wanted very much to ask her what the yippies were. He thought she would know. He thought she could explain all sorts of things to him.

Instead he watched her and the dog engage in a game of tug-of-war. Only for a moment did she let her eyes flicker across his face, and he thought he saw a hint of embarrassment in them, that she couldn't make the dog walk in her direction, that she had a pot dealer for a father, and other things.

"So, um," Alex began.

"Arnie!" she screamed.

"I was wondering . . ."

But he was too shy, and she was too preoccupied with the dog, and maybe too shy as well, and eventually she pulled Arnie in the direction of the Bowery. Alex watched them turn the corner. Arnie, previously so reluctant, was now dragging her forward.

He walked west, in the opposite direction, towards the subway. He had the pot stashed in one of the pockets of his army jacket. The sky was purple. His career as a pot dealer was getting off to an excellent start—in the upcoming days he would take each baggie and, for some inexplicable reason, wrap it up in a piece of paper so that they looked like white batons. On each one he carefully wrote out the name of the recipient in neat script as though it were a present to be handed out at Hanukkah. When he got to school he convened everyone at lunchtime and it was as though he were giving out gifts. He realized this was something his mother would do, make things nice like that, make them special, and it revolted him a little to think of the overlap of dealing pot and his mother.

The connection was weirdly present, though.

A year earlier she had found a nickel bag in one of the pockets of his army jacket one day while he was at school, and confronted him when he came home. It was the first one he had ever bought, and it seemed grossly unfair that he should be busted on his first time.

Her face was furious and grave. The nickel bag sat on the kitchen table. She had washed the jacket and found it. It sat there connecting two parts of the world that were not supposed to connect. The expression on his mother's face caused him grief. It was as though *she* was hurting herself over this nickel bag; she was making this tiny object inflict a kind of physical pain on herself that he couldn't help but feel, too.

"What is that?" she said, and didn't take her eyes from his. It was obvious she knew what it was. Yet it wasn't. His mother was so damn uncool. He examined the possibilities of an incredible fabrication. Could he say it was pipe tobacco or maybe some weird thing he had stolen from the chemistry lab? Or that he didn't know what it was? For a moment he wanted to laugh, to giggle.

"It's marijuana, isn't it?" said his mother. Her voice was flat and devoid of the slight musicality which drove him insane with annoyance and also was an essential bedrock of comfort and stability and sanity for him. Her voice was that of a prosecutor, though she couldn't even pull that off. It had too much emotion for a prosecutor. She was in an agony over this.

"Mom . . ." he said, trailing.

"Are you smoking this?" And then, very loud: "I want you to

answer me!" The voice was horrible. Huge and fiery. She trembled with rage. It cut him to some place he hardly knew existed. Again, amidst his terror, a strange desire to laugh overtook him. He breathed deeply.

"Look," he said. "This is just an experiment. Someone gave that to me. I forgot I even had it. I tried it once. All right? But I didn't like it. I don't care about it." She was listening. Her brow was furrowed with concern. It was just a nickel bag. Why was everything such a big deal! But he stayed calm. A little progress had been made, and he had to capitalize on it. There was something about the sheer intensity of his mother's focus on him that gave him the confidence of a performer who knows he has his audience's entire undivided attention.

"It was just a freak accident, me having this. I don't want it." He picked it up. "I want to throw it out." The look of relief that came over her face, slight yet perceptible, was heartbreaking. She didn't want this little bag of pot to exist any more than he did.

He went to the garbage with it, lifted the lid, and watched the bag fall into the garbage pail with a little thump, like a tea bag. Then he shut the pail. She still had that look. He opened the pail, retrieved the little pregnant envelope, and upended it, pouring the leaves down. The bag fluttered down after the pot.

"See?" he said. She had come to stand beside him. The look of pain was still etched in her brow, and around her mouth, and he was suddenly hurt and terrified by it, worried that it wouldn't go away.

"I'm sorry, Mom," he said, and was aware simultaneously of being dishonest and manipulative with her, wanting to smooth this aberration over, and also of a nearly excruciating realness of his feelings, a brightness of his own emotion which he could hardly bear. "I'm sorry, Mom," he said again, and they hugged. And then he finally was converted. He no longer wanted to lie to her, no longer wanted to later retreat into the camaraderie of a retold parental bust story with Nick and Walker, but was truly penitent. The reformist urge swept through him like fire.

NOW, WALKING DOWN Bleecker Street, he vowed to be incredibly cautious about his current stash. That night he returned home, got past his mother safely, and hid the pot. The army jacket was laid on a chair, and he watched television, a quiet Saturday night in front of the television. There was a local news program on. A special feature on a guy who went through garbage. He wore a three-piece suit and pushed his glasses up on the bridge of his nose again and again. There was a ridiculous scene of this man walking down a well-groomed street in his suit, pausing before a set of garbage pails, casting that particular kind of shoplifter's look-around before reaching in and grabbing a garbage bag, and then sprinting down the block at full speed and jumping into a waiting van that sped away, as though it were a bank robbery.

The man had just stolen some of Richard Nixon's garbage. He had stolen Bob Dylan's garbage, too. It was, he told the reporter, an important form of academic research.

"JESUS, ROY, YOU'RE famous!" Alex said when he next saw him. "I had no idea."

"This is why you have to be careful, kid. Don't go blabbing that everywhere," he said. "I don't want you ruining my reputation." But he seemed pleased that Alex had discovered this other life of his.

Over the next couple of years they became friendly, though Alex only bought small quantities for personal use. His dealing career had ended abruptly shortly after it started.

"I don't want people to think of me as a dealer," he had confided to Walker, and Walker, ever the rationalist, had responded, "Then you shouldn't sell them drugs." So he didn't.

He became an old-timer at Roy's. He accepted his lime rickeys. He occasionally saw Levi, who was always agitated about the lenient, pacifist position of the Jewish Defense League and babbling on at high speed about wire tapes, trails, the CIA. It was a peculiar mixture of radical Zionism and radical antiestablishmentarianism, and Alex assumed it was a folly. He watched Arnie the dog get older, and learned that puppy Dobermans get their ears taped because it makes them stand straight up for the rest of their lives. He watched a certain blank look of fatigue etch itself deeper and deeper into the face of the woman who had first pulled Arnie away. But he never saw the girl with the freckles again, and could never bring himself to ask about her.

Years after he had last seen Roy, Alex saw a picture in a newspaper of a man leaning out a window, firing a rifle at the police. The accompanying article explained that the man had been holed up in an abandoned building on Bleecker Street and was making demands regarding the security situation of Israel. The rifle was an AK-47. He wanted to negotiate with the State Department. They fired tear gas into the building and brought him out choking. No police were injured in his capture. It was Levi.

NOW, ON FREEZING Crosby Street, a woman desperately holding on to her dog staggered past him, and it all came rushing back and sprang up before him like a hologram. He saw Roy, and the long creaky staircase that led up to the loft, and the excited and clueless face of the boy he used to be, and the expression of that girl holding on to her dog. He saw the expression on his mother's face as she watched him pour the nickel bag into the garbage, as though by the force of her will she would make him upend time along with the nickel bag.

The woman in the peacoat passed him in the other direction, still struggling to control her dog. He felt perched on the edge of a reunion of some kind, but it wasn't the same girl, and he didn't even know what it was, exactly, that he would be reuniting with. The past refused to cohere into any explicable pattern, it merely surfaced briefly to wave merrily at him, the way two acquaintances might wave to each other from two escalators, one going up and the other down.

He wanted to say something to this woman, but couldn't think what.

"Hey!" he called out after her, and his voice echoed against the cast-iron buildings. "What ever happened to the yippies?"

But of course she didn't answer, or even turn around.

Stay

(On Falling Asleep in the Company of Another Person)

SHE WAS AWAKE WHEN HE CAME HOME. IT WAS A HOT summer night, and he had been to Blanche's.

Blanche's was a smoky bar with a pool table and relatively cheap drinks that had very little to distinguish itself from every other cheap bar in the world, except it was Alex's first bar, and like all firsts it was special. There were several things to recommend it: the noise, the smoke, the fairly regular group of youngish hipsters who could be found there, and the fact that it was on Avenue A. The entire East Village was a new world for Alex, and on almost every night since school ended he had commuted there on his bicycle from his home on the Upper West Side.

Interesting things often happened on the ride there or back. Once, at Seventh Avenue and Thirtieth Street, he saw a gang of kids pelting passing cars with orange rinds. A store that sold fresh-squeezed orange juice had put out bags of already squeezed oranges, and these kids, who were all black, with bony elbows and ecstatic smiles, were throwing them like snowballs. They threw oranges at Alex. He thought it was sort of funny, and at the same time he was antagonized, and so about half a block past them, when an orange thudded against him, he stopped, picked it up, and threw it back.

What followed was a small riot in which twenty or so kids chased him for blocks throwing anything they could get their hands on, including bottles. The glass smashed around him. Something sharp hit his shoulder. He enjoyed the whole thing.

NOW IT WAS almost morning, and his mother was working. She was sitting at the small typing desk in the study, which was surrounded by several other even smaller tables on which open books and papers were stacked haphazardly, an arrangement which made her seem like the navigator of a very disheveled spaceship, surrounded by her maps and controls. She looked up at him when he poked his head through the door.

This was their new ritual, these late-night encounters in which they each occupied a certain terrain of semiwakefulness. It was too late for it to be night, but too early to be morning. The days were hot and sweltering, except for this one sweet spot of cool that started around four in the morning and ended near seven. It was in this cool sweet spot that they intersected, as she began her day and he prepared to end his. He always found it jarring to encounter his mother in this manner; she was fragile in that newly awoken way and he was hardened by prolonged exposure to the world and its elements: the cool night air, the smell of cigarette and, more faintly, marijuana smoke on his clothes, loud music, and the twisted force field of girls. He considered the world and its elements and his mother to be two separate spheres of existence. Particularly the world of girls.

Not girls touched, but girls thought about, obsessed about, fantasized about. An actual embrace would have seemed quite wholesome and innocent compared to the images that ran through his mind all night as his eyes wandered over faces and bodies.

SHE WAS STILL moist with sleep and in her nightgown, which was made of some mysterious white cloth that cloaked her body and made it vague and shapeless, but which also had a somewhat gauzy transparency, within which the outline of her body was almost discernible. On the whole, he wished she had a more sturdy nightgown. She was as much a vapor as a person, and if she was not properly clothed then she would seep out into the immediate atmosphere and he would inhale her. He didn't want to inhale his mother.

"You're back," she said, stating the obvious. Her electric typewriter might have seemed vaguely state-of-the-art several years earlier, but now seemed antique, like a completely wrong prediction of the future. Her right index finger was poised above the keyboard, pointing down. This was how she typed. With one finger.

"You're working," he said, stating the equally obvious. In both of their comments there was a mixture of warmth and criticism. She felt he ought not to be out so late, and he felt she ought not to be working so early.

"Did you have a nice night?" she asked. There was a conspicuously false note in her voice. It was his summer of not being a high school student. He had yet to become a college student. He wasn't really sure what he was, and neither, he sensed, was she. Was she supposed to let him go be an adult already?

Did you have a nice night?

He made a quick inventory of what was false about it: (1) She was trying to sound awake. (2) She was trying to sound as though she had acclimated herself to this idea of him coming and going as he pleased at all hours. (3) She was trying to sound lighthearted and vaguely uninterested; she was affecting the casual tone of a peer, a friend, but parents are not the same as friends, however much they might approximate the role.

The stiffness of her language reminded him of the time that he had complained, at the age of six, about her bedtime stories. They were all populated by an old wizened man with a long white beard who lived in a dense forest, into which a prince or princess would wander, that kind of thing. And they all began with the phrase "Once upon a time." He found that opening gambit to be somehow false, inaccurate, insufficiently American. Even at the age of six, he possessed the uneasy feeling that his mother was out of sync and living apart from the world he was living in. He wanted her to describe a world more recognizable as his own.

"Tell me a story about Superman," he asked. There was a long pause.

"Once upon a time . . ." she began.

SHORTLY AFTER HIS father died, in those hot days of early summer, he had made her promise that she would not see other men. He did not understand sex explicitly, as he was only ten years old, or rather he *only* understood it explicitly, but he conveyed the idea that he did not want other men around.

What followed was about four more years of her putting him to bed. This was a cherished ritual of youth, though it only became exceptionally vivid to Alex after his father died. They called a putting-to-bed session a "stay." In their household, "stay" was a noun.

They talked about all kinds of things during the stay, or rather he talked and she mostly listened. He talked with his eyes closed, while he held her hand, long rambling half-asleep ruminations of the difference between never and forever.

Not long after his father died he said, "I know that at some point in the future I'll have hairy legs and that you won't make a stay anymore."

The stays did indeed last up to the advent of hair on his legs, and when they petered out, coincidentally, he rescinded his ultimatum, and told his mother that he wouldn't mind if she saw other men. But, as far as he knew, she hadn't.

How had she taken this bit of revised policy? He didn't know. She seemed to take the first ultimatum fairly seriously, because as far as he could tell there were no other men. She went on dates. But he had a very straightforward conception of dates. There were concerts and dinners and maybe even some flowers in dates. But there was no sex.

Once he had returned from school—this was after the ultimatum had been rescinded—and found a man sitting at the kitchen table with his mother. He wore a white linen shirt—not like a businessman, but open at the top, with a bandanna around his neck—and had a riotous tangle of gray hair that was tossed to one side of his head. He had—and this made a strong impression on Alex for some reason—hair in his nostrils. He noticed that on the table, in addition to the various meats from Zabar's and cheeses and bread that surfaced whenever there were guests, there was a small bowl of water in which floated rose petals. They were red.

Based on this information he concluded that his mother was in some way involved with this man. He said hello to the man, felt his own body being strafed by what, he felt, was a scrutinizing, admiring, and respectful glance from the man. He felt the appropriate action would be to show, if not approval exactly, then some sign that this man was acceptable. Perhaps this is how fathers feel when their daughters bring home dates. Alex searched within himself for the necessary magnanimity, found it, and chatted amicably for a few minutes before heading to his room. For a period of weeks, maybe a couple of months, Alex could sense this man's presence in his mother's life, though he never saw him again. He could sense it in the abundance of flowers around the house, in the way his mother got ready to go out, in a certain something about her. Then he was gone, or his aura was gone, and it was never remarked upon. It occurred to Alex that the episode might have caused his mother pain. He hated to think it, but he was sure it had, somehow.

That was a couple of years earlier. Now his mother had descended into a tunnel of work, an impossible project about the origins of World War I that was destined to turn her, he thought, into a madwoman. It was a grand and historical book. It required research, interviews. He wondered if he would like it better if his mother, instead of becoming this mad Don Quixote in a nightdress awake at four in the morning, had done the normal thing, remarried, and if now there were some strange guy with nose hair walking around the house in his underwear, living here. It occurred to him that once he was in college it would all be different for his mother, there would be no one in the house whose privacy or space or anything had to be accommodated, and she might behave differently with regard to men. On the other hand, she might just be lonely.

"Don't you have a bedtime?" he said now, leaning against the doorframe.

She laughed.

"Don't *you* have a bedtime?" she said.

"No," he said. "I'm all grown up. What's your excuse?"

She laughed again.

They stayed there for a moment, grinning dumbly at each other.

"Well, have a nice night," he said.

"And you have a nice morning," she said.

They both laughed with the peculiar camaraderie of a night watchman turning over the shift to the day watchman, with the tacit understanding that what they were guarding was each other.

Vas *Is* Dat?

THE BIG DAY ARRIVED AT LAST. ALL THE BOXES HAD BEEN shipped in advance. There was only one small suitcase to suggest that she was going somewhere—that and her two nephews, Karl and Alex, sitting over cups of coffee and talking soothingly at her about "the trip." She was wearing a floral-print dress and her nice shoes. Esmeralda, the housekeeper-turned-nurse, had helped her apply some lipstick. Finally they coaxed her out the front door of her apartment and into the elevator.

She emerged from the elevator, a nephew supporting her on either side, and stepped cautiously onto the lobby's marble floor, as though it were ice. This lobby she had walked through for thirty years was now traversed with an acute sense of ceremony, as if she were getting married. She seemed to understand the absurdity of it, the slightly royal atmosphere of a processional, with the morbid undertones of someone being led to her death, but she didn't seem to grasp that she would never see this place again. A white stretch limousine sat at the curb, waiting for her.

"Well, Aunti B," said Karl. "Whaddaya think?"

The B stood for Beatrice. Her brow furrowed, she frowned, and against this improbable facial scenery she began to laugh that particular steam-escaping-from-a-pipe laugh that someone who didn't know her might initially mistake for crying. Her laugh seemed to express a kind of relief and gratitude that against all odds the world had managed to deliver one more absurd surprise.

"Vas *is* dat?" she said.

The driver, in white shirt and black tie, came around and opened the door. For a long she time refused to get in. Karl coaxed her in his not-so-gentle baritone.

"Come on, Aunti B, we're going for a ride in a stretch limo! You'll love it! Tons of leg room!"

Alex stood there, rendered mute by the sight of this last ridiculous extravagance of Karl's, who was not content to merely hire a stretch limousine for the last person in the world who needed extra leg room, but a *white* one, as though she were going to the Academy Awards and not to a nursing home in Pennsylvania. Also, his aunt was still holding on to his forearm with her small hand, and it was as though he needed all his strength to bear the weight of this tiny woman. She started to cry. But then she stopped abruptly. She suddenly seemed quite pleased to get in the limo, and at the last second a look of impatience crossed her face, as if she had been waiting a long time for this white stretch limo to show up and it was about time it did! Esmeralda got in after her—she was going to help smooth the transition—and then Karl. He and Alex exchanged a look. Alex wasn't sure if it meant good luck, or goodbye, or neither, or both.

WHEN THE LIMO was gone, Alex went back up to her apartment. The harsh light of the hallway was replaced by the dim, dreamy morning light that made its way through the dirty windows. It was very quiet, except for the sound of children playing in the alley. He closed the door behind him, leaned against it, and marveled that the place was now his. It was the sort of one-bedroom apartment that real-estate agents, in their inflationary use of language, might call gigantic. Or *huge*. But it faced another building, and in between was an alley where the neighborhood kids played.

He stood looking over the topography of the living room. A roll of tape and scissors sat on the coffee table. Otherwise the apartment looked untroubled. His aunt might as well have stepped out for some groceries.

He took a deep breath, and with it came the apartment's distinct aroma, not unpleasant exactly, but a *smell*, something one noticed as soon as one walked in the front door, that little pheromonal clue that you have arrived on someone's turf. If it's your own smell it can be exquisitely comforting. If it is someone else's it can be repulsive. This was somewhere in between. Somehow, he thought, he would have to get rid of that smell.

In order for him to live in the apartment it had to be clean. Not just clean of dirt, or grime, but clean of *history*.

HE PAINTED THE bedroom. He chose a buttery yellow for the walls, white for the ceiling and trim. He felt grateful for the over-

powering smell of the paint. There were dark finger smudges on
the doorframes. They were where she had reached out to steady
herself day after day. He put on a layer of paint, but the dark
smudges persisted. He put on layer after layer of white paint,
until at last the smudges were gone.

Then came the living room. The obvious thing to do was dis-
pose of the rug. It was an ungodly orange, something toxic, a
color so belligerently cheerful as to be manic-depressive. That
orange rug had absorbed an enormous amount of his aunt's atmosphere. Like his aunt, it did not go without a fight. He wrestled
with it and barely managed to get it into a massive roll. It struggled against him as though it were a person whom he was trying
to kidnap. Finally he got some tape around its top and bottom.
He had it bound and gagged. He dragged it out the back door
and dropped it next to the service elevator.

In the living room there remained a desk, couch, coffee table,
bookshelves, and a bunch of lamps. It was the sort of Scandina-
vian wood furniture that was fashionable when his aunt had decorated the place in the early sixties, and it was once again
percolating into the realm of super fashionability. But Alex didn't
know that, and would not have cared. He *did* exist in the world of
irony and trends and fashion and the lovely brimming surface of
popular culture, but that was in another life, a parallel universe to
the one in which he stood. There was no irony here, only the
ghost of his aunt, and others.

He got rid of the lamps by putting all five of them out on the
sidewalk on Amsterdam Avenue in the middle of the night. Traffic
rushed by in waves. Three table lamps and two standing lamps sat
there on the sidewalk like a family, two parents presiding over the
three children. At the last moment, as he was turning away, he
saw how beautiful one of the standing lamps was—a slender shaft
of dark wood on top of which glowed the crescent of a low

moon. It looked exposed and beautiful, like a woman whose bare arms are shivering on a cool night. He took it back upstairs.

He now had one lamp for the living room. The result was dim and atmospheric.

He moved the furniture around in an attempt to make the place less her place and more his own. He took the couch and put it where the desk was. He took the desk and put it where the couch was. They switched sides and were now looking at each other from opposite directions.

ALL HIS LIFE Alex had visited his Aunti B rarely and reluctantly. This was because:

Her apartment was dark.

It had a strange smell.

She had a limp.

She was a complainer, a nag, but not in any big-picture way— she didn't write to Congress demanding the world be made a better place; she wrote to the landlord castigating him for the drip in her kitchen sink. Also, she was a glarer. Medusa had nothing on these glares.

She was the sort of person for whom the word "difficult" was used diplomatically by those closest to her; those less close used words less diplomatic.

Alex vividly recalled an argument between Aunti B and his father, years after it happened, and marveled at the power she was able to exert over his normally implacable dad, whose temper, though simmering palpably below the surface, flared so rarely. She was over for dinner—a relatively infrequent event— and had made an idle remark about the red wine. Alex didn't hear the remark, but assumed it was disparaging. Even at seven he had a keen ear for his aunt's disparaging remarks and also for the slight comic edge underlying them, as though she knew there was an element of absurdity in her constantly judging everything to be lacking. For his father, however, the humor was a little too subtle on that occasion, or too familiar, and he responded sharply. Voices were raised. Alex watched his father's neck redden in a way he had never seen before, starting just above the shoulders and rising up through his neck and then his face. It wasn't pink like a blush. It was darker, more ominous, like the red wine.

What could make his father so angry? Why would he boil over with rage like that?

There was something about her voice that naturally rose to a volume just a touch too loud, that took on a tone that was a little too insistent, and it was made even more contentious, perhaps, by that Viennese accent. She had a voice that suggested that all things being equal she would be just as happy to argue as to talk.

"Tell me something about Vienna," he once asked her.

"The Viennese," she said, "are great haters."

But she did not hate Alex. In fact her love for him was undiluted and unqualified. She lived frugally, but on his birthday and at Hanukkah he received from her a healthy check, which grew in proportion to his age, and during his freshman year in college she made a generous loan without hesitation. There was something deliciously reckless about those checks. It wasn't even the sum that impressed him. It was her handwriting. Sometimes you can tell in what spirit a check was written just from the handwriting. Her checks were always written in an unbounded spirit of generosity.

THERE WERE CERTAIN rituals observed, unintentionally, whenever he visited her. These rituals were at once a comfort and a source of agony. They charmed him and they made him cringe. They included, but were not limited to:

The Lock Symphony. She had three locks on her door, and it was difficult, for reasons he never understood, to get them all unlocked at once, so he always spent a period of time in the hall listening to the locks click this way and that with periodic tugs at the still-locked door.

The way that when she finally got the door open she would look up and then farther up, very conspicuously, because he had grown much taller than she was, and she never tired of making a display of amazement at his height.

The way that when her eyes met his she burst into that strange weeping laugh of hers.

The way she always insisted on cooking for him. Sometimes she made gnocchi, which he loved, and which, she said, her own mother used to make, and sometimes just chicken and rice, which she loved, but which her mother did not make, or at least it didn't ever become part of the ongoing commentary that took place as she cooked. "I like rice" was a refrain of hers, almost an anthem. She always laughed when she said it. Nothing could be funnier for Aunti B than the fact that she liked rice.

She seemed to take real pleasure in feeding him, but he found it excruciating to watch her cook. He would sit at the kitchen table and watch her hobble around, adjusting the flame on her old stove, stirring the pots. She couldn't touch an item of food without his imagining her limping through a supermarket, alone, picking it off the shelf and giving it a long and close inspection to make sure it was "the best." This made it impossible for him to enjoy her food, in spite of the fact that he knew how much love went into the making of it, which in turn made him hate himself for hating her food, which further diminished his enjoyment of the food. And also, he understood on some subsonic, gut level that finding that *one* excellent tomato among the many mediocre ones was among the deeply satisfying experiences that life has to offer. Yet his youthful self rebelled at the thought that these little pleasures were in fact one of life's great prizes—that, and having someone with whom to share your tomato.

The one thing that made all this bearable for Alex was that he felt that on some unspoken level Aunti B understood his feelings, and forgave him for them.

Then there was the black-and-white photograph of his father on the living-room table, at which he always stared for a moment. There was a similar picture at his mother's house, but this one was slightly different. The one at his mother's featured his father with a softer expression. This one, taken perhaps a minute before or after the one at his mother's, featured a handsome man with a lined face and black hair that was combed back over his head in what seemed a rakish manner. He was in leisure mode, but pensive. He looked off to the side, lost in thought, absent even in his presence. It seemed appropriate that Aunti B should have this one; it was as if she liked being in the presence of this brooding, ambivalent, handsome, and elusive younger brother.

She often peppered her speech with bits of German, which he enjoyed. Whenever his father had uttered a few words of German it had made Alex convulse with laughter. Why was it so hilariously funny when his father spoke German? He had heard the language spoken in other contexts, and it was the most absolutely unfunny language he had ever heard. But when his father unleashed a few phrases it sent him into hysterics. Her German had a similar if less potent effect.

Aunti B always referred to his father by his childhood nickname, "Sundy." It made Alex happy to hear such an affectionate nickname. "Sundy" was the name for that part of his father's life that was unknowable, when his father was a child and had a child's delights and a child's miseries, and it was also the name for that strange interrupted adolescence when, at the age of fourteen, his father had made a mad dash across a freezing river in the middle of the night, and then found his way across the Italian border, where he met up with his older brother Frank, Karl's father, in Turin. The whole series of events in which his father's family left Vienna, scattered across Europe, and somehow reconvened in New York seemed, in Alex's imagination, to have a zany, madcap quality.

From his Aunti B he received several verbal snapshots of his father as a child, and the image that appeared was of a self-sufficient and somewhat self-absorbed boy with a mischievous and melancholy demeanor. Apparently it was normal back then to bring your own snacks on train rides, and Sundy always arrived with a big bag of apples. The touchstone image of his father's youth was of his serious-faced father sitting on a train, shy, handsome, jet-black hair and mischievous monkey eyes, munching apple after apple down to the core.

SHE TRAVELED TO Europe often, and alone, and sent him postcards. He got a postcard from Vienna once.

"My God," his mother had remarked. "To think how she must have felt walking around that city."

"How do you think she felt?" he asked.

"How do you think it would feel to have to leave where you are from, where you spent your whole childhood, and then years later return, after all that had happened?"

"I don't know," he said.

"Try and imagine," she said.

"I can't," he said.

"Try," she said.

"That's what happened to you," he said. "You don't have to imagine it."

"Yes," she said, "but it's different." She had a slight aversion to talking about her past, which, as he grew older, he found more and more curious.

He couldn't really imagine what either of his parents had gone through before they got to America. The entire convulsion of life that took place in the wake of World War II was something he was prepared—throughout high school and even college—to pay somber lip service to, but could not really engage or grasp. Like most children of immigrants he had a primary, if unconscious, wish to not be an immigrant. He could rattle off certain facts about his parents, but they had no resonance to him. His father had grown up in Vienna, his mother in Israel, though her parents had made a narrow escape from Berlin just after she was born. He understood these dislocations, but they didn't move him. His mother knew this, and he could tell it saddened and angered and heartened her all at once. She played it cool, and waited for that surge of curiosity and gratitude that descends on children as they approach the age their parents were when they were born, and so begin to fathom the hard choices that preceded their existence.

While he was growing up, however, Alex was, as far as he was concerned, an American. And part of being an American, he felt on some level, was thinking only about America.

"Spell it," his father once said, interrupting his eight-year-old boy's recitation of the merits of the Declaration of Independence.

"Spell what?"

"This country you're so fond of."

"A-M-A-R-I . . ."

"The great patriot," said his father. "He can't even spell his own country's name."

"DO YOU *KNOW?*" Aunti B said, her cadence Viennese, Jewish, inquiring, playful.

"Do I know what?"

"Do you know who you look like?"

It wasn't troubling at first, the first hundred or so times. He knew he looked like his father. After the first hundred times, however, it became like Viennese water torture, one innocent question landing again and again on the same spot in his head.

WHEN AUNTI B spoke of "Sundy" her face became warm in a way that was incongruous with her normal, agitated persona. Alex enjoyed basking in the unqualified love his aunt was lavishing not just on himself but on this other young boy whom he did not know but who would through some mysterious act of alchemy evolve into the man who was his father. But for all the pleasures of these moments of love, he felt repulsed by them, too. They provoked in him a strange and nearly carnal disgust for his aunt, for her limp, for the sad frightened way her mouth turned down at the corners, for her accent, for her loneliness and barrenness.

The syntax of her speech was strange, and so too was the entire grammar of her existence. She had never married. She lived alone. She worked as a psychologist at a state mental institution. Alex felt sorry for the patients.

When he left her apartment, a mere fifteen blocks from his own, at the end of his infrequent visits it was always with a sense of relief. Alex would bound down the stairs and burst forth into the unruly life of Amsterdam Avenue feeling as though he had escaped.

From what?

He stayed away from her because they were of the same blood and that made it impossible for him to really take her in, to sample her being in more than the most tiny and intermittent quantities, because there is something impossible about close family with whom your life is not entwined on a day-to-day routine. They are like the sun—warm, nourishing, but too powerful to look at directly. Their secrets are at once a novelty and too familiar. They are an occasion for superficial courtesy and also the fathoming of depths in which lurks some strange shared secret of the blood; they provoke a kind of claustrophobia. Perhaps that is why Alex always preferred the families of his friends: he could swim into their waters and swim out—their secrets couldn't really hurt him.

IN SEVENTH GRADE he spent weekend after weekend at Joe Ford's apartment in the Dakota, an arrangement of high-ceilinged rooms so labyrinthine that Joe's mother, Carol, would sometimes bump into him in a hallway with a surprised expression, as though she hadn't realized he was still in the house. He often went with the Fords to their country house, a weekend farm (someone else ran it), where he was given small chores, just like Joe and his brother, George. One morning he was told to take a pot of leftover cous-cous out to the chickens. He had really loved the cous-cous the previous evening but had eaten only a civilized portion, as he was always on good behavior when a guest. In the chicken shack he stood there throwing meager amounts of cous-cous to the hysterical chickens and stuffing his face with the rest. It was a strange and pathetic lapse into the role of thief. He was stealing the chickens' breakfast.

Once, when they were eating in a restaurant one Sunday night on their way back to the city, Joe's father, Carlo, had bellowed at Alex: "Stop bending over your plate! Animals go down to their food, humans bring their food up to them!"

"All right, Carlo," he had muttered, and sat erect. Afterwards as they all ambled to the parking lot, Joe's older brother, George, had grabbed Alex's arm and hissed: "You don't call my father Carlo! You call him Mr. Ford!" He said this with a degree of hatred that brothers usually reserve for other brothers. Alex was terrified, but also ecstatic, understanding the implicit compliment he had been paid—he had become a character in the lives of the Fords, a serious competitor, a player.

His friends' brothers and sisters knew him and either liked or resented him with a siblingish intensity. Their maids knew him, and with them he always had slightly confused relations. It was with the maids that the reality of his circumstance was felt most acutely—he was neither a special guest to be doted on nor a member of the employing family. With the maids he shared smiles, or cursory nods, but with the doormen he was usually exuberant. He tended to adore the doormen, because they (literally) let him in. For entire weekends he would disappear into the homes of others. He would eat their food, watch their television, chat intimately with their parents, showering them with uncomplicated precocity, good manners, attentiveness, as though he were auditioning for the role of son. He didn't see his sleep-overs as a slight to his own mother. With her he was most at home, natural, and happy; his traveling road show was merely a testament to what a good job she had done, as he saw it. But as far as sleep-overs went, he never reciprocated. During all those years he never had one friend sleep over at his own house.

But his own home was, at least, where he lived. He could take vacations from it, but he had to return. Aunti B's house was possessed of whatever qualities his own home had that drove him so adamantly away, but he didn't live there. So he never went.

His friends' parents' eyes would sometimes come to rest on him at the dinner table as if to say: "You're still here?"

Meanwhile his aunt, who loved him, sat alone in her apartment.

And when he graduated from college and moved back to New York, he became a sleep-over artist at the apartments of his girl-friends.

One afternoon, checking his answering machine from his girl-friend Debbie's house, he found a message that began: "Yo, cuz. You'll never believe who this is."

ALEX WAS NOT the main focus of his Aunti B's love. There was always "Karly," his cousin, about whom he received periodic updates—he was still playing in a band, he was living in Brazil, he had moved to Australia, he was back in Philadelphia driving a tow truck at night and drove up on his motorcycle to stay for a week-end now and then.

When Alex's father was still alive the two families convened periodically. The grown-ups would huddle over coffee and cold cuts while Alex and Karl wandered off for long discussions which usually involved Karl, who was nine years older than Alex, leisurely holding forth on his various experiences with women, and also his various experiences with drugs, and also his various experiences with women while on drugs.

"The key to girls is that the more you do what *you* want to do, the more *they'll* do what you want them to do," he explained. "And you can never be afraid of grossing girls out. They need to be grossed out sometimes. It's good for them."

Karl always talked about his imminent stardom (he played gui-tar), and even though Alex was nine years old, and therefore already comprehending of the little deceptions older people were likely to commit towards making themselves sound happy or important, he believed what his cousin told him, and admired him for it.

The same could not be said for Karl's parents, Frank and Linda. There was always a strange distance between Karl and his mother and father. They tended to look at him with a fixedly beneficent expression, as though trying to will themselves to accept an experiment that hadn't turned out right. Frank was a successful professor specializing in childhood development, one of those ironies made extra-cruel by the fact that life, at its deepest level, *should not be ironic.* Most mornings he administered to Karl an absentminded pat on the head on his way to work, where he orchestrated vast research projects about child-rearing.

Alex's relationship with Karl had ground to halt on a cold winter day when Alex was twelve. They got into a fight at Aunti B's house. Karl had taken Alex bowling, and they had gone to Aunti B's afterwards for dinner. Everything went well until Alex was on his way out the door and Aunti B tried to give him ten dollars for a cab. For some reason Karl objected violently to this. A strange three-way fight broke out. It was one of those odd pieces of family choreography that makes no real sense, leaves no lasting marks, and yet somehow changes a fundamental equilibrium among those involved. Karl and Alex drifted apart, and once apart they drifted farther apart. There were no uncles to unite them. And after the fight at Aunti B's, there was no aunt at whose house they might convene. They simply went off into separate worlds.

Aunti B loved Alex like a nephew, but she loved Karl like a son. Alex was glad for that. She clearly loved Karl more than she loved him, if one can make such distinctions, and Alex was *happy* to make such distinctions. He was grateful someone else shouldered a greater responsibility for his crazy aunt. He was glad they had each other.

———

IT WAS A Sunday afternoon in winter and Alex and his girlfriend Debbie were lolling around on her futon, naked, with beers open, talking about Debbie's mother, who was threatening to visit. Debbie's mother lived in grand style down in Louisville, Kentucky.

"My mother says I'm a tourist in my own life," said Debbie and laughed. She laughed frequently, often bitterly, but her laugh was tentative, as if she expected to be interrupted. "She says I'm leaning back when I should be leaning forward. She says I act like I'm constantly exhaling cigarette smoke through my nose."

"And you don't even smoke," he said.

"I know!" she said. "I told you about the time she hid my college applications. She didn't even *want* me to get into Brown."

"Yes," he replied curtly. "You told me." He was sick of hearing about Brown. He knew a number of people who had gone there. There was something about Brown University that imbued their graduates with a Tourette's-like compulsion to drop their alma mater's name with absurd frequency. Debbie's mouth was set in a pout. She was an ironic pouter. But eventually the irony wore off the pout, like lipstick, and what remained was self-pity.

"The college application injustice has been combed over already," he said. "With a fine-tooth comb. And besides, you got in."

At which point, in an act of escapist desperation, Alex went to the phone and dialed his answering machine. The machine he was calling was located in his mother's house, in his room, on the bottom shelf of a night table next to his bed; it was an old clunker of a machine that clattered loudly when it rewound and played back, a sound that was audible everywhere in the apartment, so these check-ins with his machine were, on some level, the psychic equivalent of poking his head into his own home and saying hello to his mom, without actually having to say hello. He spent most nights at Debbie's.

"Yo, cuz," the message began. The voice was so low that the reverb it created was almost too much for the telephone to convey. "You'll never believe who this is. I'm calling about Aunti B. Serious shit is going down. She had a bad fall. I just got a call from the hospital. I can't get up there until the weekend, so you got to check it out. She's at Columbia Presbyterian right now. I've been on the horn all afternoon talking to doctors. They're saying some bad shit, man. She got knocked over by the wind. Right in front of the building. A gust of wind just knocked her down, man. It's fucked. Call me."

He called Columbia Presbyterian. Yes, his aunt was there. No, it was past visiting hours, there was nothing he could do. He called Karl's number. He got a machine, on which Karl's recorded voice sounded relatively sane. It struck him as intensely strange that he should have a cousin with whom he had not spoken in so many years.

"Karl, it's Alex," he began. "I'm going in the morning." Then he added, tentatively, unsure if it was a lie, "It's good to hear your voice."

ALEX WAS WEIRDLY in the mood for a hospital scene. His postgraduate existence, in which he worked as a personal assistant for a movie producer for whom he ran complex errands to the dry cleaners and walked the dog and was chastised for eating too many of the chewable vitamin C's that sat on the producer's desk, was becoming a little too *small*, and except for drinking, the comfort of Debbie's loft, and his sleep-overish obsession with her family, there was nothing to soften the edge, no graduation to look forward to or dread, no mandatory transition, no imminent waterfall for which to brace.

A hospital scene is unreal real life. All niggling concerns

about love and ambition are put on hold. The hospital visitor proceeds with the single-minded concentration of someone hacking through the jungle's underbrush where they glimpse, through the dense foliage of their grief, their own soul, and find it worthy.

THE HOSPITAL SMELLED like a hospital—like death and exposed feet. He wound his way through the fluorescent halls and came to her room. The first thing he saw was a very large black woman groaning and asleep. On the far side of the room lay his aunt. Her face was badly bruised and gaunt, her eyes were wide, panic-stricken, and staring up at the ceiling as though she were looking at the sky and seeing some terrible midair collision between two planes. Her lips were moving slightly, and when he came closer he heard she was speaking German. When he arrived next to her bed he noted, with horror, that her wrists were tied down to the bed.

The shape of her mouth and her brow held something that reminded him strongly of his father, or of pictures of his father. In the absence of the man himself, the pictures and the man became confused, as when you are not sure you remember something that happened to you when you were very young, or if you simply remember being told about it.

He found the doctor, a youngish man with wispy remnants of blond hair on his head, wire-rimmed glasses, and a long complicated nose. They sat down in a conference room down the hall. Alex immediately wondered how many people had sat in this chair and heard the news that their loved one was going to die.

"So tell me what your relationship is to Ms. Fader," said the doctor.

"I'm the nephew. She has another nephew. And a brother who lives abroad."

"Any children?"

"No."

"And that brother is your father?"

"No. My father was her other brother."

"And where is he?"

"Just out of curiosity, why are you asking?" said Alex.

"I want to know the situation," he said. He clasped his hands. "I need to know who I'm talking to."

"You're talking to one of the two people in the country she is related to. Her other nephew lives in Philadelphia."

"I see."

"What's up with my aunt?"

This, he thought, was just what he needed: to stride through halls where his small petty concerns were reduced to the appropriate size. To relinquish all the little plans, the schedules, the whole self-interested enterprise of himself, so as to do something for someone else. For a flash he wondered if being a parent was a little like this, a thousand selfless gestures, each its own reward. The prospect of death was so clarifying. His aunt had been a pain in the ass whom he visited maybe once or twice a year for his whole life in spite of the fact that she lived about a fifteen-minute walk away from him, yet now she was in trouble and he was going to be there for her. Or at least visit her in the hospital.

The doctor rubbed his hands together.

"Was your aunt ever in a concentration camp?" he asked.

"No," said Alex, surprised. "They all got out. Or the immediate family. . . ." He had a nauseating pang of doubt, about everything.

"I see. Because she is very hostile, very suspicious, she is mostly speaking German, and one of the nurses here who speaks German, says it isn't making much sense."

Alex briefly pondered the peculiar idea that by virtue of speaking German and being a pain in the ass his aunt was a concentration camp candidate. If the question was being asked, there must be some grounds for it. Perhaps all over New York there were survivors who in the tumultuous flow of life had been dignified and controlled, who had kept their death-camp experiences a deep subtext, who had lived in the present and made money and been parents and grandparents, but now with their last breaths were unleashing torrents of rage and tormenting doctors like this one.

"Generally speaking," said Alex, "she is a somewhat difficult person. But I don't think that means she has been in a concentration camp."

"But the nurse says that she keeps talking about someone and what they did to him. Do you know who she might be talking about?

"No," said Alex. "I don't."

"Oh," said the doctor. He looked pensive for a moment. Alex had the weird thought that maybe the doctor's wife was having an affair. The doctor had a distanced, abstract look in his eyes, wishful and anxious, as if he was living through some terrible episode over which had no power. Alex stared into his face for further evidence of his theory, but the doctor turned his gaze back towards Alex and his face softened into an expression people use when they have importantly bad news to deliver.

"Your aunt has Alzheimer's disease," he said. "We're going to strongly recommend that she be put into a home."

Alex took this in for a moment.

"Is that bad?" he said. "I mean, how bad is that?"

"In your aunt's case, the disease has progressed a fair amount. I would say it's quite bad."

"Jesus," said Alex. He stared at the floor for a moment and

then looked sharply at the doctor. "Is Alzheimer's disease hereditary?"

He immediately hated himself for the question.

THE TWO COUSINS had staged their reunion in a dim hallway at Columbia Presbyterian where family members sat on benches, waited, worried, collected themselves, or, in the case of Alex and Karl, became reacquainted with each other.

Alex filled Karl in on the basic outline of his life: his awful job assisting the producer, the fact that he still lived at home, his vague thoughts about film school. He told Karl he played drums in a band. Karl looked at him somberly and said, "I knew you had the spirit in you, bro. I *knew* it." His voice boomed through the cavernous hallway. Alex often wondered if perhaps playing drums in a band—which he loved doing, in part because its futility (in any practical terms) made it seem pure—was something he ought to reconsider. Karl's endorsement added considerable fuel to that fire.

Karl, for his part, was living above a beauty salon in North Philadelphia; he had been in some trouble with drugs, and he had come within one lucky break of really making it big with the Karl Fader Band. But the band had disbanded. He was on a strict regimen of AA and NA meetings and was taking courses towards a college degree. He worked at a firm that specialized in medical headhunting, a temp job, he explained, but it was better that way, "because I like the flexibility."

Karl scared him a little bit. There was something extremely volatile and untrustworthy about him. And yet Alex had to recognize a strange glowing emotion that radiated out from Karl, to which he could only offer a tentative friendliness.

"I have something to tell you, bro," Karl had said. "About a year ago I walked into Aunti B's place, and there she is with her mail everywhere. I mean stacks of it, piles of it, unopened bills, and she's just wandering around in her apartment, totally lost. I got power of attorney, and started paying her bills."

"What exactly does power of attorney mean?" said Alex.

"It means I can sign her checks," said Karl.

Alex was immediately suspicious. But why? His cousin Karl was looking after their Aunti B. No one else was going to take care of her. He tried to feel generosity towards Karl. But something held him back.

"I can see you're suspicious, which is cool," said Karl, who seemed to be really enjoying the general sense of drama. It made Alex feel ill. But at the same time he had to admit he was slightly enjoying it too.

"There's a will," Karl said.

"And what does it say?" said Alex.

"Sixty-forty, me and you."

"There can't possibly be any money to divide."

"Oh, but there is," said Karl with a big smile. "There is."

THEY WENT UPSTAIRS and took Aunti B home. She was delighted to see them both, and even seemed her old self as she left, saying goodbye to the doctor and then, as she limped down the hall, muttering, "The food here is terrible! Awful!"

Instead of arranging for a nursing home, Esmeralda, the housekeeper, was now drafted to be a full-time nurse. For her this meant nearly a thousand dollars a week. For Alex and Karl, it meant some time.

When they got home, Esmeralda cooked them all lunch. Karl made some jocular remarks to her about how good the food was, and Esmeralda smiled rather bashfully. She had a luscious mane of brown wavy hair that came down below her shoulders, and a full figure, and when she smiled a gold tooth flashed at the front of her mouth. Alex was meeting her for the first time, and her bashfulness, and the gold tooth, and her figure, caught his eye.

When the plate was set before her, Aunti B looked at it as though it were a plate of dog food.

"It's a tuna fish sandwich, Aunti B, " said Karl. "It's not going to bite you. It's good! Look." He took a bite of his sandwich. "Mmmmm."

"Tuna fish," she muttered. "Vas *is* dat?"

"Eat it, Aunti B," said Karl. There was a certain menace in his voice. She ate it.

"Terrible!" she said. Esmeralda's face hardened a little. For a moment she had been in the spirit of this family gathering, but now she was just marking time, doing a job. Alex felt her presence with a strange acuteness. He liked it.

"We have to talk about her money," Karl said later that afternoon, in a coffee shop where they had convened, leaving Esmeralda to try and shepherd Aunti B to bed.

"Why?" said Alex. "She can't possibly have any money. She has a pension from her job, and when she dies that will be gone."

"As it turns out . . ." said Karl, and onto the Formica tabletop he dumped a gaggle of bankbooks.

Alex stared at the bankbooks and marveled how an element of the surreal, of insanity, seemed to creep into everything Karl touched. Bankbooks were strange, pre-electronic, antiquated things. And so many bankbooks?

"The situation we're in is this," said Karl. "It's a situation that millions of people like you and me are in all across America. It's fucked."

Alex was highly attuned to a special dip in Karl's voice. He was being sold on something.

"She has quite a bit of money," said Karl. "At least compared to what you would expect."

"Which is a little bit more than nothing," said Alex.

"A couple hundred thou. Compared to what it costs to be in a nursing home, it *is* nothing. One or two years in a nursing home, and her life savings are down the drain. You have to go broke before the government helps, and of course they do an audit to make sure you don't just transfer all your money to your kids and then say, 'Hey. I'm broke!' But I have a plan. It's simple. We keep a detailed account in a logbook of all the time we spend there at her place, all the time we spend doing things for her, and we pay ourselves."

"How much time do you expect to be spending working on Aunti B–related things?" said Alex. "How much money could that possibly add up to?"

Karl announced what he thought was a fair hourly rate.

"Lawyers get paid that much per hour," said Alex. "Doctors. We're her *nephews,* not her psychiatrists. It's not a paid position."

"Well, bro, I'm glad you put it that way, because in a way we're both her psychiatrists *and* her lawyers. That is exactly it. I couldn't have put it better myself. And we deserve it. Do you think she saved and scrimped all those years so she could just turn it all over to a nursing home? No way, man! I already looked into it. We'll need somewhere between fifty and a hundred grand to move her into a good home. Esmeralda is another chunk of change. And the rest we split. And anyway, she *paid* her taxes. It's not like we're ripping anyone off."

"This sounds like an absurd scam. What happens when we've spent all her money and the government says, 'Sorry, guys, you don't get paid for being nice to your aunt'? And then we've got this crazy person on our hands, and she has to go to some terrible place."

"You could have the apartment," said Karl matter-of-factly. "Rent-controlled. You never know how long it would take before they noticed she's not living there. Here's the deal. You write Aunti B a check every month, I deposit it in her account, then I write the realty company a check with her personal checks, which is what I've been doing for over a year now. You haven't had a place of your own, right? This'll be your first place. You'll love living at Aunti B's."

"I couldn't possibly live in her house," said Alex. "It's *her house!* It would be like living with *her.*"

"What do you say, cuz? Are you in on this? Or do you feel so fucking patriotic that you want all of Aunti B's hard-earned money, which she fucking saved all her life to give to you and me, do you want it to go to some fucking nursing home?"

"How do you know it's for you and me?" said Alex.

"I told you. There's a will."

"What does it say?"

"Sixty-forty," Karl repeated. He slid four bankbooks to Alex, and kept six.

"All I want is my share," said Karl. "I'll give you power of attorney also and you can go down to the East River Savings Bank on Ninety-sixth Street whenever you feel like it and pay yourself a couple of thousand. That place is like going to the track. There's a hundred old people checking out interest rates and flipping their CDs. You get your share, I get mine. Other than that, we do everything the best for Aunti B. The best social workers, the best home I can get, the best everything. And what's left goes to you, and to me."

AFTER THAT INITIAL encounter they saw each other only once every couple of months but spoke regularly on the phone. Karl did weekends with Aunti B. Alex popped in during the week.

Karl's relationship to Aunti B's money annoyed Alex. Karl, even when he was perfectly sane and actually getting things done, seemed sloppy, deranged, expansive, delusional. He was able to imbue the most fundamental and simple transaction with the atmosphere of insanity. Alex couldn't get past it. He lectured himself on Karl's virtues and tried to drown out his reservations: Isn't he taking care of Aunti B? Isn't he shouldering the responsibility for her when no one else in the whole world is up to it? Including yourself!

WINTER TURNED TO spring.

Aunti B was changing in unexpected ways. There was something infantilizing about Alzheimer's; it was opening her up and, in some odd way, making her a warmer, more pleasant person.

One day Alex came over to find her standing in the middle of her orange rug, clutching a photograph of a young man. The man was earnest-looking, handsome, with wire-rimmed glasses and a touching number of pens shoved into the breast pocket of his tweed jacket.

"Who's that, Aunti B?" he asked.

"Who? Who knows!" she said, and her laughter cackled.

He went into the kitchen, where Esmeralda was washing dishes.

"How's it going?" he said.

"Oh, all right," she sighed. "She's been very difficult. A lot of crying. She wouldn't eat her lunch today."

Alex had become adept at dropping in between meals; there was something mildly revolting about watching his aunt eat.

"Who's the man in the picture, Aunti B?" he asked when he came back to the living room. She hadn't moved once while he was in the kitchen. She had stood there like a statue.

"My boyfriend!" she said, suddenly animated, and gave him a wide-eyed look of defiance, daring him to look shocked. Then she laughed. She was so inscrutable at times like this—was this perfect-pitch irony? Or had she concealed from him all these years her own erotic history, knowing a young boy doesn't want to know such things about his aunt? Had she waited until now, in her waning moments, to show him the truth, like a flasher—with intent to shock? Or was she simply loosening into Alzheimer-induced incoherence? Maybe she was just kidding.

In the darkest parts of his soul he wondered if he wished she were already dead. The doctor had been vague about life expectancy. It could be a year, or ten years. "It depends on the will to live," he had said.

So privately Alex monitored her will to live.

GETTING UP AND down from chairs had become difficult for Aunti B, so she preferred to simply stay standing. She just kept walking that strange hobbling walk, ba-bump, in circles around the apartment, using her cane as though she were outside. When Alex visited her he got in the habit of walking with her. It was like going for a walk but in a tight two-room circle.

He tried to get her to talk about her past, but it was like a ruined city to her. If she tried hard she could distinguish, among the rubble, parts of old monuments she had enjoyed, places she was happy, familiar locations in the metropolis of her personal history—the town square, City Hall, the Museum of Natural History. But there was too much dust in the air to breathe. She saw it all from above, at a middle distance. Amidst the wreckage was her childhood, her youth. Who bombed her? And what could Alex have saved before this happened, what could he have gotten out?

All these questions about his father she could have answered if only he had asked in time!

ALEX WAS SPENDING less and less time with Debbie and more and more time with his aunt. During the day Esmeralda was there, but at night it was just the two of them, and Alex felt giddy with the responsibility. Anything could happen in that apartment.

Once, when he walked in the door she erupted in a delighted laugh, and proceeded to call him Karly.

"I'm Alex," he said.

She absorbed this information for a moment and then broke into tears. But it was like a summer shower, and the skies quickly brightened. She asked if he wanted something to eat.

"No," he said.

"You must be hungry!" she said, and walked to the kitchen to do an inventory. She scrutinized the salt, the oatmeal, the packet of spaghetti, the noodles, as though she were a pharmacist looking to fill a prescription.

"I'm not hungry. I'll just eat these grapes," said Alex.

Karl always stocked the place lavishly. Fresh fruit, various delicacies from Zabar's, an abundance of cooked shrimp, her favorite. She was living more extravagantly than she ever had in her life and couldn't remember any of it from one moment to the next. But she did seem to get pleasure in each moment as she passed through it. And, he thought, isn't that almost as much as one can hope for?

Her head seemed to be getting bigger as the rest of her wasted away. He could see how a gust of wind might knock her down. It was a miracle it hadn't lifted her off the ground entirely and blown her away.

"Do you want to go out?" he asked. "For a walk? We could go down to the lobby at least."

"Out, out . . . vas *is* dat?" She started laughing her new laugh, the one she had only recently developed. It brimmed with warmth and love and tears. He had never heard it before.

"I thought maybe you want to go somewhere," he said. "Is there anywhere you want to go?"

She stood hunched on her cane, muttering in contemplation as though someone had offered her a million dollars if she could remember her high school locker combination.

"The top!" she exclaimed suddenly. A tremendous smile.

MEANWHILE, KARL WAS on a spending spree. It started innocently enough. "She should have the best bed possible," Karl had said. "She sure is going to be spending a lot of time there."

But after the new bed it was a stereo, and the week after a coffeemaker, then a television, a vacuum cleaner, new silverware, a special water filtration system. When a state-of-the-art electric toothbrush appeared, Alex couldn't take it anymore.

"You're spending her money like it's going to spontaneously combust!" he shouted to Karl over the phone.

"It is, man. It's going to go down the Medicare drain. Either she gets it or Uncle Sam gets it."

"But an electric toothbrush? She's going to maim herself with that thing!"

"It's not for her, cuz. It's for me. You got a problem with that?" It was part threat, but partly a sincere question. The sincere answer would have been yes. But Alex was not up for that confrontation.

ESMERALDA WAS BEING paid an absolute fortune for her total full-time commitment to Aunti B, but it seemed to be taking a toll on her. A certain vibrancy Alex had detected in her when he first lay eyes on her seemed to be in peril. She padded around the house in pink cotton sweatpants, a baggy T-shirt, and socks and slippers. There were moments when she looked like a patient herself, and arriving at the apartment felt like coming upon two shut-ins who were slowly driving each other crazy.

But Alex had once seen Esmeralda leave for the weekend wearing a skirt and knee-high leather boots, her hair full, her cheeks alive, her figure startlingly feminine. It was a reminder that she had a life outside the dim apartment and the care of his aunt. Judging from the vigor with which she made her exit that evening, it was a life she was very anxious to resume living.

"You should see what she does with men!" his aunt bellowed at him one day. For a moment Alex took her seriously, and wondered what the hell Esmeralda was doing bringing men to the apartment. Then he remembered his aunt was insane.

"What's going on with you and men?" Alex said to Esmeralda, who was standing in the room laughing, her gold tooth flashing.

"Do you know what she does with men?" Aunti B said again, this time in a mischievous whisper.

Alex shook his head.

"Nothing!" she yelled. "She's a virgin!"

Esmeralda laughed some more but with a hint of embarrassment, which Alex shared.

"I've got a son," she said. "How am I going to be a virgin?"

EMPTY CARDBOARD BOXES were placed here and there around the apartment.

When Alex asked Esmeralda about the boxes she shrugged and said, "Your cousin." She said it in a way that implied she had sufficient contact with Karl to grasp that he was a little out of his mind.

He called Karl. "What's up with all the boxes? It's like an obstacle course in here."

"I'm trying to get her acclimated to the concept of packing," said Karl. "The more boxes lying around, the more she'll be comfortable with the idea of moving."

This was exactly the kind of thinking that made Alex nervous about Karl. But he didn't contest him. He didn't have the vigor and energy that Karl seemed to have on the subject of their aunt. She was going to leave the dim cavernous one-bedroom apartment she had lived in for thirty years, a bodega on the corner and a housing project across the street, and go live amidst the woods and meadows and deer and bunnies in rural Pennsylvania not far from where Karl lived, because Karl wanted her to. She loved Alex, but she was obsessed with Karl. It was Karl's call.

So Alex put the phone down and decided to concentrate on the task at hand, which was to visit with his aunt. She seemed incredibly pleased to see him. She seemed to take this sudden invasion of cardboard boxes as some kind of game, and puttered around weaving in and out of them, looking up at him and laughing her sputtering laugh as though to say, "Can you believe it!" It was really nice to see her look so pleased.

Then she called him Karl, as she often did.

"I'm not Karl," he said. "I'm Alex."

She looked surprised. "Where's Karly?" she asked.

"Not here," he said.

"Not here? Why not? Vas *is* dat?"

This three-word phrase could be a statement of pleasure or of anger, or a question, as well as a multitude of variations and combinations of the above, depending on tonality and whether the accent was on the "is" or the "dat."

An accent on the "is" usually meant indignation; if it was on the "dat?" it usually implied an amorphously good-humored question within which was the suggestion that life was an unknowable mystery and one might as well make the best of it.

She wore two small watches on her left wrist.

"Why are you wearing two watches, Aunti B?" he said.

"So I can tell the time!" she snapped.

Esmeralda shuffled into the living room in her slippers, en route to another chore. She shot him a look that seemed to say, "See what I have to deal with?"

AUNTI B HAD spent two years, starting at the age of five, at a sanitarium outside Vienna because of polio. What happened in sanitariums in Austria in the years just after World War I Alex did not know. Judging from his aunt, it was nothing good. He wanted to ask her about it, but was constantly reminded that his aunt was beyond the realm of normal comprehension.

"What do you think of all this?" he asked her, waving towards the boxes that dotted the living room.

"Well," she said, without bitterness, "what can you do?"

"You could stay."

"Yes!" It seemed like a new idea. A tremendous discovery along the lines of Galileo, Newton, Darwin. Everything must be fairly novel when you can't remember anything.

She held a pair of scissors like a dagger. Karl wanted to move her out in a matter of weeks. But he had wanted to move her out in a matter of weeks for six months. It was now summer. She was staring down at the scissors as though she couldn't understand how she came to be holding them. She'll kill herself if she stays here, Alex thought, but he didn't really believe it.

HE HAD BEEN arguing terribly with Debbie. His scale of priorities was being recalibrated in ways he didn't understand, but he no longer felt interested by anything she had to say. Instead he became a regular at his aunt's place, seeking solace there the way one might frequent a bar.

Almost every day now he turned the key in the lock, pushed the door open, and entered the claustrophobic world of his declining aunt and her housekeeper/nurse. It was though a theatrical event was going on eight hours a day, and you could drop in at any time and simply pick up the plot from that moment.

Aunti B was always clutching the photograph of her young intellectual, her small bent body often contorted with tears, while Esmeralda stood before her, burgeoning out of her improvised uniform, ass in one direction, breasts in the other, robust, healthy, and helpless before this tiny woman's inexplicable rage. On one such occasion Esmeralda's eyes turned to Alex's with a mixture of relief that assistance had arrived, and embarrassment that he had walked in on such a scene.

"She's trying to kill me!" shrieked Aunti B between sobs. "You don't know . . . you know what she does to me!"

Alex strode forward and put his arm around his aunt's tiny bony shoulder. He cast a quick glance at Esmeralda that tried to convey sympathy, and was surprised to find on her face an odd look of contrition, as though she had accidentally broken something valuable while dusting.

"I didn't do nothing," she said.

"Come here, Aunti B, come into the kitchen, let's—"

"No!" A murderous cry, a primal scream of rage and frustration of the sort a baby might make.

After a few failed attempts to navigate her to the kitchen, he turned her in the opposite direction and got her into her bedroom. Whenever possible he tried to avoid this room. It smelled faintly of urine. Its one window hadn't been cleaned in years. She had gotten in the habit of raiding her drawers and throwing everything on the floor. Sometimes Esmeralda just left everything out until the end of the day, and then put it away before going home. The place was strewn with underwear.

"Please," she whispered, suddenly with real focus, real urgency, as though her crazy personality were just an act, and this was a brief moment when she could be herself. "Get rid of that woman! Get rid of her! Get rid of her!" She yelled these last words, fierce, hysterical, dictatorial, the ferocity of a monarch who had returned to retake her conquered kingdom, in this case the tiny kingdom that was her life. The queen is back, and she will wreak havoc on the nincompoops who have been doing such a bad job in her absence!

"Sit!" he said, and nearly pushed her onto the bed. She sat with a thud, and immediately became quiet.

"I'll be right back," he said.

He rushed out to touch base with Esmeralda. It was only a few steps, but he started to formulate an apology. He was full of sympathy for the woman. She was being paid a thousand a week, but no amount of money was worth being cooped up with his crazy aunt.

But when he reached her he was surprised to find on her face a look of fear and remorse and anxiety that collated into an expression he hadn't expected. It was, more than anything else, womanly, even a little childish, and in a flash he apprehended her not as a maid or nurse, but as a woman, a vulnerable and quite sexy woman.

Her breasts strained against her shirt. She looked at him with wide anxious eyes.

"Esmeralda," he said. "This is a difficult situation. I want to be fair."

Her face remained unchanged, anxious and worried.

He let his eyes stare into hers for a moment, and then he slowly and very deliberately moved them down her body, over her face, her neck, and let them linger on her two large melon-shaped breasts protruding against her pink T-shirt. Then he looked farther down, over her wide heavy hips, all the way down to her feet, which were in socks and slippers. He looked back at her eyes.

"It's not fair," she said. "She is crazy. I am doing nothing wrong."

"Esmeralda, go have a seat on the couch."

He stared at her some more. His face was incredibly dispassionate. There was a huge welling-up in his chest of varying emotions, and he imagined that beneath his expressionless gaze, Esmeralda could sense some kind of turbulence.

"Sit down," he said, more harshly than he expected.

He went into the bedroom and quieted his aunt; she was agitated and mournful. He sat at the edge of her bed and held her gnarled hand. It was a weird kind of seduction. He rarely touched her like this. The room smelled of her sour smell. He willed her to sleep, and miraculously, after a few minutes, her eyes shut. He got up and closed the door behind him. She didn't like the door closed, and it was when he heard it click shut that his blood started to race again.

Esmeralda was not on the couch. He looked around. She was nowhere. He went to the kitchen, and just then heard a sound in the bathroom. He went there and saw Esmeralda about to emerge. She had obviously decided that there was no point in sitting on the couch, and had begun to clean the bathroom. Was she cleaning to make a good impression, to mitigate his aunt's shrieking protest against her competence?

Or was there something on his face that, even in its blankness, registered with her and made her not want to wait for him on the couch?

They collided in the doorway to the bathroom. She held her blue rubber gloves in one hand, and he could smell the faint, bitter smell of Ajax. She had just washed the sink and the tub. He was aware of her breasts, how much closer to him they were than the rest of her. The fullness that had eluded him for the months that he had been lurking around in her presence was now overwhelming, monstrous, luscious; she was a gorgeous thing with blue rubber gloves. It was not a transformation he had expected, but now that it had occurred it seemed obvious and natural. Other than the blue gloves he was aware of her eyes, brown and flecked with orange. She looked up at him as he blocked her way in the bathroom doorway. At that moment he didn't look at her face but instead looked up at the bathroom mirror. In it he saw himself, and Esmeralda looking up at him. Her expression was bemused and also worried. For a moment he felt their age difference. She had mentioned she had a son, seventeen, not that much younger than he. She was firm, though, full and firm, and in profile her breasts and her hips and ass looked all the more formidable. There was something offensive and angering about them. He saw how close they were to his torso. They held their respective gazes for a long time—she on his face, his face towards the mirror, looking at her looking at him—as though they were sitting for a portrait.

"Come with me," he said, and turned to face her. He took a step forward. She took a step forward, and they bumped. It was comic. Now he didn't know where to look. But he didn't move. An image of an outrageous coupling in the bathroom was vaguely taking form in his mind.

"Excuse me," she said in a bored and almost annoyed way, as though impatient to get on with her cleaning. She said it with so much authority—the authority of someone who doesn't have time for nonsense—that he completely lost his nerve. Only the memory of her open, worried face staring up at him moments before kept him planted to the spot, resolute to go through with it. For some reason his eyes cast down to the floor where her white socks creased at the point where the slipper's thong pressed into them, next to her big toe. Again she froze, still staring at him, and he stared at her slippers—pure work clothes, totally unglamorous, tawdry really, yet charged with sex all of a sudden.

"We need to talk," he mumbled. He stepped forward again. She held her ground. She didn't want to be pushed into the bathroom.

"We need to talk," he said again, and stepped forward again. She stepped back. They were in the bathroom. He turned and closed the door. He fumbled with the lock for a second, and then another second. He was standing there with his back to her in the small Ajax-smelling bathroom fumbling with the lock which didn't work because in the thirty years his aunt had lived there she had never used it. At the last moment, as he began to feel utterly ridiculous, the lock clicked, and he turned to face her.

Her expression was now one of glowering anger. Her eyes were wide and hostile, but her mouth was a little open. It was open in a sort of shocked, surprised way, taken aback and confused. Her eyes scared him, but her mouth gave him strength.

"We have to talk about the situation with my aunt," he said.

"We have to talk about it in the bathroom?"

"We have to talk about it in private."

"What's not private enough about the living room?" she said.

He stared at her uncertainly. Alex couldn't believe what he was doing, but in Aunti B's apartment none of the normal rules mattered.

"How much do we pay you a week?" he blurted out. He was sad about the "we." He didn't want Karl involved. But of course he was; he loomed over this scene with an approving smirk.

"What does that have to do with why we are standing here in the bathroom with the door locked?" she said.

He really wanted to say something about her son. It was just a sick thought. He wanted to say, "Don't you have a son to support?" It was an inside joke, and part of him delighted in it as another part rose up in a kind of indignant fury that he might be such a bastard.

Instead he said, "We pay you well. You were making house-cleaning money and now you're making nurse money. That's about four times as much. Do you know why you're making this kind of money?"

She remained still. He realized now that from the moment he had bumped into her in the door she had hardly moved, except to step back. Not a single movement in her face or hands.

"You're making it because you are supposed to take care of my aunt—"

"I am taking care of her. I'm doing the best I can, I couldn't be doing nothing more. You know she's crazy. You know that."

"I know that, Esmeralda, but I also know that we have to do everything we can to keep her happy."

"But I'm—"

"No, listen to me. I have to do what I think is right with regard to my aunt's care. And at the moment I am seriously considering what is right. Are you the right person? I don't know."

"Listen, if you're going to fire me, then get it over with. I don't need to stand here—"

"I didn't say I was going to fire you. Did I say that? I said I wanted to talk to you. Why do you think we're in here?"

"That's a very good question," she said. She was a little indignant now, hotter and madder than he had seen her. She had always seemed so docile, a slow mound of feminine flesh moving around the apartment.

"I want to help you," he said pathetically.

"Help me? How are you going to help me?"

"Do you want to be fired?" he stammered.

"Listen, kid," she said. She hesitated after this, as though calling him "kid" was a bit too much.

"No, you listen," he said. "I've got a crazy aunt out there I'm responsible for. And though she may be crazy . . . listen, the point is this, the point is this . . ." he was sweating a little now. "The point is I like having you around here and would like to keep you around here. But if I don't fire you, I'm the crazy one. The way she's acting now . . ."

He stopped. She had gone back to her docile, quiet, and vaguely sweet incarnation. The cheerful housekeeper who was slow and had big tits. She was private again. That glimmer of anger and personality had gone away. He was confused. He wished he hadn't locked the door. He wanted to flee. The only thing that prevented him at that moment was the prospect of having to fumble with the lock again. That and her breasts. In her mode of silence and passivity he became maniacally attracted to her. He wanted to touch her. His eyes fixated on her mouth, then her breasts, and before he realized what was happening he had stared intently at them for several full seconds, in utter silence, while she stared back at him. This wasn't the smooth and suggestive and deliciously smarmy glance he had given her earlier, the raking-over, the up-and-down, the appraisal. This was just dumb staring, like a tourist standing dumbfounded in front of the small window boxes at Tiffany's, staring at the beautiful gems he would never be able to own or even touch.

"What are you staring at?" she said. It was the inevitable reprimand.

He looked up at her bashfully, speechless. He felt a wave of patheticness sweep over him. It wasn't the thought or even the act that was so pathetic, just the vague attempt, just enough to be busted, to be caught, and then no follow-through, the return to the real world empty-handed. He realized how far he had traveled to be in this little enclosed private space. Surely he would never get this far again. A renewed sense of urgency overcame him.

"What do you think I'm looking at?"

"I think you're staring at my tits." Her use of the word had an effect on him.

"That's right. I'm staring at your big tits."

"That why you locked the door? You want to do something with my tits? You think you're gonna lock me in and threaten me with this stupid job?"

"You're a very pretty lady. Do you know that?" He looked back at her eyes at last. "Very pretty lady. I would hate for you to leave."

"Well, maybe I want to leave."

"I'm not asking much."

"What are you asking? What do you want? You want to play with my tits? And then what?"

The fact that she was now doing the work for him was a great relief. She had said the word herself, "tits," and so the subject of sex had at least been articulated. She had even provided the word, in all its garishness—"tits"—the appropriate word for the situation. Neither subtle and romantic nor clinical, just matter-of-fact, an object, a kind of currency.

"Let me play with them."

"Then what?"

"We'll see."

"No we'll sees. I want to know."

Again, she was helping him. She wasn't telling him that this was out of the question. She was telling him that this was up for debate. There was some negotiating to be done.

"I want . . . I want to . . ." He couldn't go further. His lack of imagination was amazing. He had approached the bathroom with a rather specific fantasy, but that fantasy was like some rare animal that could exist only at the untenable altitude of unreality, and if it was brought down into the thicker, life-giving air of the real world it would not only die, it would utterly disappear and vanish without a trace. They were in the real world, Esmeralda and he. His sick aunt was sleeping in the next room.

"What do I get?" she said. He wanted to call time out, stop the scene, and shake her hand, thanking her profusely for her help.

"I want you to stay. I like you here. I just want to . . ."

"Say it."

He reached out and stroked one. It was firm and he could feel the weight of it. He could feel the heavy lining of her bra underneath the shirt. It seemed like a formidable piece of equipment.

"And that's all?" she said.

"That's all."

She gave him a hateful look, which he enjoyed a lot. And then she put down the blue rubber gloves and the Ajax on the side of the sink. He hadn't realized that this whole time she had been clutching them. Now her hands were free. He liked them, with their shiny apricot-colored nail polish, small and inelegant. Working hands. They found the bottom of the T-shirt and started to slowly pull it up. Her eyes stayed on his the whole time. She pulled it up to her armpits and held the shirt there, as though at any moment she would pull it back down. Her elbows stuck up in the air. Her face softened ever so slightly, and he thought he detected an inquiring look in her eyes, as though she were saying, "What do you think?"

He was slightly revolted. It was too matter-of-fact. He didn't know what drama he was concocting, but this was just too willful, and the bra, a big industrial-strength beige thing, was painfully redolent of real life. It was a little frayed, a little stained. Nevertheless he reached out and began to stroke her breasts. At first just the tops, the exposed part, and then he cupped them underneath, and lifted, wanting to feel their heft. The bra prevented this. Again her eyes modulated slightly, both a little proud and a little disdainful, as though to say, "Are you enjoying this?" and also "All this fuss over this, you idiot, was it worth it?"

"Take this off," he said.

"No."

"Take this off, I want them all, the whole thing."

"No."

"I want to see your tits, Esmeralda."

"This is them."

He pushed his finger underneath the bottom cup, underneath the heavy wire. For a moment he thought he felt a rib, and it upset him, this digging into her flesh.

He lifted the cups up, and she inhaled as though she were at a doctor's examination, and out spilled her large bountiful brownish breasts. The nipples he had so speculated and fantasized about came into view. They were lewd, her nipples, in their expanse, their screaming presence, their darkness. They quickly puckered a little in the open air. He held her breasts from underneath. They spilled sloppily over his hands. He brought his face towards them.

"Oh Jesus," she said.

"That's right," he murmured for some reason.

"Jesus Christ," she said. He stood back up and started pinching her nipples lightly, pulling them out a little so her breasts shook. His eyes went from her breasts to her eyes, back and forth. Her expression was cold now. "So you are doing this, but it doesn't mean anything," it said. She still held her T-shirt up for him, her elbows stuck out in the air. He started kneading her breasts, squeezing, stupid hand-splayed squeezes.

"More," he said.

"No more," she said. She brought her hands down. The T-shirt fell. His hands were not removed. They were under the shirt. She reached for her bra to pull it down, but he continued to squeeze and touch.

"More," he said, and pushed her back toward the toilet. "I want you to do something for me."

"What?"

"Sit."

He reached behind her and put the toilet seat and lid down.

"You want that too? You didn't say that. You're a liar," she said in a steely voice.

"Suck me."

She glared at him, sat down, her hands on her lap. He unzipped his pants and an erection sprang forward like a reptile. It stuck out at her, pink and brazen. He was at a loss as to what to do next. All facilities for speech, and even thought, were more or less down and out. And he needed her help.

"Show me," he said.

"Show you what?"

His erection diminished in the next heartbeat, and in its diminishing, it pulsed, like a diving board someone had just jumped off.

She smiled a derisive sneering smile. "You got a pretty one, though."

"Put it in your mouth."

"Oh, a tough guy. Little cousin, the tough guy."

"Please?"

"Please! Oh, you ask nice. What a good little boy."

She stuck her tongue out, as if she were going to take a lick, brought it right near the tip, and then narrowed it and stuck it up at his face like a schoolgirl. Mocking.

He reached down to her plentiful hair, full and curly. His hand burrowed deep in it, held her tight, and pulled her towards him.

"Uh oh!" she said. How this had all become a big joke he didn't know. "Tough guy! Here he comes!"

Then he heard the sound of the bedroom door opening, followed by the distinct shuffling sound of his aunt walking, that heartbeat shuffle step, her bad leg dragging a little. She took in the empty room. Then the phrase, unmistakable, comic: "Vas is *dat*?"

Emphasis on the "dat," connoting curiosity, surprise, though not yet alarm. She was looking out at the living room and, for the first time in months, finding herself alone.

His heart jumped, his brain traveled at lightning speed from his penis to his head, and, finding itself there for the first time in fifteen minutes, it was amazed at the horrible damage it found, the absurd wreckage of its dignity and sense of self. Why was the housekeeper sitting on the toilet?

He heard more scraping of the leg, the little banging of the cane, the cadence of that limp, and then his name: "Alex? Alex?"

Esmeralda gave him a big smile. "Tough guy!" she said. "What happens now?" And she laughed a horrible shrieking laugh while she adjusted her bra and stood up. From beyond the door he heard the scraping stop and the sudden stillness of his aunt standing alone in her own house, aware of something else alive and near her, like an animal in the forest who senses some danger, but doesn't know from which direction it comes.

GRADUALLY THE EMPTY cardboard boxes filled up with possessions. Karl packed up her pots, pans, clothes, and silverware.

The books were a different story. Alex went through them with her one by one. Some were in German, others in English.

"What do you think of Kafka?" he asked, holding up *The Trial*. "Kafka?"

She shrugged her shoulders and narrowed her eyes in a vague imitation of someone about to humbly express some talmudic wisdom.

"Kafka," she said. "Kafka is Kafka."

He thought it was a pretty good answer.

"WHAT THEY DID to him! What they did to him!" His Aunti B was screaming and weeping in the middle of the living room, a moist dot of humanity set on the expanse of her awful orange rug, holding a photograph in her hand. Alex stood helplessly before her.

Esmeralda poked her head in from the kitchen and shrugged. She looked at him with eyes that suggested both that she somehow was willing to forgive him and that he shouldn't even *think* of trying it again.

"Who is that man?" he said. There was the young man in the picture, her young intellectual with the pens in his breast pocket. He thought of the doctor's question about concentration camps. "Who was he? Who were *they?*"

It was all gone now. The treasure of his aunt's biography had disappeared, and yet the person still stood before him with tears in her eyes.

THE DATE WAS set. During the last week before the move he slept over several times. He had broken up with Debbie, remorsefully, but with a sense of relief. He went from sleeping over at his girlfriend's to sleeping over at his aunt's. He slept on the couch. Aunti B kept impossible hours. In his sleep he heard her shuffling around the apartment. In some odd way it comforted him, knowing that she was still there.

Once she prodded him gently with her hand in the middle of the night. Very gently. His eyes cracked open. She was a dim figure in the dark. He could see her outline, that bent posture. She prodded him again, more like a pat, as if she were plumping pillows.

"What's that?" she said.

"It's me, Aunti B," he said.

"Me?" she said. And started laughing. It was weirdly sweet. But she was out of her mind.

"I think it's a cat," she said.

THE DAY BEFORE her departure all that was left on the bare living-room bookshelf was the picture of his father. It was the last thing to be packed. Since Karl had done all the packing, Alex thought it was curious that it was still out. Was it for her benefit? For his? It didn't occur to Alex that Karl had left the picture out for himself. That Karl himself stared lovingly at it, and grieved for his uncle, whom he had known twice as long as Alex.

In the picture, the face was in semiprofile, his father's eyes looking away.

Alex tried to position himself in the corner of the room, where he thought his father was looking. He slid over as far as he could go, trying to get in range of his father's gaze, but those eyes evaded him. Aunti B watched him, amused, and blurted out a few words in German. The one word he recognized was *Meschugge*.

The next day he and Karl escorted her through the lobby, a royal ceremony which seemed to amuse her until she saw the huge white stretch limousine that sat improbably at the curb, Karl's last irrational extravagance.

"Well, Aunti B!" Karl exclaimed. "Whaddaya think?"

Even now at the last possible moment Alex struggled with his ambivalence towards Karl. Who needs a white stretch limo to take his tiny aunt to a nursing home? But he made himself forgive Karl, even appreciate him, and even experience, beneath the muffling layers of confusion, a glimmer of love. Leaving home forever is something you only do once. Take a white limo. Why not?

When at last she got in, the last thing he saw of her was her lame leg still hanging down from the door. She struggled to pull it up into the car with the rest of her. That exposed leg with the special shoe. It was a chilling sight.

When the limo turned the corner, Alex went upstairs to his new apartment. He took a deep breath and closed his eyes. The place smelled exactly as he remembered it from when he first walked in as a child. He couldn't imagine the smell ever going away. A boy's shriek arrived through the window, and then it was quiet again. Very quiet. He could hear his heart beating, he could feel it, and with a shiver it struck him that it was the exact same cadence as her halting step.

Say It with Furs

WHEN THE BUZZER RANG, CHRISTINE WAS IN HER PAJAMAS, leaning against the kitchen sink, sipping tea, and indulging in a careful reconstruction of the Gum Incident. The buzzer made her jump. She had been in deep space, staring at the small wooden night table that had sat for years next to her bed, supporting an infinitely long procession of Kleenex boxes and also a highly impractical lamp that was supposed to look like an old candelabra, and whose three candle-shaped lightbulbs—each supported by a candlestick with fake wax artfully dripping down the side—produced just barely enough light by which to read. She kept the candelabra on her night table because it sometimes made her feel as though she were living in an old windswept mansion filled with ghosts. Other times it made her feel as though she were living in a tiny studio apartment decorated with stuff from the Sixth Avenue flea market.

She had been obsessing about whether to keep or get rid of the candelabra. The night table had already bitten the dust in the private inventory she was making. She had been obsessing about whether to keep or get rid of nearly everything she owned ever since she decided, once and for all, to move from New York to San Francisco, where she could start a new life, more or less, and rid herself of the oppressive layers of her own history amidst which she had been living for the last ten years. She had decided this, once and for all, that morning. It was her thirty-fifth birthday.

The one slight hitch to her plan was her boyfriend, Alex. He played drums in a rock band and was ten years younger than she was. For a whole year they had been having a relationship, and she loved him, and yet their relationship had become static, frozen with warmth. It would have ended soon anyway. It was just a matter of telling him. Leaving town, she thought, will make it easier.

The buzz—an incredibly loud, grating, and unpleasant sound—made her whole body twitch, as though she were falling backwards in a dream, and had jerked awake a split second before impact. The tea spilled. It burned her hand on the soft fleshy part just below the thumb. She switched the mug, which had little bunnies on it, from right hand to left, brought the injured part instinctively up to her mouth, and gave it a long restorative suck. Then she moved towards the intercom.

"Hello?" she said into the intercom.

"Delivery!" came the voice over the intercom. It was female and, for a delivery person, unnaturally cheerful.

———

ON THE OCCASION of Christine's birthday, Alex had reserved a table for two at her favorite restaurant, Nadine's. It was a dark, romantic place on Greenwich Street, not far from her home, lit by a series of crystal chandeliers over which the owners had draped a light gauzy material which made the chandeliers, and the place in general, feel dreamy, like a faraway memory even while you sat in its midst.

They had eaten there a number of times together, and Alex had stared at Christine's large, delicate hands as they fluttered about in the dim light with a strange animal gracefulness, coming to rest now and then on the table's darkness, against which they seemed all the more radiant and beautiful.

Alex's next step in planning the birthday, after he made the dinner reservation, was to pay a visit to the Ritz Thrift Shop on Fifty-seventh Street just off Sixth Avenue. The Ritz Thrift Shop sold new and used furs. It had been around for years, and Alex had seen its commercials on television when he was a kid. Even then the commercials had seemed ancient, conceived and produced in some prehistoric, pre-ironic, pre–animal rights era, and long before Alex developed an ironic, retro-appreciating bone in his body he sensed a thrilling bit of artifice in the black-and-white commercial. A well-dressed, elegant woman walked down the sloping incline of Fifty-seventh Street wearing a knee-length white skirt and white gloves, and a nice fur coat that came down just below her waist. Her brown hair was in an elaborate bun. Though there were no pearls visible, it seemed likely that she owned a very nice double-strand necklace. Her pretty face was set in the blank but slightly expectant expression of someone who knows quality when she sees it, who likes to see it, and who knows she will shortly be seeing a whole lot of it. As she walked down the street a demure male narrator extolled the virtues of fur, and of the Ritz Thrift Shop as a place to buy it, new or used, and in the end there was a shot of her entering the store, a refuge of good taste and style at reasonable prices, while the announcer said: "The Ritz Thrift Shop—where you don't have to spend a million to look like a million."

Alex had already closed the door to his apartment, ready to head out to the Ritz, when something came over him and he dashed back in, flipped through the yellow pages, barked some instructions to the voice on the other end of the line, recited his credit card number and Christine's address, and then headed uptown feeling vaguely pleased with himself for his inspiration.

Beneath his smile was a terrible panic that the woman he loved would leave him. He had no guile or cleverness or subtlety or strategy with which to confront this mortal threat. He only had one big idea; it was blunt, bludgeoning, and simple: he would love her more.

"I'M NOT EXPECTING anything," said Christine into the intercom. Then she added: "What are you delivering?"

"It's a surprise," came the voice.

"I'm on the fifth floor. I'm sorry, but I'm not expecting anything and I can't come down right now."

"I'm supposed to come up," said the voice. "It's a surprise what I'm delivering."

"Can you just tell me what it is? Are you from FedEx or something?"

"I'm supposed to just show up at your front door and surprise you, ideally, but if you have to know in advance, the thing that I'm delivering is, like, basically, me. I'm a singing telegram. If you buzz me in I'll come upstairs."

She hit the buzzer and stared with a sort of numb horror at her night table. The Gum Incident was exactly the sort of minor travesty that she wanted to delete from, if not her memory, then at least her immediate surroundings. The man who had been chewing the gum was just a footnote to the story. She had met him at a bar years ago, and they had ended up at her house, where they copulated drunkenly. He left the next morning, acting cordial and friendly. They never spoke again (because of the gum incident) even though he called several times and left messages.

After the Gum Incident man left that morning she had padded around her tiny apartment in socks feeling besieged by conflicting feelings of pride and revulsion. She had been working, at the time, as a legal proofreader on the lucrative graveyard shift, so she had her days to herself. But the nocturnal schedule got to her sometimes. She had been in a miserable lonely funk in the preceding weeks, and was proud that she had galvanized herself to go out into the world and find company. She had gone to a bar with a friend and let herself be found by this reasonably attractive man.

But she also felt disgust at having slept with him right away. It was a moral issue, though not in the normal good-girl-versus-slut terms. She thought of it more in food terms: daintiness versus gluttony. Sleeping with this anonymous man was like binge eating. She could have had a small portion of making out passionately at the bar where they met, or a more substantial heavy grope session on the street, against a building, in the shadows, which might have been sufficiently filling. But she wanted to finish everything on her plate, and so she brought him home and let things take their course.

She had been in a good mood after he left, though. But then a mystery of sorts had come into her mind. While he was making love to her the man had been chewing gum. He had chewed gum throughout the whole evening, and she had commented on it, saying he looked really good with his jaw muscle clenched, which

to her amazement he took seriously, forcing her to add that when
he was at the other end of the chew cycle, with his jaw slack,
he looked a bit slow. She was hoping he'd lose the gum, but he
didn't.

The mystery was that after they had done it, when he was
lying beside her, breathing heavily and with an amazingly lewd
look of satiation on his face, he was no longer chewing gum.

She began to wonder what had happened to the gum. Had he
put it behind his ear? Had he executed a deft jump shot into the
trash bag over by the sink without her noticing? Was it in storage
in some corner of his mouth?

She had pondered it all morning, and then reflexively and
without any rational thought she walked over to the night table
and ran her hand along the underside. She almost felt ashamed
for even entertaining such a thought; he had been nice and well-
mannered, after all. The night table was a nice piece of furniture,
not some temporary plastic thing a college student had dragged
into a dorm room. She felt disgusting to even suspect that he
might . . .

There it was. Soft and moist. She removed it and held it up for
inspection. It looked like a tiny brain. He must have reached over
at some point, while he was inside her, and stuck his gum underneath her nice wooden night table. He might as well have stuck it
on her forehead.

Now she glared at the little white intercom box on the wall
with the irrational feeling that anyone who laid eyes on the night
table would understand the whole sordid history right away.

ALEX WALKED FROM the subway down the sloping incline of
Fifty-seventh Street. He wore black jeans and a white T-shirt,
over which he wore a black V-neck cashmere sweater, his favorite

item of clothing, something so dear to him that in spite of the gaping holes at the elbow he wore it with pride and felt utterly confident that it made him look as cool as it was possible for him to look. On his face was a five-o'clock shadow which had taken three days to accumulate, and the blank but expectant expression of someone who wanted to buy a really nice, and original, and memorable, and daring, and also useful gift for the woman he loved, but who didn't want to spend too much money to get it, and who was also racking his brains for the memory of any remark his beloved might have once uttered in passing that would suggest a deep emotional connection with beavers, minks, lynxes, or foxes, which would incline her to exclaim with horror when presented with, at her birthday dinner, a muff.

The very word made him happy: "Muff."

He had become obsessed with muffs. The idea of Christine's long fingers, so quick to get cold, swaddled inside a big warm ball of fur pleased him enormously. He took long loping strides down the hill, staring at the sidewalk, as appealingly preoccupied and lost in thought as the woman in the Ritz Thrift Shop commercial had been appealingly empty of all thought save one—to visit the Ritz Thrift Shop.

He instinctively looked up across the street to take in the Russian Tea Room's red awning. He used to go there on his birthday. He would sit there amidst the red banquettes and bustle. On every visit he carefully read the menu before making his usual order of blinis and caviar to the attentive waiter in his high-necked authentic Russian jacket, and later he would marvel at the deft wrist movement with which the waiter would personally roll his first blini, a demonstration whose effortless perfection he could never match with the remaining blinis. How earnest and touching those dinners had been!

But Christine's birthday dinner would not be about those emotions. Hers was a completely different way of experiencing things. Even the most straightforward moments with Christine always had a twist. In the middle of fooling around, for example, she sometimes looked at him with a pained, almost tragically wistful expression, as though this were the last time they would ever be together. It was with such an expression that she had told him, just weeks earlier, in bed, "I love you."

He found her expression when she said this incredibly sexy but also complicated, because he sensed she was being theatrical, that she was creating a little bit of false drama for the sake of play. It was as though there were, in her mind, an urgent scene unfolding, something out of a Russian novel, in which one of them would shortly be boarding a train to a far-off place, and this was the last tryst fate was affording them.

There was also the suspicion, always in the shadows when he was with Christine, that she really was thinking their relationship was coming to an end, and that these were their last moments together. He had felt lucky to be with her in the first place, and like many people who feel that their lover is somehow a gift of fate, he had the uneasy feeling that his luck would run out.

He thought of her saying those words: I love you. She rarely said them. Walking down Fifty-seventh Street, he marveled at that moment of pure unbridled feeling to which she could provoke him, the incredible pleasure of it.

"I love you, too," he had said, and he saw her face change ever so slightly. A tiny shadow came across it.

A YOUNG WOMAN, extremely tall, stood before Christine in an absurdly garish outfit consisting of short pants, a red satin shirt, and a puffy down jacket (blue). She was on roller skates (white), which partially explained her enormous height. Her hair was blond and pulled back in a ponytail. She exuded vigor and good health.

"Hi," she said. "This is from . . ." She consulted a piece of paper. "Alex. Ready?"

Christine stared up at her with stunned fascination. "Okay," she said rather softly.

The woman in the satin shirt took out a harmonica and blew on it once, producing a single note. Then, armed with that clarifying middle C, she launched into "Happy Birthday to You."

Christine held on to the doorknob. The occasion of her birthday, combined with her decision to move, and the strange earnestness of this woman's cheer, and the fact that it was Alex who had conjured this up, unleashed all sorts of strange emotional energy in her. She began to cry. Her eyes got puffy. A tear rolled down her cheek. By the time the song was over it was near her mouth. The singer's bright smile evaporated when she saw it.

"God, I'm sorry," she said. In the absence of her clear bright voice the only sound was her roller skates rolling back and forth on the hallway's linoleum floor, making it creak a little.

"Excuse me," said Christine, sniffling.

"Oh shit," said the woman. She stamped her roller skate on the floor. "I'm not cut out for this job. You're the second person who's cried on me this week."

"It's not your fault," said Christine. "You were really good."

"No, you don't understand, I have that effect on people. I've talked about it with one of the other girls. She's been doing this for nine months and no one has ever cried on her. I've been at it for three weeks and I've had four of them. It must be something about my personality. People take one look at me and they burst into tears." She looked stricken.

"It had nothing to do with your personality at all," said Christine. "It's just I'm not used to surprises, I don't take them very well. . . ."

AT THE RITZ Thrift Shop, the phrase "Miracle on 57th Street" was embossed in gold script on the two glass front doors, though the gold had chipped and faded, and the script in which it was written seemed quaint and out of date, an old-fashioned notion of elegance. Beyond the glass door was a vast stretch of wall-to-wall carpet, which once upon a time might have been white, or perhaps ivory, but was now decidedly gray. The store was filled with ancient-looking sofas and chairs whose pillows were tired and deflated. Two men stood in the middle of the store with their hands behind their backs, like guards at a museum which no one ever visited. One was bald, in a blue blazer and sharply creased gray slacks, with a handlebar mustache. The other was shorter, in a tan two-piece suit, and had an outburst of frizzy gray hair that leapt off his head.

"May I help you?" said the bald man with the handlebar mustache.

"I'm looking for something in fur," said Alex. "Preferably used."

"Well, you've come to right place!" said the man with the frizzy hair. He laughed nervously.

The shop was mostly empty, though Alex noticed an older woman sitting on one of the sofas with an impatient look on her face. The one thing that seemed conspicuously absent from the store, besides customers, was fur.

"Are you hiding the fur?" he asked.

"It's in a vault," said the bald man curtly. "Was there anything in particular you were looking for?"

Alex looked around the store. There was a black security guard standing behind him by the door, slowly rotating a toothpick between his teeth. "These past years must have been tough," he said. "With the anti-fur people, the protests and so forth. Women getting attacked for wearing fur. I want you to know I'm not one of those people. I'm not a fur terrorist, in case you were worried."

"We weren't worried," said the bald man.

"Spray paint!" shouted the woman on the sofa.

All three men turned to her. She stared back at Alex with wide incredulous eyes to which a great deal of mascara had been applied.

"Mrs. Gluck had an incident," said the frizzy-haired man.

"It's madness, insanity! Right on Sixty-fourth and Park. A lunatic with orange spray paint. A woman! Can you imagine?"

"We're cleaning it up, no problem," said the frizzy-haired man to Alex in a confiding tone.

"What exactly did you have in mind?" said the bald man.

"It's not for me," said Alex. "In case you were wondering. It's for my girlfriend. And I'm not interested in a coat. I wanted to look . . ." He hesitated. "I was thinking about muffs."

To actually pronounce the word in the hallowed decrepit confines of the Ritz Thrift Shop, whose sexy television advertisement had made such a deep impression on him at the age of eight, thrilled him. It was perhaps the first time he had said it out loud since the idea came to him, and probably one of the few times in his entire life he had had the occasion to use the word—"muff"—in a literal, practical, unironic sense. Everyone seemed cheered by the word.

"A muff!" said the frizzy-haired man.

"That's nice," said Mrs. Gluck from the couch. "You don't see muffs as much as you used to."

"Al," said the bald man, for the first time dropping the guarded, formal, and even stand-offish air that he had possessed since the moment Alex walked into the shop, "show him our muff selection."

"I hope you've got some in orange," said Mrs. Gluck. "That's the color of the spray paint that's on my mink. Orange!"

"It's going to be all right, Mrs. Gluck," said the bald man, a little sternly.

"A stripe, like a skunk!" she continued. "I walked into the Regency looking like an orange skunk."

The bald man turned at the waist towards Mrs. Gluck without actually moving his feet, which, Alex noticed, had been planted to the exact same two spots on the faded white carpet since the moment he walked in the door, as though years ago the carpet had acquired a terrible pair of stains, and store policy dictated that every day an employee had to stand for the whole day with a foot on each one so as to cover them up.

"Mrs. Gluck," said the bald man, his shiny bald head lowered a little so his eyes were looking out from under his brow, his handlebar mustache looking strangely like a weapon with which he was taking aim. It was the tone of voice bartenders famously use for their regulars who are at risk of being asked to leave. Then he turned back to his cohort and said, "Al, why don't you get Renata to show the gentleman our muff selection."

They walked to the back of the store.

"You know, you were not out of line to make that clarification," said Al under his breath. He moved with brisk steps that for some reason did not propel him any faster than Alex's more languid pace. "Bud always gets a little tense when he sees an unfamiliar face. Not that we don't want some unfamiliar faces!"

They walked up three steps to a smaller area, set off from the rest of the store, where a large bin sat, and where a metal rack held an array of new muffs. "Renata!" he called out. He waited a second, and then hurried through a doorway above which was a sign that read "Repairs."

Alex stared at the muffs. They looked like the things one finds furiously spinning at a car wash. They bristled with newness. Most of them were a color which he could only define to himself as "blond." None of them was what he had in mind. The muff idea was becoming a failure. Alex felt a trickle of grief the way one might feel a raindrop fall down the back of one's collar.

"I understand you're looking for a muff," came a voice by his side. It belonged to a young woman with curly black hair and thick eyeliner and tight black pants. She was stylish in a contemporary way that for a moment Alex had a hard time reconciling with the interior of the Ritz Thrift Shop.

"They're so crazy disorganized," she continued. "There's these," and she gestured to the rack of blond muffs, "but they're not too nice. Do you like them?"

"Not really," said Alex.

"Yeah. Neither do I. But over here, this is where the good stuff is." She walked over to a box Alex hadn't noticed before, something like a wooden laundry hamper for fur, which was filled with muffs. She began to pull them out one after another, providing a running commentary.

"This is sort of fifties slinky; this one's crazy sixties; this is all beat up, you'd have to restore it yourself; I love this, it's beautiful, but between you and me I think it's in less than ideal condition. But what glamour! So thirties glamour! Is that what you're looking for?"

"I was just thinking muff. I didn't have a more vivid picture in mind," said Alex. But then he realized he did have a vivid picture. And it *was* thirties glamour. "Will you try on that muff?" he said.

She did.

"What kind of look does she have?" said Renata.

"It's hard to explain," said Alex.

She cocked her head as though she were relinquishing her own personality and making herself blank, a mannequin onto which the customer could project whatever image he wanted. It was amazingly effective. Suddenly, in a flash, Alex saw the muff as it would look on Christine. It was sleek and elegant.

"What kind of animal?" he said.

"Fox," she said. "The best."

ALEX'S RELATIONSHIP WITH Christine was a beautiful dream, but also an extremely anxious one, because just as some dreams have, within them, a built-in awareness that *this is a dream* and at some point it will end, thereby giving the dream world a peculiar kind of deadline, a ticking clock against which the dream's action has to race, so Alex's relationship with Christine had within it a kind of time bomb, a self-destruct mechanism whose ticking was a constant reminder of the finite quantity of their love.

Maybe it was that she was so much older than he was (though she didn't look it). Or maybe it was the blank wondrous gaze she sometimes bestowed on him, as though she couldn't believe she would be visited by such a nice twist of fate, but it was nevertheless a visit.

He delivered the box to Nadine's in advance and left it with the bartender. Then he went to her apartment building. He had said he would pick her up at eight, and when he looked at his watch he saw he was exactly one minute early. The watch had been a gift from her on his birthday almost exactly six months earlier. It was sporty, digital, and not particularly expensive. He loved it. Alex had never worn a watch in his entire life, but kept it on his wrist at all times, day or night, except for showers.

He decided to wait the one minute until eight precisely. He stared at the list of names beside their corresponding buzzers. There were a series of black sticker strips, produced by the kind of handheld machine that punches out the letters one at a time. He stared at her name, Bancroft, its letters now faded because she was one of the more senior tenants. He knew she wanted, in some diffuse way, to leave New York. How could you argue on behalf of New York? he wondered. If you grew up there it was one thing, but to arrive from somewhere else . . . what was to prevent you from leaving for a more sane and practical environment? And he couldn't make the only argument he could think to make: you can't leave New York because I'm here!

He thought about the muff, how it would look on her, and speculated on her mood.

Today marked the end of the six-month period when she was ten years older than he was, and began the period when she was eleven years older. It was a Wednesday and he hadn't slept with her since Saturday, and had not seen her since Sunday night, when, in spite of his cajoling attempts to change her mind, she had said she wanted to spend a couple of days alone, sleep alone in her bed (a fair request, he rationalized, because no matter how well they snuggled it was a single bed and he was a big guy and anyone should be forgiven for wanting to sleep alone on a single bed now and then), and generally collect herself. That he should be the occasion of her becoming scattered was either a good sign or a bad sign, depending on his mood.

AT THE RESTAURANT, her steak consumed, Christine took a sip of red wine and, putting the glass down, proceeded to make a sheep sound.

"Mahahha." A little lamb sound. She took a pleasant sip of her red wine amidst the kooky and subdued festivity of Nadine's.

"Oh my God," he said, delighted. "Not the lamb sound."

Now she made a deeper, more feline sound, more like an ominous purr, not a kitten, a leopard.

"Jesus! What was that?" he said. "That was terrifying. Go back to being a sheep."

"It's not a sheep," she said. "It's a lamb." Then she made the sound: "Mahaha." Then she smiled at Alex. She liked it when he responded to things she did. His face sometimes took on that look of dumb delight people have when they watch fireworks. She affected him that way. It worried her, though, to think that for anyone else in the world, including the perplexed-looking couple sitting next to them, that sound would mean nothing except, perhaps, that she was weird. Well, she figured, she *was* weird. When she was happy, she made lamb sounds.

It had been a lovely dinner. She described her surprise and befuddlement at receiving a singing telegram, related the emotional complications, and both she and Alex laughed gleefully, their comprehension and appreciation of the general absurdity of things in perfect synchronization. These moments of synchronization frightened her. His laughter was infectious. He had a way of simultaneously teasing her and complimenting her—with his laughter, his attention, his lustful eyes, the bright flare of surprise that lit his face when she did unexpected things—that she delighted in. The thought of its absence sent a pang of fear through her. It didn't linger. It was a single sharp jab of pain inside of her, something inexplicable, incurable. She hadn't told him about what thoughts the singing telegram had interrupted.

The Gum Incident was the most obvious example of something she had been feeling more and more strongly for a couple of years—she was like a house that had been overgrown with vines. Her own history had crept up around her and tied her down, made her earthbound. She wanted to fly. She wanted her life to change. And in her imagination this change would come about via a kind of hurricane that would sweep her away, unmoor her, change her life. There was the possibility, the vague hope, that the hurricane would come in the form of a man, that he would sweep her off her feet. But she was prepared to be her own hurricane, to do it herself. Alex had been a lovely breeze. But his love felt like another constraining vine wending its way around her. It didn't feel liberating. It was at the opposite end of the spectrum from the Gum Incident—more beautiful, connected, real— but it was on the same spectrum. He was part of her past even while sitting across from her, even when inside of her. But she couldn't tell him any of this. He was too young to understand this restlessness, which is different from youthful, meandering, exploratory, all-the-time-in-the-world restlessness. Hers was an urgent restlessness: now or never.

She rehearsed the words in her mind: *I'm going to move to San Francisco.*

What! he would say, another huge firework thudding into the dark sky. *Why?*

"Now what?" he said now, with a jokey petulance. "What's the matter?"

"Nothing," she said.

"You looked . . . like you saw someone you knew a long time ago just cross the street."

"I was just thinking," she said.

"Well, never a dull moment, baby," he said now, his face softening to a smile. "I've got something for you, too."

He jumped up from his seat and went to the bar, returning with a big box.

"Close your eyes," he said.

"Alex, what are you doing?"

"Close your eyes," he said again. She closed them. "Put out your hand. Palm up." She did so. She could hear the sound of the box open, and the soft ruffle of that tissuelike paper that is used to cosset shirts and sweaters in boxes. Except the box was a strange round shape. This was going to make her announcement about leaving more difficult. She steeled herself for it; maybe over dessert, she thought. And then she had a bizarre thought. Maybe he was going to give her a ring. Was Alex going to propose? Was the box an elaborate fake-out? He would ask her to marry him and half the restaurant would turn to see what she had to say in response and she would blurt out that she wanted to break up and move three thousand miles away, thereby causing a level of emotional carnage in the restaurant that would stream through the gossipy tributaries of these other people's lives for weeks and months to come.

"Happy birthday," he said, and as he said the words a soft furry thing descended onto her hand, enveloping it. She opened her eyes. Alex sat across from her, beaming, and on her hand, precariously balanced, was a black fur thing that bore a very strong resemblance to a dead animal.

"What is it?" she said, a little mortified.

"It's a muff," he said. "For your hands."

The extremely unwelcome words "anal electrocution" flashed through her mind, courtesy of some anti-fur literature that someone had once thrust into her hand on a street corner. She stared at it. She could feel her mouth drop open. She pushed one hand into the enclosure, and then the other. It was warm in there.

"It's sort of an antique, I hope you don't mind. It was the nicest thing I saw. They don't make muffs like they used to. Well? Well? Is it too weird?"

"No," she said. "It's beautiful."

She stared at him, stricken, thinking of how to break the news.

Alex saw that Christine had a strange expression on her face. She was clutching the muff with both hands, holding on to it for dear life. Her white fingers dug into the black fur. His body tensed with expectation, not knowing what was going on.

"Christine?" he said. A huge wave of panic crashed against him. She saw it in his face. She knew he sensed her impending detachment. Yet rather than retracting into himself, pulling himself upright and standing on his own two feet, he was instead throwing himself at her.

"Oh, Alex," she said. It was, he thought, the most deliciously complicated statement, partly patronizing, partly a cry for help. They sat there in silence for a moment.

He leaned in towards her across the table, and it was as though he were flying at her through the air, and she felt like a trapeze artist who won't extend her arms at the crucial moment. You can't really catch other people, she thought. If they're going to fall, they fall.

"Christine," he whispered, and, bracing himself on his elbows, he leaned forward to kiss her on her forehead.

Personal Style

ALEX FADER SAT ON SALLY BROWN'S COUCH HAVING THE
following thoughts: She's beautiful. She's beautiful. She's beautiful.

"Everyone from Yale is jealous of you," Sally was saying. "I just
talked to a guy who went there and all he could talk about was
you." Her voice was low, almost sultry, except when she got
excited and it leapt to a high register.

"I didn't go to Yale," said Alex, emerging from his reverie. He
mentioned the name of his considerably less distinguished college.

"That's what I meant," she said, unfazed.

"Why would anyone be jealous of me, anyway?"

"Because of what a *success* you are!" she said. Her voice leapt up on the word "success." "I mean, how many people have made a movie at such a young age? And been written up in the paper? How many people have done that?"

He was tempted to point out, somewhat tersely, that what he had made was a short *documentary*, which, though it was a movie, wasn't really a *movie*, in the usual popcorn-eating sense of the word. He was also tempted to point out that hundreds if not thousands of people his own age had made things and been written about in the papers. He was tempted to point out that she was behaving like a grandmother who takes exaggerated delight in every accomplishment of her grandchild. He was tempted to point out many different things, but didn't. Instead he sat in a docile stupor on her couch, looking at her.

Sally belonged to that class of men and women (though mostly women) who were associated with all the city's great charities but who, aside from substantial outlays of cash, projected an atmosphere and ambience that was the exact opposite of charitable. Most of these women were very old, and though Sally was still in her late twenties, he wondered if she pretended to be old (and a little senile) to better fit in.

She cocked her head a little to the side in a manner that reminded him, for some reason, of an absurd movie he had been dragged to as a kid, *Benji*, about a dog with a personality so intense that it was able to communicate with humans with its facial expressions. It wasn't that she looked like Benji. It was that she looked like she *owned* Benji, that Benji was her dog, whose intense, questioning gaze she was now returning. She seemed to be expecting him to say something.

"I'm not so young," he said. He was twenty-five. "And also . . ." He was going to continue with a series of self-deprecating and down-to-earth comments, but lost his train of thought.

The couch on which Alex and Sally sat was a white pillowy two-seater. Sally was sitting about as far away from Alex as possible, reclining against the far armrest, and Alex might have thought that she had concocted this whole meeting for some strange anthropological reason—a field trip in which the field came to her—but for her two bare feet, which were comfortably propped up on his knee. She wore faded blue jeans with a hole in one knee the size of a dime, and a silky white button-down shirt with the top three buttons undone.

Alex was wearing a blue blazer with gold buttons and a white button-down shirt whose sleeves were a little too short. And black jeans. They were new, so he hoped they registered not as jeans, but as black. He was striking out for new ground, clotheswise; like Sally's couch, the blazer was unfamiliar territory. He had recently decided to stop dressing like a graduate student who also played drums in a rock band (his friends, whom he barraged with postcard invitations to every show, told him that when he got carried away, which was more or less always, he looked like the drummer in the Muppets) and start dressing like a serious filmmaker or one of those neat but slightly raffish television reporters who knock on the doors of ne'er-do-wells, camera crew in tow, and confront them about their misdeeds.

This was exactly what he had done in his short documentary, *Petty Cash*, which retold the story of his expulsion from the Wave Hill School, in eleventh grade. His crime was having started a renegade newspaper, the *Student Herald*, whose first issue had a front-page headline which read, in a type size usually reserved for the outbreak of war, "Student Faculty Animosity: Whose Fault Is It?" Alex's crime had been greatly compounded, in the eyes of the administration, by the fact that he had obtained, through completely honest and legitimate means (he insisted until the bitter end), the mailing list for the entire school, as well as the school's bulk mail stamp, and had sent out the premier issue with its inflammatory cover story along with a passionate piece of fund-raising literature to every parent in the school. Even this infraction against the established (in 1907) order of the Wave Hill School might have been survivable but for the fact that Alex, as both author and editor of the newspaper and the accompanying letter, had managed to average about three spelling mistakes in every line, and so to go along with some very generous checks he received from a few progressive and open-minded parents, the school was inundated with irate letters and phone calls demanding to know what kind of school was this that they could have an illiterate going unnoticed in its midst? What kind of education were their kids getting in return for these astronomical fees?

"You know who I liked the best?" said Sally. "The science teacher, what's-her-name. She was so intense, talking about her son. Her eyes had this, I don't know, pooling effect. Like she was on the verge of tears but stoically holding back. I loved that."

The whole event had been a gruesome episode in Alex's life, and it seemed deeply perverse to him that it should in some way be responsible for landing him on Sally's couch. His documentary approached the whole affair in the spirit of an investigative report, as on *60 Minutes,* into a long-covered-up crime. Alex appeared on camera dressed in a jacket and tie, made some pre-liminary remarks about the time and the place and the cast of characters, and then embarked on a quest to interview the key players, almost none of whom had any desire to be interviewed by a formerly expelled student. It became, almost by accident, a farce; after being politely rebuffed by his old nemesis, Mr. McPherson, he found out where he lived and staked out his drive-way. For some reason there is an enduring *Candid Camera* kind of delight in seeing people being filmed who were not expecting to be filmed; to see their discomfort, the way they draw themselves up, to see their faces make calculations, get their bearings, and try and behave in a proper manner. Mr. McPherson declined to be interviewed, as did several other administrators—serious, tweedy men who took their jobs as educators seriously, and who had seriously presided over Alex's breach of etiquette, decorum, criminal law, and, most maddeningly to him, "the spirit of community that is so important to Wave Hill," as Mr. Laverman, the most tweedy and bow-tied of the bunch, had put it to the assembled culprits and their parents on the first day of the proceedings, with all the sick glee of a torturer dripping a little hot wax on the bare asses of his victims before getting down to the serious business of pain administration.

The one person who had agreed to go on camera was Ms. Sanchez, the biology teacher, who had testified on his behalf at the trial, making an incredibly serious and even passionate argument that he was, basically, a good kid and deserved a second chance, even if he had already had quite a few second chances. Ms. Sanchez was a Spanish woman with large, heaving, and rather firm breasts and deep, melancholy eyes, the former of which caused Alex to frequently excuse himself in the middle of class to alleviate the monstrous sex fantasy that proceeded unabated from the moment he laid eyes on her at the start of every class, and the latter causing him a weird sensation of shame and pleasure when he returned to his seat, human again, and she cast him a peculiar glance over the rim of her glasses, which always slid down to the end of her nose when she taught, that suggested she knew exactly what he had just done, and didn't mind.

Ms. Sanchez had given him a very undeserved good grade in vertebrate anatomy the previous year, mostly because he had done so well on the year-end cat-brain dissection project. He had done so well because one day he arrived in class early, went up to one of the stinking buckets of formaldehyde in which the cats were stored, removed a random cat, and traded it for the botched Frankenstein experiment of a cat that was in his bucket. He got lucky; he got a perfectly dissected cat brain.

Ms. Sanchez's emotion on his behalf at the trial was replicated in an unexpected way when he interviewed her for the documentary. She had been its one heartwarming feature. On camera she explained that a few years prior to when he knew her she had lost a son. He had died when he crashed a motorcycle he had borrowed from a friend. Her melancholy eyes filled up as she told the story. It made him feel ashamed to be devoting all this attention to such a small gripe, such a petty complaint about what, in the big scheme of things, was a very small bump in life's road, and yet she gave the film some real authority. She was still upset about "what they did to you," as she had put it.

"They" became his prey. Particularly Mr. McPherson, dean of the upper school, who had been angling for principal and seemed to think that in squashing the *Student Herald* insurrection he was making a name for himself as a law-and-order sort of dean. Alex became a dogged reporter; at one point McPherson was seen pathetically jogging down a leafy suburban block only to have Alex jump out of the bushes in jacket and tie, microphone in hand, and start jogging along with him, asking pointed questions about the specifics of the trial. Mr. McPherson's response, amazingly, was to break into a sprint. He outran Alex and his camera crew. It proved to be the weirdest and funniest footage of the documentary, McPherson's white-soled sneakers flashing smaller and smaller as he receded in the distance.

The whole experience of making the movie had been extremely painful and unfunny on some level, and the project was driven by a sort of zealous and, some of his friends and professors pointed out, unhealthy desire for revenge. Alex's response was that he was not vengeful. But he felt there was a lot to be avenged.

There had been, back in eleventh grade, a trial. He and his cohorts—Phil Singer, Arnold Gerstein, and Jack Eisner—had to sit alongside their parents on several occasions after school and face the inquisition. It was mass humiliation. In the end, Gerstein, Singer, and Eisner were subtly abused by not getting into the college of their choice the following year. But Alex, because of his long track record as a disruptive force and an academic underachiever, was booted outright. For years afterwards he found himself imagining clever ripostes and new philosophical defenses he could have delivered to the committee. In real life he had begun with a spirited defense and ended with a mumbled contrition and an appeal for amnesty. Then he slunk out of the school for the last time with his furious, white-lipped mother, who, to his delight and grief, reserved her anger about the whole situation almost entirely for the bastards who ran Wave Hill, with only a little left over for him.

Petty Cash, humbly screened along with the other graduate projects, had been seen by a journalist who was writing an article on the state of New York's private schools. It was one of those part-news, part-lifestyle articles that manage to make a certain schadenfreude-sensitive segment of the population react as though the dentist had accidentally drilled through a nonanesthetized tooth. The journalist featured the documentary prominently as an example of the malaise that existed beneath the glossy surface of private school life. There was a photo of Alex. The whole article had a seismic importance for the exact amount of time it was on the newsstands, after which it completely vanished. But an afterglow had lingered around Alex for a few more weeks, at the tail end of which he met Sally.

"You're a public figure," she had remarked to him when they first met, a twinkle in her eye, as though she might be kidding, or she might not.

It occurred to him that Sally was probably McPherson and Laverman's idea of a dream student. She was everything they wanted their lives to be like. She was the fantasy to which he was ghastly reality, the counterpoint.

So his presence on her couch had an almost political or anthropological aspect to it; he wanted to get inside this strange creature and understand the mechanics of her thought, of her existence, to see how much irony and facetiousness she attached to the act of appearing in majestically expensive jewels at benefits for the needy (not much, he thought). Less philosophically, he just wanted to get inside her. He wanted to perturb that placid elegant surface and watch her turn into an animal. He wasn't a hunter, literally or in that figurative way that people sometimes use for men chasing women, but there was an element of blood sport to this visit.

As he sat on her couch and saw the ease with which she threw her bare feet up on his lap, however, it occurred to him that if there was a hunter in the room, it was probably the person not wearing shoes.

NOW HE RECALLED that line about his being a public figure—its inscrutable mirth—as he sat on her couch. At the moment, however, there was no public. There was a room with green wallpaper and small framed lithographs of horses and other vestiges of a certain preppy kind of wealth; there was a white couch with a rather stunning woman with shiny brown hair and green eyes on it; and there were Sally Brown's two bare feet. She was speaking, and his right hand rested calmly on her left ankle as though it were the most natural thing in the world.

He had never before touched her ankle, or even seen it, as this was only their second meeting. The first one had been two nights earlier at a party that was filled with people whose presence reminded him of freshly minted coins. He had always felt disdain for these shiny people, and was amazed and appalled at how eager he was, once in their presence, to be mistaken for one. He had met Sally just moments after entering into a conversation with a tall blond model he had just been introduced to and in whose presence he had developed, for the first time in his entire life, an utterly debilitating stutter. His conversation with the model—or rather his brief session of stammering at her before she smiled and walked away—had gained Sally's attention and, he thought, respect. In the same way that a sleazy real estate developer secures a loan from one bank on the strength of a loan he has secured from another, he had somehow secured the interest of Sally Brown.

He had heard of her. She possessed a certain amount of gossip-column notoriety and a cold, slightly cruel beauty which looked good in pictures, and better in person. She was rich. She wrote about clothes. Her eyes had the piercing judgmental quality of someone who makes important decisions—like what dress to buy—frequently. They had chatted in a coy insubstantial way that Alex enjoyed a great deal. A man ran up to them, a drink in one hand and a small Instamatic in the other. "Sally!" he called out familiarly, and snapped a picture. She turned ever so slightly towards the man and smiled just as the flash went off. Alex blinked.

Eventually they had held hands, and she had almost let him kiss her on the lips as he put her into a taxi, turning her head at the last second.

"Why don't you call me and we can have tea," she said instead. Which was how he had ended up on her couch, without the aid of alcohol, and only his rational faculties to fall back on. He weighed the situation.

On the one hand, Sally's position at the far end of the couch, her beauty, the florid swags of cloth that hung down from the ceiling, the address (Park Avenue), the tray of tea she had brought out for them to sip (a drink would have held more promise), and the small amount of time she had allotted this meeting (six to seven) all suggested to Alex that this was a mistake in the cosmic order of things, that he didn't belong here, and that Sally would soon end the meeting as quickly and circumspectly as possible.

On the other hand, there were her feet—two innocent and unassuming repudiations of all the above objections. They were pretty feet, but not perfect. The arch was nice, the bones delicate, but the toes were slightly bulbous at the ends and were spaced a little strangely. They were, to their credit, devoid of all the abused, exhausted, *footsy* qualities that feet often have. Both of them, like the rest of Sally, seemed to have recently emerged from a fragrant hot bath and been swaddled in something spectacularly smooth and luxurious.

"Alex, are you listening to me?" she said. "You've gone all glassy-eyed on me." She took her feet down from his lap.

"I was listening to you," he said. "I was also trying to remember something. I can do several things at once."

"What were you trying to remember?"

He couldn't remember. "This room is like one big four-poster bed," he said.

"Do you want a drink instead of tea?" she said. "I have whiskey."

"No. This tea is very nice." He reached forward and picked up the cup and saucer. It had little flowers printed on it. He felt like a gorilla who has had an object of sophistication tossed into his cage, and whose reaction was being carefully monitored by scientists in white coats with clipboards. He took a sip, and his hand shook slightly as he brought the teacup back to the saucer; the pieces of porcelain quivered against each other before settling, producing a faint ringing sound.

"Where do you live again?" she said.

"On the West Side. Uptown a bit from here," he added vaguely.

"I was just on the West Side today! They finally opened up the Seventy-ninth Street transverse they've been working on for so long and so I thought I would take a look. I went all the way to Zabar's!" She made it sound as if she had been on a safari.

"Go on with what you were saying before," he said.

"You don't even know what I was saying before," she said.

"You were talking about how much you hate that woman," he guessed.

"Right. Well, anyway, I just think it's absurd that she's been made a contributing editor at *My Cell*," said Sally, mentioning the name of a hip new fashion magazine. "I mean, she doesn't even write anything. You know, I'm a contributing editor at *My Cell*. Did I mention that?"

"Several times."

"Don't be snide." She put her feet back on his knee, though this time she didn't cross them at the ankles and they lay there like two slats, waiting to be touched.

He was amazed at his ability to be slightly rude to her, and knew he must somehow keep it up at all costs.

She started in on how unpleasant this other woman, the socialite, was, how she only threw parties and meanwhile here was Sally slaving away in front of the word processor. Alex now had a hand on each ankle. He squeezed gently and methodically, left right left right, and watched the effect of each squeeze manifest itself in the slight movement of her toes. If he squeezed hard they splayed a little. Eventually he squeezed too hard and Sally said, "Stop it," and took her feet down.

"And so then my mother calls and says, 'Honey, you looked just wonderful in that spread in the magazine. I never knew you wore top hats out at night.' And you know what that means, don't you? Don't you?"

"No, I don't. What does it mean?"

"It means she actually mistook her for me! It means my own goddam mother actually thought she was me! And meanwhile I was on the other page in this nice white dress and, and . . . oh, I hate my mother!"

At this moment Sally sat forward abruptly and her loose white shirt parted. The inside half of both her breasts—which were quite full and, apparently, bare—briefly came into view. Alex apprehended them at the same time that he saw a remarkable thing happen at the corners of Sally's mouth. A veritable avalanche of saliva came forward, bubbling out at the corners. Only at the last second did she catch it and suck it back in. It was quite disgusting, the very first unattractive thing he had seen of her, and the combination of this slightly gross physical mistake (maybe she drooled while she slept) and the incredible sight of her breasts and the beauty of her face and the greenness of her eyes and the buoyant bounce of her shiny brown hair, and also the thought of what it might mean that she had invited him over for tea and was padding around barefoot and braless and in a loose white button-down shirt with the top three buttons undone confessing to feelings of dissatisfaction and pain—all this conspired to give him an erection.

It rose up beneath his black jeans without any regard to decorum or tea rules, and Alex sat back and closed his eyes and prayed for it to go away.

"Oh God, look, I've freaked you out. I guess you see all this has nothing to do with Emily Peters, it's all about my mother. I have a difficult relationship with my mother."

With the word "mother," Alex's erection went away. He sat back up, struggling a little with the pillows. When he was upright he looked at Sally, whose feet were back on the ground and whose face was near his.

"You have very beautiful eyes," he ventured.

"Thank you," she said. They stared at each other, with lust, with love, with curiosity, Alex wasn't sure. Then Sally jumped off the couch and went over to a little rolltop desk in the corner of the room on which she had a computer turned on and began to furiously pound something out on the keyboard. This went on for about thirty seconds and then she sat back down on her side of the couch.

"Did I inspire you to write something?" he asked.

"No. I just wrote a few sentences about Miranda Frasier's jewelry the other night. I'm doing a piece for *My Cell*. It's due in a week."

"What's it about."

"Personal style. The way people look. The way they act. They way they combine all these different elements into a personal style."

"I think you have a really nice personal style."

"Thank you, Alex," she said, and she sat up and smiled what seemed like the most radiant and suggestive smile he had ever seen. She sat straight up and brought her face very close to his, as though there were a very small message spelled out on the tip of her nose and she wanted him to read it. He leaned in a little, narrowing the distance between them so that he could almost feel her breath.

"I think having a personal style is almost something you can't even pay attention to," he murmured, as though in a trance. "It sort of just happens. One day you're walking down the street and you glimpse yourself reflected in the window of some store . . ."

His hand found hers on the couch and he began squeezing it in the same palpitating way he had squeezed her ankle. He was almost whispering now. His hand and hers meshed perfectly. Their hands fit so well it felt matrimonial. ". . . and you have this spontaneous reaction, when you see this thing reflected in the window, you think, 'I'd like to have that, I'd like to own that,' except you already have it. It's you."

Her eyes looked into his, moving a little as they focused on the left one and then the right one, and she was smiling a little, as though enjoying herself tremendously, and then a most important decision was upon him: Should he try to kiss her? And risk spoiling this perfect moment with Sally Brown? The famous socialite who was in *People* magazine as one of the fifty most beautiful women of the year and who had taken an inexplicable liking to him at a party and was now gazing lovingly into his eyes and holding his hand in her apartment where she had invited him and made him tea?

Or should he play it safe and preserve this moment forever in the realm of the possible, the present tense that hovers just before another more exciting present tense that hasn't yet arrived? But then he would risk missing an opportunity to kiss her, to touch her breasts, to discover the exact shape and color of her nipples, to listen to her breath, to feel her hands on the back of his neck.

Maybe, he thought, his whole appeal to her was as someone a little rougher than what she was used to, a little less bound by social convention, someone who would make the pass, who would kiss her deeply, who would enter several different parts of her body at once and generally molest her and fuck her and use her, and after all hadn't all that saliva come frothing forward in her mouth? Didn't she have these desires like everyone else? Wasn't she a grown woman, an adult grown-up lady in the world who had a grown man on the couch with her with whom she was entangling her sensitive, warm, and well-washed extremities? Would she ever forgive him for this moment lost?

Years of experience with women, years of lustful passes, of attempted seductions, of earnest caresses that led to further caresses—all this fell away in just a few seconds, and what remained was a tender reed of inexperience going back to age twelve, when a young girl's moonlike face hovered before his much as Sally's hovered before his face now. That first kiss had been a mild disaster, and somehow every bit of skill in the art of the kiss acquired since then had suddenly disappeared, and he was stuck in the position of instantly learning the entire alphabet all over again so that he might construct a rather complicated sentence.

From somewhere in the depths of his soul, the tribunal that makes these decisions returned from its private chambers and rendered judgment: better to have tried and failed than to spend the rest of your life wondering if Sally Brown had wanted to fool around on her couch and was waiting for you to start. And so, with the eloquence, grace, and cunning of the his former twelve-year-old self, he closed his eyes, pursed his lips, and stuck out his pointy love-seeking head.

Sally performed an effortless feint; not even a cheek was available. He withdrew and opened his eyes. Her expression was remarkably unchanged.

"It's cold and flu season," she said.

Instinctively, they both leaned back into their side of the couch, letting the pillows envelop them slightly. Alex felt the burn of humiliation across his neck and shoulders, but he struggled to keep his expression as implacable as hers.

"I don't have a cold," he said matter-of-factly. "I take a vitamin C every day. Sometimes twice a day."

Much to his amazement, she propped her feet back onto his

lap. He glanced down at them momentarily, but they had lost their sexual charge. The gesture seemed almost sisterly.

"If I think I'm getting a cold I start taking echinacea and goldenseal like crazy," she said.

"I'm not getting a cold," he said. "I'm perfectly healthy."

"I think you're right about personal style, about how it should seem really casual and accidental. Except it takes a lot of effort to appear casual. People who have personal style have to work hard at it. It doesn't just spontaneously combust, it has to be developed."

"Some people spontaneously combust," said Alex.

Shortly thereafter Alex excused himself to go to the bathroom, where he was seized with a torrential coughing fit. He pushed his face into a towel and coughed vehemently, then he washed his face, wetted his hair a little, and went back to the couch. He tried to remember what it had been like with Sally before the attempted kiss, in the realm of Maybe, but couldn't. All he could recall was that there had been a casual and even a somewhat cruel element to his behavior towards her when they first met. He had recognized the necessity of maintaining the threat of cruelty, or at least indifference, but now he had dropped the ball. You can't be cruel to someone after you've tried to kiss her and failed, he thought. As a sort of self-punishment, he returned to the subject of clothing.

"You know what I find very difficult?" he said. "Deciding about the blue blazer thing. Like this, for example." He held out his arm.

"It's nice," she said, a little uneasily, as though she suspected him to be on the verge of a long speech.

"This is a nice jacket. Paul Stewart." He gave her a knowing look. "The thing is, is it really . . . me? I mean, is it my own personal style, or is it someone else's? I'm not sure. I usually wear black jeans and a T-shirt with a sweater over it."

"I think men look good in blue blazers," said Sally. She was clearly trying to lighten up the moment. Her voice had a ring of impatience to it, as though she were saying, "Pull yourself together, goddamm it."

"But the question is, does the blue blazer look good with black jeans?" He gave her the penetrating look of a prosecutor.

"It's all right with black jeans. Blue jeans might be better, if it has to be jeans," she said.

"And how about the shoes?" he said, kicking one foot up in the air. "White socks with black shoes. A disaster if you ask me. Yet, you ask, why am I wearing them?"

"I'm not asking."

"Wait! We are onto something. Don't you think black shoes and white socks are a bit extreme?

"Extremes are good," she said. "Though maybe you should try black socks."

"I've been intending to drop this white socks thing for years. Years! Why haven't I?" His voice was charged now, full of fire.

"Alex, I think you look nice. You shouldn't worry about this. Worrying is not a good personal style."

"I sense a personal style crisis coming on," he said glumly.

"I'm going to dinner soon," she said. She smiled at him. It was a smile that had leveled men more confident and self-possessed than Alex, and Alex, one leg still extended in the air, was no match for it. The leg came down. "Ansel is coming to pick me up, it's a long-standing date. He's just the most incredible man. He just got back from Istanbul and is going through his third round of chemotherapy and is forty-two years old and is just amazing. Anyway, he's coming by soon. In fact I think I've got to get dressed now."

"All right," he said. He stood up. "Let's do this again soon." He went over and picked up his leather jacket and started to put it on. "This jacket doesn't go very well with the blazer, does it?" he said. There was a pathetic ring to his voice.

"You need a topcoat," she said in her sisterly tone. He felt himself start to tremble. His career as a Freshly Minted Coin was, apparently, in its concluding phase. An image of the scolding tribunal of Wave Hill administrators passed before him. She kissed goodbye on the cheek.

"Wow, you have I think the smoothest skin I've ever felt. It's quite an experience," he said.

"And you're a little unshaven," she said, smiling. It was a completely unreadable smile, friendly in a generic sexless way.

"Bye," he said.

"Bye," she said. "Hope to see you soon." She closed the door.

The vestibule had mirrored walls, floor to ceiling, and as Alex stepped towards the elevator he saw a thousand versions of himself moving alongside, each one depicting a man with a blue blazer sticking out unattractively from beneath his black motorcycle jacket. It was a most unwelcome sight. He stood there for a few moments, then looked down at his shoes, which seemed misshapen and in need of a shine.

He walked over to Fifth Avenue and then into dark, lamp-lit Central Park. He liked the park at night, its emptiness, its slight menace. He walked to the gravelly jogging path that snaked around the reservoir. The water was a vast black mirror. The lights from Central Park West and Fifth Avenue glimmered on its surface, and he stared at their reflection. Each shimmering speck on the reservoir was a home, a life; they glittered like stars, but like a star they were all out of reach.

Caller ID

PANIC AT THE VIDEO STORE. TWO MINUTES TO CLOSING, and no decision. Melissa had been standing shoulder to shoulder with Alex in front of the new releases. Now they split up, heading down separate aisles. She paused in front of Classics, and before she could even decide what decade she might be interested in visiting, he returned clutching a box, looking pleased and, she thought, a little cruel, as if this was going to be a movie that would somehow edify and enrich her, as opposed to make her happy.

"Have you ever seen this?" he asked. He held it up.

"No," she said. "I haven't." She wanted to add that there was a reason she hadn't seen it, which was that she wasn't that interested in the Vietnam War.

"Closing," yelled the clerk. They both turned to look at him. He was an avid hockey fan. This, she felt, detracted greatly from the cinema-appreciating vibe of the store. He glowered at them in his blue Rangers jersey.

It was a chilly autumn night and the wind was gusting. He pulled her along brusquely, his arm around her shoulder, and she ducked her chin into the collar of her coat. One hand held the collar against her mouth, the other was pressed deep into her pocket, balled up in a fist. The short walk to her house made her long for the couch, and when they finally arranged themselves there, she felt a great sense of relief, as though everything up to that moment had been preparation. Now, on the couch, indoors, the night could begin, and their distinct, hardened, separate bodies could relax, commingle, and begin to entwine.

She was in her underwear and a T-shirt, with black socks pulled up over her calves. Her work clothes were in a pile on a nearby chair. Alex was still in his jeans, a T-shirt, and work boots.

The one unfortunate aspect to the situation, from Melissa's point of view, was the video: *Apocalypse Now*. Other than a brief shot of Martin Sheen's bare ass, she was finding it a bit abstract. But she knew that he wanted her to like it, so she leaned into his shoulder, pulled her feet under her, and watched. She could feel the warmth of his chest. He was a warm person, literally.

THEY HAD BEEN together nine months. In the beginning they went out often. There was something exhibitionist about their ventures into the world together, as though they wanted to show each other off, and to revel in their newfound status as one-half of a pair. But lately they'd been spending more and more time at home, *her* home. She had made an effort to make her living space accommodating and pleasant; it was soft-edged, pillow-strewn, and a bit peachy in atmosphere and color. His place was either barren or pristine, depending on how you looked at it, and their time there was a bit like time in a motel room—exciting, theatrical, and alienating.

Then the phone rang, and Melissa cocked her head at the sound of it, not wanting to walk the ten steps into the kitchen and wanting in equal measure not to subject one of her friends to the humiliation of babbling into the answering machine while the two of them listened.

"I'll get it," she said in the middle of the second ring, and got up from the couch.

"Do you want me to press pause?" said Alex.

"No, I'll just be a second," she said.

The voice on the phone belonged to Rodney Donoghue. It took her by surprise and made her shiver. It was deep and low and much too intimate.

"Hello, Melissa, it's Rodney," he said. "I'm just calling to say hi, see how you are." He had a way of pronouncing the most innocent comments in a sordid, suggestive manner, as though he were stroking her ass while saying it. This sort of duplicity was, she had come to understand, his specialty—high-mindedness and cordiality providing a thin gloss on his weirdly obsessive and unpleasant nature. His faintly Southern accent was particularly useful in this obscuring cause.

"Hi," she said, and instinctively glanced at Alex to see if he had registered any anxiety, any falseness, in her voice. She thought she sounded shrill and self-incriminating, but Alex just stared at the screen, watching Martin Sheen sulk on a boat going up the Mekong River.

"I'm just calling because I've been thinking about our last conversation," Rodney said.

You mean the one where I said I didn't think you were behaving properly and that your behavior was in fact offending me and that I wanted you to stop touching me that way, she wanted to say.

"Uhm, yeah?" she said instead, and concentrated on the background noise—a faint hiss—trying to figure out if he was calling from his cell phone again. When he had last called she had talked with him merrily for an hour, feeling the peculiar liberation and freedom that comes with the implied distance of a phone conversation, only to have him blurt out: "I'm in a car right in front of your building. Why don't I just come up and we can continue this in person?" She had been so flustered by this that she agreed.

"I thought the conversation didn't really go the way it should have," he said now, "which was unfortunate given that we normally have such a fine rapport."

He was a television talk show host, of the highbrow variety. Rapport was his specialty. She had spent several years of her life concluding many of her evenings lying in bed and watching him nod intelligently at one important, fascinating, and powerful guest after another, interrupting them with penetrating questions and lulling her with his deep, comforting, and faintly paternal voice. Who could blame her for being excited when she met him at a party?

She had rehashed this line of thought many times—*Her Innocence at the Beginning.* They had met at the party for the New York Film Festival, where she worked as a publicist. She had placed numerous calls to his office repeating the invitation at the instruction of her boss. So it was natural that she should introduce herself. They had chatted amicably and he had listened attentively and nodded as she spoke—just as he did on the show—and she had felt the particular thrill of that rapt, attentive expression he always bestowed upon his guests.

"You're a very intelligent and perceptive woman," he had said at one point. "I'm curious to hear suggestions you might have for people on my show." She was aware that he was flattering her. She didn't mind. She was flattered to be flattered.

"Uhm, I'm sort of watching a movie," she said now.

"Which movie are you sort of watching?" he said.

"*Apocalypse Now*," she said.

"You can hit pause," he said.

She wanted to snap something rude and witty at him.

"I'm just going to watch the movie now," she said instead. "Why don't we speak later." This was as terse as she could be without being conspicuous.

"All right. I really wanted to say that I'd like to see you again. I don't want there to be any awkwardness between us because of my last visit. I enjoy your company and also value your opinions. I'm doing a one-hour special on Rembrandt and I thought you could have some input, maybe even help produce. It's all very preliminary."

She was amazed to note her body stiffen a little when he said all this, as though she were a cat being stroked. Her intellect registered the falseness, but she had heard him utter so many words with that homespun Southern accent of his, addressing the guests on his show, that she was instinctively pleased to have such good company in being deceived. She flashed to another moment of weakness, when she had ushered him into her apartment, as though he were there all the time. In a sense, he was. Something very similar to the body that had stood before her had been in her apartment countless times before, but it had been confined to the square television screen. It had been unsettling to have it before her in all its ungainly life-sized reality.

She remembered the weird way his body had occupied space in her apartment, sitting right there on the couch where Alex now sat. It was so strange to see Rodney there, in his suit and tie, smelling faintly of cologne. She didn't smell the cologne until he got near her, and right away she could picture him applying it, standing in the mirror and letting his face go slack with admiration while thinking: Women love this smell.

He had said kind intelligent words of praise to her, loosened his tie, and then he had put his hand on her thigh and stroked it. There was so much gross sexual energy in that single caress that she had almost allowed him to continue. The idea of letting this overly suave, self-possessed, attractive, and successful older man barge into her life and fuck her, thereby letting his already distorted ego pump even farther out of shape at his success with her, was so repulsive that her mind froze in a kind of fascination when considering it. He stroked her thigh several times and moved closer. She was under a kind of spell. Fortunately, the cologne was nauseating. It was a metaphor for the whole situation. There was something rank, false, and toxic about this man. She slapped his hand away and asked him to leave.

"All right," she said now. "I'll talk to you soon." Her voice softened at the very end, as though to leave the door to Rodney open just a crack. She put the phone down, aware of her moment of duplicity.

She went back to the couch, where Alex sat slouched, clutching the video remote, and as she leaned back against him, she was aware of how much she hoped he had noticed something. She wanted him to call her on it. He was always getting into moods and sulks. What she wanted from him was some rage, threat, and anger. She wanted action.

Alex, without looking at her, pressed rewind. Images flickered backwards on the screen. A boat raced backwards down a river, led by a man water-skiing backwards.

"You missed some good parts," he said. "You should really see the whole thing straight through." He put his right arm around her, and casually pulled her against him.

"Who was that on the phone?" he asked nonchalantly.

"Jim Milford," she lied, citing an old friend from college who was familiar to Alex as Just a Friend. She was a terrible liar. Whenever she attempted it she tried to remember what she normally sounded like, and drew an utter blank, and was thus forced to impersonate a self she couldn't imagine. The words slipped out and she glanced at his expression to see if there was a flicker of suspicion. She half hoped to find it.

There was nothing but Alex's slack television gaze, focused on the screen, and for a brief moment she hated him for his inertia even more than she hated herself for her gullibility. For a split second she considered blurting it all out, but then decided that would be ridiculous. She hadn't done anything wrong. Besides, Alex hadn't earned a confession. She wasn't going to do all the work.

ALEX KEPT HIS cool. There was nothing to be gained by expressing the intense pang of anger and fear that had shot through him when he heard her voice dip and observed her body twist slightly, turning away from him just before she put the phone down. And now this outlandish lie about who she was talking to, her voice trilling upwards, her nostrils flaring, her desperate glance to see if he noticed. He had always cherished her sincerity and in a way he was touched by this transparency. But he was also furious, disgusted, frightened, and all the emotions that had been coursing through him for weeks were further inflamed by this new complication. He had come to see Melissa as the indispensable shock absorber between him and the world. He didn't want this buffer, but at the same time, he didn't want to be shocked.

When they met, he had fallen into her soft gaze, her sensitive hands, with a sense of relief. He loved her emotional and wary eyes; he had seen them before. She had gone to the high school that had taken him in for his senior year, and they had talked in the school's lobby. She had been a freshman. One faintly memorable conversation, interrupted for about a decade and picked up again at a party. Senior/freshman. The dynamic still percolated. When that sense of relief ended after a few months he waited for a spark of engagement to succeed it, he waited for it ripen. She was, theoretically, perfect. Why didn't he want her more? What was he waiting for? For her to push him. For something against which he could push. For fear, really. He seemed to have a taste for women who could frighten him a little, one way or another. But the spark hadn't come.

Meanwhile, he sank into her house, her pillows, her; he experienced this as a narcotic, not as love. It removed him from life as opposed to bringing him closer to it. That was his worry, at least. That, and the concern that, as to a narcotic, he was becoming addicted to her. He felt the swell of anxiety that comes with dependence, as well as the resentment. He depended on her even for housing at this point. His own home was strange to him. It was a place where he changed socks. Even these had migrated to her fluffy apartment.

"Baby," he said, summoning the paternal attitude he often assumed when he wanted to calm her down and do what he wanted. "This is a really good movie. You have to concentrate a little, but it's worth it."

"Okay, honey," she said. She looked into his eyes in that way of hers—trusting, sweet, soft, and open, but spiced with that tiny but fierce self-preserving instinct, within which, he thought, was the ability for deceit. He admired that. He liked it when she was strong.

Then he remembered the betrayal he was sure he had just suffered, and was seized with a blinding desire to slap her across the
face. He wanted it both ways. He had no idea what he wanted. In
the midst of his confusion he was determined to be calm and bide
his time.

He tried to resist the pleasures that the night had to offer—her
kindness, softness, the sweetness of coupledom—but could not,
and eventually, as sugar turns into energy, his anger and irritation
transformed itself into lust. He began stroking her hair and kissing her neck. Their bodies melded into one another. She received
his touches with a weird energy that stemmed as much from relief
as from desire.

The sounds of a Wagnerian opera underscoring a helicopter
attack on a small Vietnamese village filled the room. At first he
found the war sounds to be an interesting juxtaposition, but then
they became distracting, and, grappling for the remote, he hit
pause and threw it on the floor with abandon. They started
touching and kissing again and soon were having an amazingly
desperate encounter on the couch, with his pants around his
ankles. For some reason he liked doing it with his pants around
his ankles. Then the pause automatically ended, and the movie
picked up right in the middle of Robert Duvall walking around
with his bastard expression and cowboy hat saying, "I love the
smell of napalm. It smells like . . ."

"I don't believe it," he said, a little embarrassed, as though
someone had in fact walked into the room.

"Victory," said Duvall.

He had to grapple to find the VCR's remote control in order to
stop the video, and then a game show popped on the TV, necessi-
tating a frantic search for the TV's remote control to quell the
horrible screams of game show pleasure. By then there was almost
nothing left.

"I'm being destroyed by technology," he feebly joked. For a while they just lay there next to each other, breathing. Gradually, they recovered, and began again. There was some nugget of panic and desperation in his chest—triggered by the frantic search for the remote control, the brief attack of the shrieking game show, the hushed sound of her voice on the phone—but his insecurity made the sex better, as though he wanted to devour her and thereby be assured that no betrayal was forthcoming. At the end of it he noticed her cheeks were bright pink. He was never completely sure that this actually meant that something had happened, but he always took it as a personal triumph.

Afterwards, she went to the bathroom, and he stood, pulled his pants up, and went to the kitchen counter, where a gaggle of electronic devices were pushed into the corner—phone, answering machine, and a small white gadget she had recently purchased, Caller ID. This little white box registered the number of the person calling you, and the name, on a small LED screen. He hit the last-call button and a number popped up along with a name: *R. Donoghue*. What a clever little device, he thought.

She had told him it had been an impulse buy at Bed, Bath, and Beyond. "They had it right by the checkout counter and I thought what the hell, nineteen ninety-nine, it could be interesting," she had said. Perfect that a store specializing in the pleasures of the home and hearth, a place devoted to the comforts of couples, should have such a suspicious device stuck there as an afterthought, as though the hour or two their patrons had spent contemplating the pleasures to be had using their fluffy white towels, cuddling in flannel sheets, cooking on immaculate Teflon, was the perfect setup for a pang of paranoia: what is really going on with the person with whom all this comfort is to be shared?

He stared at the number on the little gray screen. He heard the faint sound of a toilet flush, and, like a shoplifter who stuffs something in his pocket without thought, only to feel a sense of shock at what he has just done and a simultaneous sense of its irreversibility, he picked up the phone and dialed the number. There was something perverted and betraying about this gesture just after sex, this little bit of romantic espionage. But then he had been betrayed, too. Or had he? He hovered on the edge of hateful seething feelings that, in truth, had no real basis. And if he hung up right away, they never would. Some self-preserving instinct told him to do so; the part of him addicted to the soft warmth of her, the fluffy-towel loving part of him that wanted pleasure and comfort and softness in the world told him to hang up and be done with it.

But there was another force within him too, destructive and condemning, an Old Testament fire-and-brimstone force that said life should be hard, that wanted to punish.

She came into the room in her nightgown, a powder puff of loveliness. She gave him a mildly quizzical look when she saw him on the phone.

"Hello," came a voice after the second ring. "Hello?"

Alex nearly laughed at the obviousness of it. If one went to Central Casting and said, "We need a voice for the Other Man," this is what they would send over. It was ridiculous. The only weird thing was that there was something familiar about it. He looked at Melissa standing there, looking at him, and felt horrible, at last. It was a kind of catharsis, to be such a shit that he no longer hated her, but hated himself, instead. In feeling guilty towards her he could cleanse himself of his anger towards her. He put the phone down in the middle of the third "Hello?"

"Do you want to watch the movie some more?" she asked. She was being accommodating.

"No, hon. That's fine." He went and hugged her.

"Who was that?" she said softly.

"My answering machine."

They got in her fluffy bed and cuddled. Then they rolled onto their backs and turned on the television. Alex stretched his left arm straight out and cracked his wrist. It was a brisk motion—the snap lent it an air of precision. Melissa had come to recognize this simple gesture as a sign that something was bothering him.

"What's wrong?" she said.

"Nothing," he said.

But she didn't believe him. She experienced that crack in the same way a swimmer treading water in the ocean experiences a strange bit of turbulence just beneath the toes, where the water is cold and dark.

He brought her close and held her. His moments of disgust with her were often followed by remorse and relief, as though only at the last moment had he stopped himself from smashing a precious object to the floor.

They held on to one another, flipped channels, browsed through countless voices and images, shared the remote control, both secretly thinking that the television was killing them, that they should get out more, out into the world against which they could define themselves, and when the remote was in his hands he happened to come across Martin Sheen, of all people, being interviewed on a talk show of the high-minded variety, by a man whose loquacious Southern accent was vaguely familiar.

"Let's watch this for a while," he said.

Seconds of Pleasure

KATRINA ARRIVED AT THE GALLERY TO DISCOVER A DENSELY
crowded room whose walls were painted in chocolate. The smell
of chocolate was overwhelming. For once it was impossible to
attend an opening and ignore the art. A small sign in one corner
said that Cadbury had cosponsored the event. A sign in another
corner announced that viewers could lick the art, but at their own
risk. No one was licking the art.

She scanned the room for Nina. Nina had a way of looking at
her with twinkling admiring eyes and a permissive smirk. She
made her want to divulge. They had met at St. Paul's and been

great friends; then there was a long slow death of their friendship. At university Nina had flourished. At university Katrina had met Sam. Nina had become a wit and Katrina had become a wife. But in the last year they had become friends again in a sudden burst.

But Katrina didn't see her, she saw no one she knew. The faces were harsh in the glare. Already she felt the sudden loss of sexual self-confidence that comes with not being married. She sat down on a bench in the middle of the room and hid.

ALEX FADER CLOSED his eyes and smelled the chocolate; its intensity was almost sickening. He opened his eyes and stared at the deep brown wall of chocolate. He peered at it the way people at a museum come right up to a painting so they can see every microscopic nuance. Some parts were very brown, other parts were milky. It had been brushed on, like paint, and he could see the brushstrokes.

He'd been in London for five days, but he had not yet managed to leave New York. Arriving in a new place makes you think of where you have left. You look inward, backward, or spend all your time reading a book explaining what it's like to be where you are. Alex understood this impulse in himself and he tried to resist it.

Once, when he was eleven, his mother had taken him to Israel, where he had been in complete and utter thrall to a book about the Beatles. On a bus, as he continued to press his nose into the book, his mother had cried out, "Oh Alex, look!" He had looked up. "That's Mount Olive over there." He stared at the stone wall in the distance, took in the sunbaked scenery. Then he went back to the Beatles.

Now he stared at the chocolate wall and thought: Oh, come on! Life is out there waiting for you! Engage! He turned to face the room.

He saw an attractive woman, stylish, wearing sleek black clothes, sitting alone on a bench in the middle of the room, and something about her cheeks, the way they were bright, and a certain nervousness about her hands, made his eyes rest upon her. He sidled up to her and saw a strange mark on the back of her hand.

"Excuse me?" he said, gesturing to the back of her hand. "What's that?"

He looked more closely. He took her hand in his and examined it. "You have a dinosaur tattooed in red on the back of your hand. That's very impressive. Do you mind if I sit next to you?"

"It's not my bench," she said. "But it is my hand," and she withdrew it.

He asked her if it was a real tattoo.

"It's fake," she said.

He took a quick appraising glance at her. She wasn't that pretty. His eyes roamed the crowded room and then settled back on her.

She was, suddenly and incontestably, beautiful. Her cheeks and lips had the high color of someone who has just returned from a long walk in the cold. There was a trembling liquid quality to her lips, which were a deep, natural red. Her eyes had within them a certain judgmental distance which suggested that she felt that human beings were irreconcilably alone, that they could never be anything other than alone. There was something about her that would always be "I," never "us," and this made him feel lonely. The loneliness caused him pain. He found the pain delicious.

"Are you the artist?" he said.

"No," she said.

"Friend of the artist?"

"No. Have you been in London long?"

"What makes you think I'm newly arrived?"

"Just a guess."

"Why the dinosaur?"

"It was my son's doing."

"Oh," he said, and looked a bit shocked.

KATRINA STARED THROUGH this interloper, grateful for the cover, nodding and smiling a little on the strength of the conversation's rhythm, not the content, and looking out for Nina. This man's face reminded her slightly of her dog, Abner, a long-faced whippet with soulful, questioning eyes that were always at their most perplexed after he had been barking, as though he himself didn't know what had come over him. On the strength of this resemblance she felt some vague goodwill towards this American. Then she mentioned Patrick, and he changed a little, and this change got her attention; he became a person, curious and pensive and real. She was suddenly able to pay attention to him.

"Have I said anything that has disturbed you?" she said. She noticed that he was wearing a candy necklace wrapped around his wrist, two strands of edible color. She hadn't seen one of those in years.

"No," he said. "Want one?"

"Is that something you wear regularly?"

"No. And I have no excuse for it. I mean, I can't say my daughter put it there or anything. I don't, I'm not . . . Want a bite?" He held his arm up the way men do when they are about to go for a stroll with a woman and want her to take their arm; a formal, old-fashioned, polite gesture, except he was offering candy off his wrist. "They're good," he said. "Go ahead. Really."

She leaned over and carefully, using only her teeth, bit off several of the candies. A half circle of yellow pastel fell off her lips, and she caught it in her palm. It looked like a Valium. With a quick flick of her tongue she retrieved it into her mouth.

"Thank you," she said. They were good. Delicious. "How long are you on vacation?" she said.

"I'm not on vacation. I'm never going back to New York." The words surprised him; they were exhilarating. He felt wonderfully confident. He glanced at her to see if she knew this easygoing person, this casual confidence, was a sham.

She didn't.

SHE DID.

"That's too bad," she said. "Because everyone will like you much more if you're on the verge of going back to wherever it is you've come from."

"I'm leaving on Saturday," he said.

"Very good."

"Really? So, in my last days here in London, would you care to recommend some activity? Perhaps over a drink?"

"Is this an invitation?"

"I suppose so. I'd like to have a drink with you, somewhere away from all this chocolate."

"Would you?" She looked at him with a smile. It was a funny idea, that she might get to know this stray, random bit of Americanness. She regarded him as one might regard an interesting piece of driftwood washed up on a beach—might it look good on the mantel?—before deciding it was simply not worth carrying back to the house.

"I would," he said.

She looked at him. His eyes were green. For a brief moment she felt something recoil within her, not in horror or displeasure, but in the way that one shivers when stroked lightly in a sensitive place. It was intimate and strange and unsettling.

At that moment Alex experienced a hiccup in time; it was as if his own life were on film—not video, not digital, but actual movie film—and there had been a bad splice which had briefly ruined the illusion. On the other side of the splice, she looked different. He wanted to be with her. He stared at her, thinking, Is this real?

He was vaguely aware of his friend Harry's voice nearby. Was he willing to risk humiliation and press the point further? He stared at her closely.

"You're staring," she said.

"Do you want to get a drink after this?"

She started to look away, but didn't. Her eyes stayed on his— they were *dark* green, a little hooded; she had a weird vision of him years from now, his forehead deeply lined, his eyelids heavy, the lines around his mouth making him seem a little sour, a little sexy, a mouth like overripe fruit suggesting both wisdom and sloth. The sort of man you would want to keep your daughter away from, and also the sort of man to whom your daughter, per- versely, might be attracted. The sort of man to whom *she* might be perversely attracted. But this was twenty years down the road. Now he was just a boyish American. She didn't like boyishness. And she didn't like Americans.

"Can't," she said. "Sorry. Have plans."

He stared at her, the rejection burning inside of him; a thin layer of moisture materialized on his chest and back, a cold sweat. His new self had crashed and burned.

A woman approached from the side and called her name. "Kat- rina!" He had that, at least, her name. She stood up and he stood with her. The woman's long arms wrapped around Katrina, her fingers clutching at her thick black hair, pulling it into her neck. When they stopped embracing, Katrina turned to him.

"Nice meeting you," she said, and walked off.

The room swirled around him, smoky and chocolaty and foreign. He wandered outside for a breath of air. And there were Katrina and her friend, talking. He felt acutely embarrassed that it seemed as though he were following them. But there was nothing to do. He stood there and watched. She peered at him, a curious fearful glance, and then she and her friend turned and walked into the damp night.

HER DINNER WITH Nina was a delicious solace. One of the compensations of breaking up is taking stock of that which is *yours*, having for so long shared that which is *ours*. Nina was hers. Nina made her laugh, and didn't mind when she cried. She hadn't cried, but it was nice to know she was allowed.

Now, as she returned home, she remembered the taste of that cheap candy bracelet the American had offered her. She re-saw the whole scene as though there had been a small camera hidden away somewhere, like the ones in a bank, monitoring the crowd. For weeks her mind had been reeling with thoughts of divorce lawyers and court cases, so it fit right into the prevailing mood. She saw herself in slow motion, bending forward to his out-stretched wrist.

ALEX HAD A theory about success in the respective realms of personal and professional life: one is up when the other is down. But the year after he broke up with Christine proved his theory wrong. His love life was awful, and his professional life was awful; he couldn't even get work with any film crews in spite of the fact that all of Manhattan that summer had become a movie set and he couldn't walk down the street without tripping over cable wires.

The worst of it had been the day she left; he carried her bags downstairs, then he went back up to her vacant apartment and carried the tiny single bed, now naked and bare and seedy-looking—as stripped beds always look—downstairs. The bed on which they had cuddled and slept and fucked and groaned and stretched now rested—per the landlord's instruction—against the side of the building.

Breaking up as friends is a miserable thing. It usually means one person agrees not to express the contempt that accompanies disinterest in exchange for the other person's not breaking down in a hysterical lump of grief and begging.

As is usually the case in the friend style of breaking up, Alex and Christina hadn't even had a terrible fight; the balloon didn't burst with a jarring pop, it slowly deflated until it was a shriveled lifeless scrotum of a relationship and then they said goodbye with the understanding that across the expanse of the entire United States, they would be "friends." He made himself look away before the cab turned the corner; he didn't want to see the back of her head vanish.

It was, in a suitably cinematic moment, drizzling. He walked through the rain for a while chanting: "It's over! It's over! It's over!" Then he went home and began reading *Anna Karenina*. At the time he thought it would be like having a whole new relationship, but by the end he decided that he had simply wanted to read about a woman who was in love, having spent all this time with a woman—his own girlfriend—who seemed clearly not to be in love. It was also possible that he wanted to read about a woman throwing herself under a train.

ALEX SPENT MOST of his time that first week in London drunk, and London, in turn, seemed drunk with him. Every day the newspapers carried some ridiculous headline splashed across the front page. A government official spearheading a campaign called

"Back to Basics" had been caught in bed with another man. He claimed he was economizing on hotel rates.

Alex's most intimate encounter had been with a Pakistani mini-cab driver who explained that though he had been born in Birmingham, he considered himself Pakistani. "The English are pissheads," said the driver. "They get their wages on Friday and by Monday they've spunked it up the wall."

Alex had just been fired from the one well-paying job he had ever held, at a television news magazine. He took some consolation in the idea that he had no wages, therefore, to spunk. He was spunking his savings.

The small flat he had been lent on Fitzroy Square was depressing. The fold-out mattress sat on the floor taking up most of the available space, so he wandered down to the local pub or to Maison Bertaux, a tiny pastry shop in Soho in whose upstairs room he gorged on eclairs and so many pots of tea that he left trembling. Then he went to the French House and eavesdropped, waiting for his friend Harry to show up and tell him where that night's social event was.

When he wasn't drinking, he was eating. He was possessed by an insatiable hunger, and ate all the time, mostly at Lazzaro's, the small desolate sandwich shop down the block. Mr. and Mrs. Lazzaro waited with stoic patience for the customers to come in. But the customers had gone elsewhere. Alex sat in their sandwich shop and immersed himself in his book—*The Savage God: A Study of Suicide*, by A. Alvarez. He wasn't suicidal, but someone had told him the book had excellent insight into the English. He sat in Lazzaro's for hours reading about Sylvia Plath, another American in London, gassing herself.

"The young," wrote Alvarez, "are great attempters."

"Yes we are!" Alex said out loud to the close, warm room that smelled of bacon grease and baked beans, in which he sat as the only patron. There was a stirring behind the counter. Harry had informed him that Lazzaro's had once been a thriving establishment, with lines out the door at lunchtime. The problem lay with the new arrival down the street, Rive Gauche, a fashionable French sandwich shop. Through the large picture window Mr. Lazzaro had a clear view of the line extending out from Rive Gauche's front door. His wife sat at the back of the shop, waiting to wait on someone.

After several greasy breakfasts at Lazzaro's, Alex decided to sample Rive Gauche. But when he walked past the corner he made eye contact with Mr. Lazzaro; Alex saw his proud forlorn face glance up from his paper, observe another defection to the enemy, and look back down at his paper without so much as a twitch. Standing in that window Mr. Lazzaro looked like a diorama in the Museum of Natural History: *Old-fashioned sandwich shop proprietor, extinct.*

Alex felt a chill of guilt, and about-faced into Lazzaro's. It was a kind of refuge in there, with its smell of frying bacon and the condensation on the windows and the gloomy expectant face of Mr. Lazzaro as he lifted his eyes from the newspaper and took in the line down the block outside of Rive Gauche.

BEFORE ALEX GOT the job at the network he had picked up odd jobs on film crews and worked as a temp. He spent a great deal of time with his friends, drinking, talking, wandering around, and pretending—in that particular way of people who are not old and cynical and worldly and who haven't really seen anything and don't know anything—to be old and cynical and worldly and to have seen everything and to know it all.

The truth of the matter, Alex thought, was that he was a philosopher. He didn't believe that the person who ends up with the most toys won. He wanted to be a pleasurist; he wanted to be a sensualist and a thinker. He did! He was spiritual that way.

He thought being in love was the highest state of existence. And in terms of his cinema (the word of choice for those who think about making films but, for the most part, don't), he was at once fascinated by and revolted by his own mother's intense interest in matters of great historical weight. After his dad died, her dancing had slowly receded and, with equal slowness, a whole new career had emerged that was a surprise to everyone who knew her. It was one of the great professional non sequiturs: modern dancer (professionally trained) historian (self-educated). Her eight-year pilgrimage of self-education had resulted in a huge scholarly book about moral choices in pre–World War I Germany, a strange, original book that was almost academic but for the fact that she wasn't an academic. It was a brilliant book that emerged with the force of an underground river swollen by the melting of glaciers, and Alex, for all his considerable pride in her, *just couldn't stand it.* The success delighted him. But the *weight* of it, the emphasis on moral choices, the valiant expression on his mother's face when she worked.

Alex liked the trivial. The small. The eccentric. But he was not a trivial thinker. He thought there was something sublime about the trivial and small, which held clues to the larger structures of life. He resisted the big picture. He was a big picture resister!

KATRINA CAME HOME late. She walked past the kitchen, already set up for the next morning's breakfast, up the stairs to the second floor, where the vast sitting room and the adjoining study sat quietly in the darkness; the third floor was the family floor, and above that was a suite of guest rooms. She poked her head into Patrick's room. His bed was empty. She went to her own room and found him sleeping in her bed. Before Sam left, Patrick would sometimes come to the bed, but would always let himself be led back. Now, seeing his mother alone, he just got in, and she let him stay.

She spent some time in the bathroom and debated whether to wake him and take him back to his room. She decided against it and slid in next to him. He was six. There was a lot of time to draw certain Oedipal lines in the sand.

She lay in the dark, staring at the ceiling high above her, with Patrick breathing softly nearby. Two years earlier they had renovated the house, and her bedroom was now two stories high. It was very dramatic, and unfortunately it was also very lonely. It been intended as a kind of sanctuary for husband and wife, but now it was a kind of cathedral to her singlehood.

ALEX HAD BROUGHT all his investigative skills to bear, and at last he got Katrina's phone number. She told him politely to go away. He put the phone down and, with nothing to lose, called right back.

"Don't be exasperated," he said. "It's just that you are the most striking, interesting person I've met in London and I'm leaving in a couple of days and I would like to take you to a brief dinner."

There was a long pause.

"Do you promise to be brief?" she said.

IT WAS THAT spectral time when the day is over and the night has not yet begun in earnest. Patrick, barefoot and in pajamas, peered into his mother's room with the stealthy air of a burglar. He had just emerged from a long fragrant bubble bath and was in no mood for bed. His mother was sitting on a small chair in front of the dressing table, her face reflected in a large oval mirror, putting on earrings. An hour earlier he had sat next to her on the carpeted bathroom floor, naked and shivering, and watched as she knelt beside him in her bathrobe, her dark hair pulled up, the soft back of her neck visible with its wispy hairs, a yellow bottle of bubble bath in her hand. They watched the bath fill up together, the white bubbles getting frothier and higher, and when he got in she scooped up a handful and put it on his head. Then she left him alone in the bubbles.

Now she was dressed up. Her body was full and curvy and warm. He padded up behind her very quietly, feeling the soft carpet between his toes, until he could see her face in the mirror. Both her hands fiddled with the little diamond earring in her right ear, and her head was tilted to the side. Their eyes met in the mirror.

"Hello, Poopsie," she said. "What are you doing?"

Patrick broke out into a giggly smile revealing a big gap where the front teeth should have been, and his body convulsed as though ten people at once had poked their index fingers into the ticklish parts of his body (almost everywhere), and then his face quieted and became solemn and watchful again.

"Nothing," he said.

"It's time for bed," she said, as he knew she would. She fiddled with her earring some more. Patrick watched, tilting his head to the side and staring with renewed interest at his mother's face in the mirror, as though his mother were a different person seen sideways.

"Are you going out?" he asked, still sideways.

She said yes.

"Where are you going?" he asked.

"Out with a friend."

Patrick understood "friend" to mean someone other than his father.

ALEX COMPOSED HIMSELF in the soft London air. The door was black and forbidding, with a huge brass knocker in the shape of a fist.

Each house on her block looked like a fortress; hers was the largest fortress. The very sound of her neighborhood was faintly military: Maida Vale.

He was let in by intercom and stood quietly in the foyer. He bent forward to read some of the invitations propped up on an antique table, but at the last second he suppressed his natural instinct to pry and averted his gaze to the floor—neat, attractive planks of narrow pale pine, unblemished and tastefully fancy. Then he looked up at the mirror above the table. Its frame was ornate, gold, garish. Within the frame stood a man in a blue blazer and white shirt, trying to be himself.

Alex ran his hands through his hair, raised his chin up and then lowered it. Trying to be yourself was difficult, he thought. He made a series of funny faces: a monster, a frightened child, a clown.

In the kitchen was a big round table that was already set for tomorrow's breakfast. There were three settings. A family-size box of Rice Krispies sat in the middle of the table. High on the wall was a large pair of antelope antlers.

"Just a minute, Alex," Katrina called out. "I'll be down in a minute!" He heard the sound of footsteps, like a distant stampede. Her son. The sound of pounding feet made him shudder.

He glanced at the foolish-looking man in the mirror. What was he afraid of? First dates are so ridiculous, he thought. You are either insanely optimistic or insanely pessimistic. He was, at the moment, the latter. Here is a woman with a whole galaxy of life surrounding her, evolving, in motion, and he was a mere asteroid hurtling recklessly in her direction. The proximity to her atmosphere was causing him to heat up. He would probably combust upon entry.

He remembered Ashley, his first First Date. She was a preppy, shy girl with blue cat-eyes who had caused a minor uproar in high school when, as a freshman, she was rumored to have slept with a senior and in the middle of the act whispered, "Hurt me." Ashley's father had met Alex in their living room when he came to pick her up. He had a square jaw and a firm handshake. In spite of all this manliness, Alex remembered a look of worry on his face: Please don't do anything unpleasant to my daughter, it seemed to say.

Later that night he and Ashley had sat on a stoop drinking from a quart of beer and attacking one another with deep clumsy kisses, and he had put his hand under her clean white tennis shirt and pushed her bra up over her brand-new breasts and was a little rough with her; he pinched her a little, not out of some subtle calculation, but just because he didn't know what he was doing. She groaned with pleasure, a noise that was womanly and real and sexual in a way he hadn't really experienced yet, which frightened him and excited him and also, for some reason, brought that expression on her father's face racing back to mind. Alex had, in fact, done something unpleasant to his daughter. And she had liked it.

That was over ten years earlier, at the end of high school on a stoop in Brooklyn Heights. For the ensuing decade his dates had been tinged with the knowledge that he might do something pleasantly unpleasant to someone's daughter.

And now, as he listened to the tiny footsteps upstairs, he experienced something of a revolution—there would be no father to see him off with his date, but there might be a son. Could he bring himself to do something pleasantly unpleasant to someone's mother?

Yes, he thought. He probably could.

He heard the voices, faint but growing stronger:

"Mum, can I stay up longer?"

"Mummy, why can't I stay up?"

"Mummy, I want to stay up! Please don't go! Stay and read me a story! Where are you going? Mum!"

She came into view for moment at the top of the stairs, and then her son tugged her back out of sight.

"Upstairs and into bed!" she said. It was the voice of motherhood, at once adamant and pleading.

"Mum, can maybe I go to the sweet shop and get more licorice tomorrow? Please!"

"Mummy, don't go, wait, one more thing, I want to tell you something! Mummy!"

She came down the stairs looking amazingly sleek—black skirt, black stockings, white shirt under a dark gray cashmere cardigan. Her clothes were tasteful and muted and expensive. A young boy in pajamas jumped around at her heels. Her eyes passed over Alex briefly, hardly acknowledging him; she was lovely in this strange moment of two worlds colliding. Her lips were full of life. Her mouth yielded no more than Mona Lisa's. When he had first met her he had thought there was something fiery and threatening about her, as though her radiant smile could change into something vicious at any moment.

But she was different now, with her son in his green pajamas with little frogs on them, his face bright with energy and enthusiasm. He was barefoot, well scrubbed, that special post-bath prebed too much energy. Alex knew the mood. He had specialized in it himself.

How obstinate he had been about not going to bed! "But Mom!" he had insisted. "I'm a night person!"

Those occasions when Alex's mother went out for the evening rushed to the surface of his consciousness, not as an idea, or an image, but as a smell. He remembered the lovely smell of her lipstick, and the perfume she used to wear. He would press his face into the softness of her neck and inhale. Then the faint sense of terror at her departure would give way to a delicious sense of opportunity, to play with the baby-sitter, to roam free in the house.

What he didn't remember, and what he tried to reach back to now, was whether he had had any sense of what his mother was up to on these nights out. After his father's death he had administered a stern injunction to his mother: she was not to remarry. He had forbidden other men! How had he come up with that?

At fifteen, five years after the proclamation, he retracted it, almost bashfully, as though he couldn't believe the audacity of his younger self. She had looked at him with one of her lovely and mysterious expressions that suggested that one could concurrently grow wiser and more incredulous as life progressed.

Watching this unlikely couple descend the stairs, Alex instinctively retreated a little into the kitchen doorway. When Patrick was almost at the bottom of the staircase, still yelling proclamations and making deals, he saw Alex and was suddenly gripped by an intense bout of shyness.

"Patrick, this is Alex," she said.

Alex waved. The boy moved closer to his mother and stared.

"Mum, I have to whisper something," he said, his eyes still on Alex.

She bent down and put her ear next to his little red mouth. He pressed his whole head deep into her neck as though he could hide there, and whispered. He received a kiss, and then scampered back upstairs into the realm of the nanny and bedtime.

She was wearing perfume. Alex held the door open and followed Katrina through it into the night, sniffing slightly at the fragrance that diffused and expanded in her wake, as though expecting it to be familiar.

———

"THAT WAS AN interesting kiss," she said much later, on her couch. The evening had been bearable, she thought. Just. He seemed to think he was charming, which was tiresome. He wasn't charming, she thought, just energetic. He talked *at* her and insisted on buying the dinner, as though some Thai place in Westbourne Grove was an extravagance. "I hadn't found you very attractive until that kiss," she added.

He pulled away from her on the couch and smiled the serene and slightly giddy smile of someone who has just attained a small amount of power.

"It was an arrogant kiss," she continued. "Are you confident too? Or just arrogant?"

His smile went away and he stood up from the couch, which was enormous, and took a few steps into the middle of the room. It was an intimidating room, lush as an opium den; thick curtains hung from the ceiling to the floor, and a round mirrored ball, a witch's eye, she explained to him, hung from the ceiling, providing a fish-eye view of everything in the room no matter where you stood. The house, like the woman, exuded good taste, refinement, wealth, and weird secrets.

"Come back," she said, and he came back to the couch and sat as far away as possible.

"Maybe it's going to be impossible to actually have, you know, to do it with you," he said. "It just occurred to me that I might not be able to do it."

"Why not," she asked. She was very cool and calm and clinical as she said this, and he decided right then that he wasn't attracted to her, which was a shame, because he had hoped, while in London, to sleep with a woman with a British accent, or to meet someone who would evoke normal human sentiments and feelings of cozy intimacy and with whom he might start figuring out what he was going to do next, and for a moment this woman had promised both.

"Because if we, if I have with you, you know, if we . . ."

"Fuck," she said. "If I fuck you, is what you're trying to say."

"If I fuck *you*, let's make it clear who is doing what here. If I fuck you—if you want to use such language . . ."

"You're the one who says fuck in every other sentence," she said.

"Yes, but I don't use it to describe the actual act. At least not on a first date."

"On a first date you just stutter and look down at the floor until the person you are talking to figures it out?"

"What I was going to say was I don't think we can, you know, do it, because if I fuck you then I will be fucking someone's mother."

She gave him one of those devastating little smiles. "And I'll be fucking someone's baby," she said.

"I hadn't thought of it that way," he said.

He looked down at the floor, then at her. They sat in silence for a few moments, looking searingly into one another's eyes, building each other back up with sincere looks of mutual appreciation and interest, and then he jumped on top of her. It was a predatory, almost athletic jump from the other end of the couch, and she shrieked and coiled up in the corner in a mock display of reticence and fear, and he reached his hand behind her neck and grabbed her hair, the short hairs at the back of her neck, and forced her mouth to his. Then he pulled it away. Then he brought it back. They kissed like this for a few minutes, his hand turning her head this way and that as though it were a diamond and he was inspecting every facet, kissing her lips, cheek, eyes, neck. She offered just enough resistance to make him feel it was a violation, which he liked. His thrill at this sensation was enhanced by the fact that he knew she was playing along. He wasn't even sure what, exactly, the game was, but they were playing. He started to feel very happy, making gentle forays with his tongue into her mouth, grazing her lips with his and then forcing her mouth open.

After a while her hand reached down towards his crotch on what struck him as an information-gathering expedition. It made little pats and squeezes, and his erection went away because it felt scrutinized. He pulled away from her. She lit a cigarette.

"Can I go get some Rice Krispies?" he said after a little while. "I'm suddenly in the mood for Rice Krispies."

She stared at him incredulously.

"Sure," she said after a moment. "You go and get it."

He stood up and she watched him walk across the room, picking his way around the scattered debris—the small sneakers flung here and there, the puppets and dolls lying like casualties on the floor—and watched him descend the staircase. He had an elegant neck and loose limbs and big hands. But the obviousness of some of his gestures—and also the lascivious greedy look that sometimes flashed across his face—mitigated his elegance and contradicted it. But then, she thought, he was an American, which she associated with Broad Gestures.

She found his request for Rice Krispies both charming and perverse. It was charming because it suggested a certain honesty and desire to be comfortable, and she wanted him to be that, having lived in what she thought was a dishonest and uncomfortable situation for some time. But it was perverse, she thought, because she had a little boy in the house, and here she was faced with the prospect of another baby who demanded Rice Krispies in the middle of the night, an extra-tall one with a capricious cock and questionable manners.

PATRICK WAS FAST asleep just then—mouth slightly ajar, breathing steadily, and vividly dreaming. He was dreaming of his father.

His father on the beach, lifting him up. His father tosses him in the air. The sound of waves and screams of pleasure. And then he is in the water alone. The waves are high and it is hard to breathe. He calls out but is choked by a mouthful of water. It is a dream, he tells himself, but the taste of the salt water is real and convincing, briny and sharp. He tries to call out again, and again his voice becomes muffled by water, his breath is deprived, his legs kick against nothing but cold water, which is colder down below, where the monsters lurk, and then he awakes with a gasp in the dark.

There was light outside the room. There was always light in the vastness of the house, and it always beckoned him. The texture of the carpet was extremely palpable beneath his feet. It was only a few steps down the hall to his mother's room, but when he pressed the door open—it glided open with a outrageous creak, as in a haunted house—he saw an empty bed. Instinctively, he went downstairs. He paused next to a painting, a self-portrait by his mother, and waved at her. He headed down another flight. Then he heard something in the living room and instead of continuing all the way to the kitchen on the ground floor, he stuck his head in and saw his mother lying on the couch underneath a strange man, whose posture was that of a beast about to devour its prey.

There was something about the way they were so close that reminded him of his dream. A choking feeling. He could see the top of her head moving. The man seemed to be moving his mother's head with his hand. He turned to scamper up the stairs.

AFTER ALEX HAD gone to the kitchen, Katrina lay on the couch and thought of Sam; she tried to get past the frustrated, gloomy, perplexed face that had silently berated her for the last year,

berated her for her distance, the ever-thickening glacier that had
sprung up between then. Beneath the anger was a faint, pathetic
perplexity as to why this had happened. It was a question she was
in no real position to answer. Something in her had withered, and
he had failed to see it until it was much too late. When Sam
awoke to the fact that something in his wife, some important part
of her, which was also an important part of *them*, had irrevocably
died, he sprang to action. But it was too late. By then she had
engaged in her one indiscretion, her one indulgence, a brief high
that was followed by a terrible black depression. The confession
just made everything worse. When Sam grasped that his marriage
might well be over, he evolved into the wrathful figure who had
very unsilently berated her through the holidays, who had
screamed and shouted and called her a whore while Patrick stood
at the top of stairs crying. Somewhere beneath all that was a more
open, loving face, stern and paternal but also soft, the one she
had spotted across a room when she was twenty and thought,
instantly, "Well, I could marry that." It was difficult to reach that
far back. She didn't think she could ever get back to that old version of Sam. And anyway, he certainly couldn't. You can't go back
to your old selves, she thought. You have to keep inventing new
ones. Or at least you have to try.

IT WASN'T DIFFICULT for Alex, downstairs in the kitchen, to
imagine Sam's face. He had gone to the fridge for milk, bowl of
Rice Krispies in hand, and had been brought up short by a series
of color snapshots haphazardly stuck onto the refrigerator door.
Scenes from the beach. One featured Katrina from behind, looking out at the rolling blue surf in a black one-piece bathing suit
(exceptionally nice ass, he noted). In another a man—somewhat
handsome, a bit rough, with blunt features and dark coloring—

stared at the camera with a faint smile at the corners of his mouth, holding an earlier version of Patrick in his arms. The husband, thought Alex, the father. The abundance of Katrina's life intimidated and fascinated him. He had never slept with a mother before. He stared at the photograph and wondered if this was a brief fling, something to pass through, or if he would stay awhile in this woman's life, visit her house, get to know Patrick on the stairs.

SHE HEARD ABNER approach, his tag jingling delicately as he hopped onto the couch where Alex had been. He lay on his back and spread his legs, revealing his lean, taut whippet stomach, and looked at her with a preposterously excited expression, tongue hanging out, waiting for her foot to begin its massage in that special place. These demanding males, she thought. She moved her silk-socked foot over him. Abner's hedonism was inspiring. Perhaps she should treat herself to a big American, the way one might treat oneself to a big milkshake at the end of a long day or, in her case, the end of a long marriage.

Alex returned to the living room with his cereal and ate. "The milk in England is incredible," he said. "These are the best Rice Krispies I've ever had." She smiled and lit a cigarette. He watched her smoke and she watched him eat. He was hunched over, savoring. Pulses of revulsion and attraction moved through her. Her husband was a fastidious man. The idea of cereal at night, let alone in the living room, would have revolted him.

"Why are you still hungry?" she said.

"I was nervous over dinner," he said.

"And now you've relaxed. I suppose that's good. Just don't get too relaxed."

"I don't think that's likely," he said.

Her husband had been tense, coiled, and expectant, but at the same time possessed of a certain ease. This man was easy in the way her husband had been tense, and tense in the way her husband had been easy. She wondered if every experience she was going to have for the rest of her life, every amorous encounter and every sexual one, too, would be subject to comparison with her husband. She knew she should try to resist this impulse. In comparing her lover to her husband, both, she suspected, would always fare poorly.

When he was done he moved over on the couch and tried to kiss her.

"Don't," she said. "You have to leave now."

"Just a little," he said.

He tried to kiss her some more but she moved her mouth away. Her face now had a tragic aspect to it—as though the two of them were subject to forces beyond their control, forces they had no choice but to accept, huge structural Romeo-and-Juliet, Capulet-and-Montague forces—and the implication that there was more going on than just a man and a woman on a couch, that there was a whole complex narrative into which he had tumbled, fascinated him and turned him on.

She wouldn't let him kiss her. Then she let him. He thought of the picture on the refrigerator, her husband, the man who for years had roamed these rooms. He thought of her boy, of all the other people in her life, if he would meet them, get to know them, if he wanted to. Particularly the boy. He thought of the son while he kissed the mother.

SHE FOUND PATRICK sleeping on the staircase. She shook him gently and said, "Poopsie, are you all right? Are you having bad dreams? What's the matter? What happened?" She stroked him, and when he didn't answer, she hugged him. She was his again, and he was enveloped by her and he let her stroke him and coo at him and escort him gently back upstairs to bed, towards that space, tiny as a universe, occupied by just the two of them.

ALEX SAT IN Lazzaro's and soaked up its conciliatory atmosphere of decline.

He was racing through *The Savage God*. It wasn't as though he were suicidal. He had a somewhat dyslexic response to substances, and this was true of printed matter as well—inspirational material made him despair, and writing that embodied or anatomized despair tended to cheer him up.

Alvarez quoted Cesar Pavese: "Every luxury must be paid for, and everything is a luxury, starting with being in the world."

Sitting in Lazzaro's he was in the grip of that pure kind of despair that contains within it, *that gives birth to*, a vertiginous happiness, a boundless sense of life's possibilities.

Feeling in love with the world all of a sudden, Alex stood abruptly to pay. Mr. Lazzaro looked up beneath heavy-lidded eyes that for the first time seemed to acknowledge the customer standing before him and said, "Not to worry. The world isn't going to end today."

Not to worry? Alex was halfway down the block when he realized that Mr. Lazzaro must have thought that his one regular customer was about to kill himself. His laughter echoed throughout the strangely vacant expanse of Fitzroy Square.

ALEX CALLED HIS mother.

"Mom!" said Alex. "I love London. I'm running around having a great time. I don't really know what I'm doing. But it's fun."

"It's a transition period," she said.

For days afterwards he was quietly infuriated. Transition to what? What time wasn't a transition period?

KATRINA WALKED ACROSS the dark room, her shoes clapping angrily against the floor. Each step took her farther away from him, and yet with each step the sound became louder, as though she were getting more and more upset. Then she reached a lamp and turned it on, and the bare bulb flooded the room with a harsh theatrical light which cast long shadows across the unknown territory of their second date.

"Don't look," she said. "You promised." She hadn't planned on taking him here, but she hadn't wanted to say goodbye outside the restaurant, and she couldn't bear taking him back to her house.

"What am I supposed to do, keep my eyes closed?" he said. He looked. She'd told him she was a painter and that she would take him to her studio, but she wouldn't show him her paintings, and he couldn't ask to see them.

The room was large and mostly empty, but its emptiness had character. The wood floor was spattered with paint. The walls were ocher, but patches were chipped away revealing the white plaster beneath. There were interesting moldings that looked as graceful as musical signatures, which were also damaged and interrupted in places. A wounded chandelier, its crystals dulled, its complex web of lights tangled, hung low over a round wooden table on which sat a solitary bowl. The bowl should have been filled with plums or peaches or grapes, a still life in waiting, but it was empty.

The sounds of long-ago parties wafted through the room's stillness, and from the bed over in the corner—plain, low to the ground, covered in a gray blanket, a monkish looking thing at once austere and illicit—there emanated moans of adulterous pleasure. It was a room whose general sense of fabulousness was enormously enhanced by the feeling that whatever excitement had once taken place here had been horribly and brutally inter-rupted, and had remained in this interrupted condition ever since.

"What happened to the walls?" he said.

"Didn't we have a deal?" she said.

"What was the deal?"

"That you would shut up."

Her hostility, he felt, was promising. If someone takes you home and is rude to you, he felt, that means they're already hat-ing you for what they are about to let you do.

She put on opera. He debated whether to complain. It was too tragic, too mournful, the place was enough of a stage set to begin with, and this made it seem as though just beyond the huge win-dow that overlooked the garden, out there in the dark, there were rows of patrons sitting quietly waiting for the action to begin. He imagined being on the outside looking in; it wasn't hard. In her presence he felt like an intruder. He wondered how the scene would look without sound.

He collapsed on the ratty couch and regarded the various paintings that sat stacked against the walls, face forward, some old and dusty, others so new their staples gleamed.

"Is there any chance . . ."

"No," she said.

He laughed.

She sat on the far end of the couch.

"Has anyone ever told you that you are very attractive when you are annoyed?" he said.

He moved across the couch and kissed her gently on the mouth. To his surprise, no insult was forthcoming. A gusher of confidence erupted within. He kissed her again, less gently. He was slightly rough with her breasts, he squeezed her ass lasciviously, he ran his hands up over her pants legs, all the way up, and though she struggled, which he liked, she also relented, which he liked even more.

After a while, they moved to the bed, and when he passed the stereo he hit stop, and the tape clicked off, leaving the room painfully silent, which he regretted, because the small thudding sounds of their shoeless feet on the floor seemed embarrassing. But then the embarrassment went away. Clothes were peeled off. Her kisses were nervous, needy, voracious, ambivalent. The opera was still playing in his head at thunderous volume, and at the same time every ruffle of the sheets, every gasp, every sticky separation of their lips and caress of her cheek, brushing her black hair out of her eyes, all these sounds were as clear to him as if an ultrasensitive recording device were positioned next to them and he were wearing headphones. He felt closer than close.

To his surprise, at the key moment, she turned herself over and presented him with her ass. He positioned himself against her and felt the terror of a skydiver, that gravity-defying leap, but he steadied himself and went in, slowly in, all the way in, to the delicious accompaniment of her animal groan.

Disgusting triumphalist feelings surged up in his chest as he began to move, letting his hips and the very top part of his thighs bang gently against her ass and relishing the juxtaposition of the motion: it was gentle; it was a bang; it was bangishly gentle; it was taunting, rapacious, malevolent, tender; afterwards, he thought, maybe she would show him her paintings; he had a medieval vision of himself marauding into the enemy's castle, a thick animal hide covering his shoulders, and raping the queen; when he was done he'd eat some mutton off the bone. He didn't know what mutton was, but seemed to recall reading about it in some Arthurian fable. England was all about mutton. England, he thought—what a wonderful place to fuck!

Then something went wrong. What was the matter? He was *not*, he told himself, having a suddenly prudish and judgmental reaction to fucking on the second date. He had wanted this! It was something else. Now things were going wrong very quickly. He felt the despair of a young boy who, having had the training wheels removed from his bicycle, pedals off furiously and realizes after just a few seconds that the machine is beyond his comprehension, and he will fall.

With razor-sharp reflexes, he blamed her.

She had maddeningly unfamiliar tendencies, he rationalized. Her mouth, for example. The expression on her mouth had excited him from the moment he first saw her, and he had looked forward to how it would look when he was inside her. At first he couldn't see her mouth at all, as it was buried in the pillow. Then he glimpsed her in profile and her expression was that of mild disappointment, the expression of someone who has ordered the endive salad only to be given the mixed green.

Or maybe it was the expression of the dieter who has snuck into the kitchen at midnight and, in the middle of stuffing her mouth, glimpses herself in the mirror.

She lay on her stomach, hands protectively near her face, very still.

She was barely tolerating him, he thought. She had brought him back here; she had agreed to let him kiss her and pull her clothes off and get behind her. But her heart was not in it. He had looked forward to what she might be like, to some resistance, to a giving in, but he wanted her to *enjoy* giving in.

Then, when it appeared things could not get worse, when he had pretty much lost all hope, and the surging pride in his chest had turned to a puddle of shame, and he was slipping out of her, she started to cry.

He rolled onto his back next to her and lay very still, listening in silence to her tears.

He wanted to say: "Honey, what's the matter?"

But he didn't. He suspected, and feared, that her reply would be something like: "A man I don't know well or like very much, but decided to sleep with just for fun, on a whim, because I decided that there was a shortage of whimsy in my life, can't even keep an erection inside of me. What do you think is the matter?"

Or: "Don't call me honey."

So he said nothing and listened.

She became quiet. They lay next to each other, not getting close, but not getting far, either.

"Are you all right?" he asked.

"Yes," she said. "I don't know what the matter is. I'm sorry." Her voice had a softness to it that he hadn't heard before.

"You know, we've been playing this game in which hostility is sort of a turn-on," he said. "But there is something incredibly heartbreaking about you that I really like. I don't mean heart-breaking as in sad. I mean it as in human."

"That's nice," she said. "But you don't know me."

The blanket was bunched up at the bottom of the bed, and her whole body was exposed and naked in the dim warm light of the lamp. Her back moved up and down with each breath. He could see the outline of her ribs, and the soft, round bulge of her breasts pressing out from her side. He tried to think of what to say. In the dim light he was reminded that she had a very nice ass. It was exposed and facing upward, and moving ever so slightly because of her quiet breathing. It was round and full and provocative and taunting. It was like a separate entity altogether. It seemed to be saying, "This ridiculous woman up there is weeping, but I'm game. I'm ready. Here I am."

He ran his hand over it, northward. He ran his hand over it, southward. He went on like this for a long time, every now and then letting his hand roam flamboyantly up between her shoulder blades. Eventually something in her relaxed as he caressed her like this. She lay on her stomach, facing away from him, and he sat propped up on one elbow, observing the whole thing, and after a while they both became hypnotized by the motion, and the whole world became reduced to the small area of her ass and lower back over which his hand moved. And then she began to push her ass up in the air, ever so slightly, almost imperceptibly, like a cat arching its back in response to being petted. He struggled to his knees behind her. The bicycle worked!

As a courtesy, he came on her ass. He was unclear if it was pregnancy that he was being practical about, or if it was just some strange sense of politeness, or some instinctive wish to mess up that smooth surface he had caressed for so long, but it was aesthetically pleasing as hell. The only problem was that, because he not only felt it but saw it, the pleasure of the moment was complicated and a little corrupted by pornography.

When he pulled out and observed the helpless-looking bit of white stuff squirt on Katrina's ass he had a confusing sense of déjà vu, as though he had seen this exact moment before, which in a sense he had, because pulling out and coming on a woman's ass after fucking her from behind is one of the great stock shots of porn movies (plus, he *had* done it before, but somehow it was the pornography that seemed familiar). Suddenly he was outside the scene completely, watching it with a director's eye, making judgments about what he saw: the size and shape and general character of the penis, the ass, particularly the way the ass moved and shook while it was being fucked, and the glistening white stuff.

He didn't even see it with the eyes of a director; it was more like an editor trying to figure out how best to use the available footage.

SHE FELL FORWARD slowly. She felt him wipe her ass with something. Then he wiped himself. Then she saw a crumpled black sock go flying off to the side of the bed.

The fact that he had just wiped his come off her ass with a black cotton sock confirmed her sense that this was an extremely sordid interlude. That she had just been fucked by a man *while he was wearing his socks* was too revolting and depressing to think about at the moment. She would lie very still and hope that the whole thing would, with the passing of time, improve and become tolerable. She closed her eyes. He lowered himself next to her, and at the last moment she opened her eyes a tiny bit, if only to make sure that she didn't get bashed in the face by his broad shoulders, and accidentally caught a glimpse of the bereft balled-up black sock sitting stickily on the floor.

They lay in silence. She could feel his chest going up and down. She began to pay attention to him, still with her eyes closed. She was looking out for smugness, or for contrition at not having made her come, or at the least for some awareness that women come at all and this was something to be taken into account. She couldn't detect any of this. Instead she felt a deep physical somnolence overtake the man next to her. His breathing steadied. His body, which had been giving off heat, began to cool. Like a meat-drunk animal, he fell asleep quickly.

There was only one sock on the floor. The other was on his foot. If there is anything worse than having just been fucked by a man wearing two socks, she thought, it is a having just been fucked by a man who is falling asleep *while wearing only one*.

Now, she thought, *now*. Make this the exact moment you decide never to see him again. Here is a piece of evidence: heed it.

Yet there was something about this man—the intensity of his gaze upon her; his oblivion to the delicate intricacies of her life, her world—which made him seem ordained somehow, an opportunity to be herself without the oppressive weight of her own context.

There was nothing to do except sleep. Later on she would figure out if this was a regrettable one-night stand. Or maybe it wasn't a one-night stand. Maybe it was a two-night stand.

AT THE NETWORK, in New York, Alex had enjoyed a brief but ecstatic honeymoon when he was first hired. He bought rounds of drinks for a bar's worth of people on his expense account and treated his friends to lavish dinners. For a flickering moment he was—to use the word his senior producer favored—"hot."

He had been hired to produce quirky, off-beat news stories, "essays on film," and had come up with a good one right off the bat: the Rainbow Man. He of the rainbow-colored wig and floppy mustache who seemed to have the best seat in the house for every major sporting event of the seventies. The Rainbow Man had gone from a groovy, disco-loving stoner making thumbs-up A-OK! signs at the camera in the seventies, to being a religious fanatic in the eighties, to being a convict in the nineties. He was now in jail, serving a life sentence for having held a hotel maid hostage in an attempt to "create a major worldwide media event and get God's word out."

It made for a great segment. There was something deeply satisfying and exciting about seeing video clips of those old sporting events, glimpses of the Red Sox's Luis Tiant doing his bizarre windup and then throwing a fastball at home plate (behind

which sat the wacky Rainbow Man). Or Tom Landry pacing stoically up and down the Dallas Cowboys' sideline (and the Rainbow Man leaping around like a freak in the front row behind
him, giving everyone in the vicinity high fives). An old Bud-
weiser commercial in which the Rainbow Man had a bit part was
dredged up, and it was amazing to perceive how strange and
funny the commercial now seemed, with its earnest "This Bud's
for you!" chorus; the theme of the commercial was "This Bud's for
all the fans." Hence the Rainbow Man's brief cameo in it, the ultimate fan.

All this old footage was juxtaposed with a long-faced man in
prison garments, telling his story, as well as footage culled from
Hard Copy and other real-life crime shows showing his final
standoff with the police—after hours of negotiations, they
threw a percussive grenade through the window and led him out
shirtless and in handcuffs. He was just another of those peculiarly American creatures: the conspiracy-minded loner, caught
in his own paranoid fantasy world, who finally explodes with
violence.

The Rainbow Man, it turned out, was a shy son of an alcoholic
father. His dad had died when he was young. He married young,
and when his marriage fell apart he went on a year-long television
binge that ended in the strange bit of inspiration that he should
devote his life to attending sporting events in a rainbow-colored
wig and making what he referred to, with touching stiffness, as
"positive hand signals."

He was a sad piece of meaningless junk, made by television, for
television, around which all sorts of effluvial junk had collected,
and Alex's piece was yet another ring in the concentric rings of
television junk being broadcast into the world twenty-four hours
a day, no doubt spawning absurd visions in some television-
obsessed loner who would, in a year or a decade, pop up behind

home plate and declare himself Rainbow Man II. It was depressing, on some deeper level than Alex even understood at first.

After a few weeks of Alex's doing nothing, his senior producer, a tight-lipped English woman with short blond hair who spoke in the clipped, businesslike manner of someone whose time is very scarce, called him into her office. "Rainbow Man was great," she told him. "Can't you do more stuff like that? You could do the Where Is That Weirdo Now? stories."

He returned to his desk and sat there like a zombie.

KATRINA WAS IN her kitchen making dinner. Alex had come over late. Patrick was staying with Sam. Three nights a week she was alone, her son at her husband's new apartment ten minutes away.

She had made some pasta with a little garlic and olive oil, and thrown some coriander on at the end. Alex had brought a bottle of white wine. There was something improvised and relaxed about having him at the table; she was at ease with him, and he delighted in the scene because, he told her, it made his awful fluorescent-lit hell at the network seem like a bad dream that was now over and could be forgotten. The large set of straight black antelope antlers hung on the wall above the sink like a giant quotation mark.

"Is it weird being here without your husband and Patrick?" he asked her.

"Yes," she said. "Extremely. But there has been so much strangeness in these last months, it's hard to focus on any one part."

"Is it hard to focus on me?"

"Oh, I see," she said. "Now we get down to it. It's about you."

"Not true!" he said. "I'm asking about you. I'm trying to figure you out."

"Don't try," she said.

"All right. It was just an experiment," he said.

"Am I an experiment? Your English experiment?"

For a moment she looked a little rueful, as though someone had once whispered to her everything that would ever happen to her, and now she had no choice but to be a one-woman receiving line for the events of her whole life, greeting them as they came through the door. It was an expression that already, days into their acquaintance, evoked in him a mixture of sadness and exasperation and sexual excitation. It suggested she had found a way to keep everything at arm's length so as to neutralize it, but was sad that so much of her life was at arm's length.

He pulled her chair over to him with her still on it.

"Come here," he said.

"I already am here," she said.

A strangely vacant room was adjacent to the kitchen. There was an expanse of empty wood floor; a television and some chairs in one corner; a hamper of toys in another; and a red leather couch with brass studs gleaming against the far wall. In a less grand house the couch might have dominated a room, but here it sat unobtrusively.

"What's the couch for?" he asked.

"It's a sofa," she said. "What are sofas usually for?"

"It looks sort of lonely over there. Like no one ever sits in it. It's too far away from the television to watch from there. There are no other chairs. It's incongruous."

"You're right," she said. "It was a wedding present from a distant relative of Sam's. We used to change Patrick on it. I don't know. It's just there."

"A couch for a baby. Interesting."

He stood and walked over to it. His shoes clacked on the wood floor. He noticed that the general spaciousness of her house had the peculiar effect of making everything theatrical. He looked back into the kitchen where Katrina sat, in different light.

"What are you doing?" she asked.

He pulled the couch to the center of the playroom. It slid easily on the smooth wood floor. The dark red leather was cool and smooth and knowing. Then he went and took her by the hand, brought her over to it, sat her in the middle, and took a few steps away, as though to get some perspective on this new arrangement. She sat with her knees close together, her hands folded in her lap, and looked at him with a certain expression that seemed to say, "All right, I'll play."

Eventually he walked over to her, sat beside her, and started stroking her hair tenderly. He planted soft kisses on her temple, her cheek, her ear. He whispered, "Baby, it's all right. It's all right, sweetie. Baby . . ." It was as though he were consoling her.

A kind of melting look came over her face, barely scrutable, as though she had lost her will; it was at once emotional and a form of numbness, as though she had been wondering if he would express this particular mixture of malevolence and love, and now that he had she was helpless to do anything but let it take its course.

He undressed her, stroking her and kissing her in this slightly perverse, paternal way. A couple of times he stood up and walked a few steps away to examine with perspective this work in progress. Her vulnerability, this trancelike state she seemed to be entering, had sent him into a stratosphere of excitement that made him feel as though his head and chest and limbs were all filling with helium and preparing to float away. The entire density of his body was concentrated into one part that strained violently against his pants.

She let him get very close to her, not just physically, but in another way, too. It was almost too much to bear. At times he circled her like a lion tamer walking around his star lion, who sat perched, utterly still, at once docile and dangerous. When it was over they lay entangled and fell asleep.

SHE WOKE UP first. She tried to rouse him gently. Then she just tried to rouse him. He refused to wake up.

"You cannot sleep here naked on the couch!" she said, irritated.

"I'm sleeping," he murmured, still sleeping.

"You have to get up. Come on!" The sheer impatience, the comfortableness of it (because there are certain kinds of impatience that are a form of intimacy), and her imperious English accent all conspired to open an eye.

"Please just let me sleep a little longer," he said, one eyed.

"No. Anyway, I can't leave you on the couch."

"My bed where I'm staying is a rag on the floor with an awful wooden bar that goes across it. Just let me lie here for another hour."

She said no, but saw that the eye had already closed.

"Oh God," she said.

She put him upstairs. She took him to a spare room with a mattress on the floor. The ceiling slanted down to a dormer window. She threw a sheet and a blanket on the bed. He held her by the waist, tightly, and tried to kiss her, but she turned her head.

"Go to sleep," she said. She seemed truly irritated that he had refused to leave her house. But sort of amused, too.

He fell asleep in the strange room, smelling his fingers and smiling.

HE WOKE TO the sound of footsteps somewhere in the house. It was cold, and he had pulled the blanket and sheet up nearly over his head. The small dormer windows admitted just a little light into the low-ceilinged room, which, other than the bed, was empty; the dim light made the day, and all the life it contained, seem like a distant, far-off thing. No one in the whole world knows where I am, he thought. He fell asleep again feeling thrillingly alive.

He awoke again to the sound of footsteps. They were light but very nearby. His eyes cracked open but he didn't move. There, in the doorway, standing stock-still, was a young boy. His hair was brown and curly. He stood motionless, staring at the lump under the blanket.

"Nanny?" he said, half a question, half a statement. He said it in a slight whisper, as though he were trying not to wake the person even as he was. "Nanny?" This time a little louder, more commanding.

He approached, one step after the other, a little jerky, like a marionette. His small figure loomed up next to the bed. A little Goldilocks, thought Alex, wondering what this napping non-nanny was doing in his house. But it was the baby bear who did the wondering . . . so Alex would have to be Goldilocks . . . his mind jangled in its half-awake state trying to straighten out what it meant that he had cast himself as Goldilocks. Meanwhile he remained utterly still until he couldn't bear the suspense any longer and opened his eyes, though he didn't move.

"Hello," he said.

The boy took in this new bit of information for a moment, swaying back on his heels as though a gust of wind had passed across him, and then he stood straight again and said, "Where's my nanny?" He was a bit demanding, even accusing, as though he suspected that she had been stolen.

"Downstairs, I think," Alex replied. The boy rocked back and forth, looking at him for another second, and then spun around and stomped out of the room.

———

KATRINA CAME UP a little later.

"My son has informed me that there is a strange man lying in bed upstairs," she said.

"Are you coming to evict him?" he said.

"I'm investigating," she said.

"He asked what I did with his nanny."

She lay down next to him. It felt very safe up here. Almost immediately he became excited. They pulled each other close. Then, with so little bashfulness it was almost perfunctory, as though she were doing some housework, she pulled off her pants and got on top of him, facing away. He had never been in this position before, and at first he looked down at what was happening with interest and also a sort of detached pride, because it felt as though his erection was something apart from him entirely. He felt the pride of a racehorse owner watching his horse come down the home stretch leading the pack. And he was intrigued by the shape of her back and the way her hips moved; they had an engorging motion, as if she were devouring his cock. He put his hands behind his head and let her do everything.

But gradually a strange and somewhat rejected feeling came over him; it was insulting to be reduced completely to a thing upon which this woman could gyrate. She seemed to be getting a considerable amount of satisfaction and pleasure from it, but the fact that he was almost entirely out of view—only his shins, ankles, feet stretched out before her—began to seem like an insult. I'm being used, he thought. For a moment he thought this was funny. Then it became less funny. His erection, sensing the slight, began to go away. He sat up sharply, pushed her forward onto her elbows, and suddenly who was using who had been rearranged into a more palatable arrangement. But the voracity of her hips stayed in his mind.

————

SHE MADE HIM a breakfast of fried eggs and tomatoes. Sitting there in the kitchen, Alex felt a familiar, sleep-overish sense of delight in this immersion in someone else's life. He munched his thickly buttered toast in the sun-strewn kitchen, and glimpsed the peculiar dance between Katrina and her household staff. It was that strangely revealing noninteraction between employer and employee, intimate and yet utterly distant. While Lisa, the nanny, was afforded a kind of respect, Emily, who was the housekeeper, was merely tolerated. Emily had light coffee skin, and her high, prominent cheekbones were sprayed with freckles. Her movements were rushed and unruly. She had a raw and wild beauty; there was a fearfulness and apprehension in her eyes, and he wondered if it was Katrina's sharpness that had instilled it. No, he thought, probably something much deeper. Amidst the cacophony of information Alex was absorbing, there was something conspicuous about the way Emily moved around the house; worry, anxiety, and sex emanated from her in equal quantities. Lisa ignored her subtly, speaking to her occasionally in Spanish, not unfriendly, but distant.

Katrina ignored her completely on the surface, but Alex could sense an impatient disdain that passed from Katrina to Emily like a fine mist that glistened on Emily's skin.

Compared to the help, Alex was being treated like a king by Katrina, the subject of enormous attention, even a tiny bit of deference. Yet he couldn't help note that he was nevertheless comparing himself to the help.

The day was bright when he left. There was an acknowledged sadness at parting that marked a new level of intimacy for them. She said goodbye from the kitchen. Their kiss was perfunctory yet somehow charged; he wondered why she didn't come to the door to see him off and then it occurred to him that it would be scandalous for her to kiss him out in the world's eye; she was still married to someone else, after all. He walked towards the Warwick Street Tube trying to suppress the raging sense of glee and joy, holding it down not out of any sense of humility or sense of proportion, but for purely pragmatic reasons. The feeling reminded him of the wildly ecstatic posture he had had when he got his job at the network. The way he walked around his apartment with his arms aloft, like a victorious Muhammad Ali. Of course this is happening to me, he had thought. Of course! It was pure hubris, and he had been punished for it.

Now he tried to keep the feeling inside him down to a buzz, a hum, not a raging torrent but a manageable current of electricity.

TWO LOVEBIRDS WERE added to Katrina's household, and an African gray whose shrieks were terrifying. The lovebirds were a big hit with Patrick, and the cat, Marvin, who sat for hours staring up at the cage.

AN AMERICAN WAS added to the household.

AT THE NETWORK'S offices, he and the other younger staff had mere cubicles, but the more senior executives and producers had their own offices with doors that locked. During the day he sat dumbfounded at his desk, unable to motivate on any project, a Bartleby the Scrivener of television news. At night he roamed the halls and touched, gently, the office doorknobs, testing to see which were unlocked.

Many were unlocked. He would step inside, close the door behind him, and, in the humming fluorescent light, stand amidst the productive debris of someone else's life.

Other people's lives were so full! So much chaos, so many strands of different enterprise.

He discovered a small room devoted exclusively to copy machines, one of which was a sophisticated color copier, and he spent several hours pressing his face and hands and feet and elbows and chest and bare ass against the smooth warm glass of the copy machine, watching the machine spit out color renditions of these body parts.

Months went by. Eventually he began staying the night.

He slept on a long couch in the lunchroom and was woken by the cleaning ladies. There were few windows at the office, and none near his cubicle, so time for Alex became a weightless, fluorescent-lit, undefinable thing. In the morning he washed in the men's room. He began having fantasies of moving in completely.

All things considered, it took them a surprisingly long time to fire him. He was given two weeks to leave. He developed a fantasy of smuggling bricks and mortar into the office and building a wall around his cubicle. He calculated that he could build it over a weekend. People would arrive at the office and instead of being gone, he would be living in an impregnable brick structure. He started perusing the aisles of supermarkets with on eye on survival food. He would stand in front of the canned corn and think:

A hundred cans of giblets. But maybe some creamed corn as well.

But I hate creamed corn.

But won't you get sick of regular corn?

I've never gotten sick of regular corn before.

But you haven't had to live on it exclusively for weeks on end while living in a brick cubicle!

He did not, in the end, buy any creamed corn. Or regular corn. He purchased no corn whatsoever. He left quietly, though not before one last nocturnal wander during which he slipped color copies of his body parts into other people's files. His foot, his elbow, his ass. He seeded these images in places where they might not be found for days or weeks or years. Each person got only one, and he imagined a long unconnected litany of private puzzlement as they were gradually discovered.

THE HUSBAND, SAM, was one of those enterprising English men who had turned his family's old money into new. He had a chain of specialty shops all across Europe that specialized in spy equipment: "Sleuths."

Alex paid a visit to the main store, which was just off Baker Street, right in the heart of Sherlock Holmes territory. Amid stores that sold every conceivable object onto which Sherlock Holmes's name and likeness could be stamped was something that appeared to be an electronics store. The logo was a silhouette of a Holmesian man with a top hat smoking a pipe. The name suggested something playful, innocent, a place of fun and fantasy. "Sleuths."

What dark fantasies!

Alex had wandered into the place, and there found a paranoid's dream (or nightmare). Pencils that could take a picture, video cameras shaped like a pack of gum that could zoom into a nostril. Katrina's lifestyle was riding high on a global surge in voyeurism. Alex chatted with a salesman, who informed him the chain was expanding into America, where the demand for surveillance equipment was even stronger than in Europe. Everyone was an amateur spy, an amateur documentarian. He should really be stocking up, he thought. Here before him was the next great leap in his creative life: the whole world was one big stage set for an ongoing *Candid Camera*.

All this surveillance equipment cast Katrina's home in a new light. He loved the hushed isolated feeling of being at Katrina's house, roaming the master bedroom, the guest rooms, the bathrooms, all covered with a thick, sound-absorbing carpet, but he could never fully escape the feeling, having visited this store, that the deposed master of the house had, as a parting gesture, wired the place with video cameras and recording devices, heat monitors, who knew what else, and was now parked in a van down the street, jerking off in a masochistic frenzy in front of a video monitor, watching his wife fucking another man.

SHE TOOK HIM to a party. It was their first social event together. She briefed him about the hostess while she drove, and he got the general idea they were headed towards something fancy, so when they arrived he was surprised to discover that the hostess, an elegant older woman, had started a company that made mulch, and the guests, upon entering, were handed plastic bags with a small amount of mulch in them. The mulch was fragrant in a nice, fertile way. If another product had been involved, then the event might have seemed crass or commercial, but there was something wholesome about this little bit of fecund earth in a plastic bag. The mulch gave the gathering a pleasant, amiable, almost giddy atmosphere. People held glasses of champagne in one hand and their plastic bag of mulch in the other, and talked feverishly to one another.

He drifted away from her, wanting to let her roam a little, to talk to people unencumbered by introductions, and also to see how she looked at a distance, across a crowded room. From certain angles she was not beautiful. And from certain angles she was. Her taste in clothes, Alex felt, was impeccable. She had, as a rule, a wild, combative look in her eyes, as though she dared anyone to make trouble for her, which only heightened her moments of softness and tenderness. She was lovely when she laughed. Her hands flitted nervously up to her hair. She had mentioned that after giving birth her hair had all fallen out. He felt a kind of pride in knowing why her fingers kept reaching up and rearranging her hair, where the habit began.

He moved through the rooms. There was a fake invitation on the face of everyone in the room, he thought. So many of these people knew each other, had fucked each other's wives and husbands, had been once cruel or once kind to each other in long-ago incarnations. They had seen each other's fortunes of wealth and happiness fall and rise and fall and rise. He felt the closeness of this world and its strange element of cruelty, which excited him. He made small talk with an attractive blond woman about mulch. He joked with her, he tried hard to make her laugh and eventually succeeded. He thought he saw in her eye a look that said, "Why are you doing this? I know you're not sincere."

She was Argentinean, she said.

"But you have an English accent," he said.

"I was born in England," she explained.

"So you're English, really," he said.

"No. I'm Argentinean."

"Both my parents were from somewhere else, but I grew up in America so I'm American," he said.

"That's not the way it works here," she said.

"IS IT POSSIBLE," she inquired on the drive home, "for you to talk to a woman without shamelessly flirting with her? It's kind of pathetic, you know."

He laughed at this.

"Three things," he began. It was, she thought, one of his more irritating qualities, announcing how many points he was about to make before he made them.

"One, I was just talking to that woman. And I'm charmed that you care, two. And three, there is, I admit, a tiny part of me that really liked being insulted," he said. "But it is a tiny part! And the rest of me is at any moment going to rise up and smite you, or smote you, or whatever happens in the Old Testament . . ."

"You're the Jew. You're supposed to know what happens in the Old Testament."

"There you go again!" he said, laughing with exasperation. "You can't help but be insulting. It's some genetic thing programmed into English people!"

"I just said you were a Jew. It's your choice to take it as an insult."

"I was just having a good time, for God sakes. Why is that so unseemly?"

"It's just that you're so *boyish!*"

THEY WENT TO the movies. Five weeks had gone by since their initial meeting. Alex had twice changed his ticket and couldn't change it again. He was leaving in three days.

Katrina navigated her car through Bayswater. It had begun to snow. The flakes turned to wet when they hit the street, but in the air they seemed fat and substantial. She drove up a winding ramp that led to the parking lot of the Whitehall movie theaters. Big improbable flakes descended rapidly. He leaned over to look at her watch. She could smell him. All afternoon, after Patrick had been picked up, they had marinated in her bed. Just when they should have gotten up to get dressed they embarked on a particularly ambitious encounter. It involved lotion, and unnatural acts, and then he went too far and she screamed and curled up in a ball saying "That hurt!" again and again and laughing, and he laughed too, both of them rolling around laughing hysterically. And then they jumped up to race to the movies.

"Hurry up," he said. "We're late."

She squeezed the car into a parking space, feeling irritated with his demanding tone. "We're late," he said again. "Hurry."

When they got out of the car he took her hand and started running through the snow. She wore a hat, and held it with her free hand. When they got inside they discovered the movie had sold out. They wandered back out towards the car, through the snow-dusted parking lot, with wide amazed eyes, as though they had never seen snow before. Her cheeks were flushed. In the middle of the parking lot he hugged her tightly.

"I never run," she said. "I never run like that."

"But that was fun," he said. "Wasn't it?"

She nodded, yes, it was.

He made her stop walking and looked at her face. Snow fell around them.

"I love you," he said.

Something passed behind her eyes.

"I love you, too," she said.

HE STAYED IN London for six weeks, until his plane ticket could be extended no further, and then there was a tearful farewell, and vows to reunite as soon as possible.

She gave him an envelope with a note in it when he left.

"Open it on the plane," she said.

He was giddy with anticipation, but also dread. Part of him looked forward to some effusion from her about how much she loved him, or wanted-needed-thought-about him. Another part of him wanted her to keep her distance, wanted her to stay cool, was rooting for some terse witty phrase. He waited until the seat belt sign was off before he opened it. There was no note. There was just a rather stylized photo of the red leather couch, its brass tacks gleaming in the sun. His heart leapt.

———————

HE HADN'T REALLY believed that she would agree to visit him in New York, and so he threw himself into the task of convincing her with easy abandon, as though it were a joke, and he was teasing her. So he was shocked, elated, and, he had to admit, almost disturbed when she responded to one of his invitations by saying yes. Patrick would be spending spring break with their father. She would visit him.

Confronted with the awesome task of being her host, he set about planning activities: walks in the park, restaurants, museums.

But when she finally arrived at his front door she fled past him and flopped facedown on the bed and refused to look at him for a long time. "This is too weird," she said.

Finally he got her to look at him, and they began their reunion on the tiny single bed that had once belonged to his aunt.

They took a walk. He should have known right away that something was wrong by the way she dealt with red lights.

She dealt with red lights by pretending they did not exist, and at the slightest opening wading into the avenue.

"Honey," he said, pleading, "Baby. Please. The red light has nothing personally against you. It is not an insult. You have to respect it. We don't have zebra crossings the way you do in London. The cars here don't stop!"

"I've been to New York" was her cool response.

His plan for their first full day together was not realized. It turned out she had friends in New York. They met one for lunch at a fashionable restaurant he had never been to before, though he'd heard of it. Then they met another at a gallery he had never been to, and together strolled to yet another gallery he *had* been to. She was obviously dear friends with the owner; it was obvious by the way he burst forth from that hidden back room, cordoned by a velvet rope, and gave her a hug.

Later that night she took him to a restaurant he had never been to but had read about in magazines and met more friends of hers. Their eyes were bright with excitement and a kind of amusement. He remembered how exciting it can be to see someone you know from home in some faraway place. It's one of those irrational but powerful forces, like the excitement of hearing your favorite song, which you own, on the radio.

He introduced her to some of his friends with great pride, and kept casting her surreptitious glances, to see if she was appreciating them, as though they were artworks to be marveled at.

But now, through her eyes, his friends seemed more like boys than men. What was it about American men that made them so attached to that glorious moment when they first become grown-ups but don't have to actually behave in a particularly grown-up fashion? There was something maddeningly blithe about them, immature, reluctant to take on responsibility.

"I want to take you to the Russian baths," she said. "Have you been?"

AS WAS THE case with nearly every other establishment she had taken him to, he had not. And as was the case with nearly every other establishment she had taken him to, it was a strange fascinating place that he berated himself for not having known about.

The Russian baths consisted of a sauna, a steam room, a plunging pool of cold chlorinated water, and the main event, the bath itself—a large, furnace-heated room with concrete tiers on which people sat. He was familiar enough with the sauna and steam rooms of the various sports and health clubs; he hadn't forgotten the Harmonie Club's sauna with its well-fed, middle-aged patrons. But those places were meant to cosset, soothe, and keep life at bay. The Russian baths had a kind of raw brutality that seemed to say: "Bring it on, give me all you've got."

Entering the Russian baths was like entering a dungeon full of writhing tortured bodies. The floor was made of rough stones. The heat slapped his face and singed his ears. The room was full of people wet with their own sweat. It was standing room only. Faucets spewed cold water into buckets, which people would hoist over their heads. Their flesh was lurid under the bare light-bulbs. Everywhere there was skin: black and brown and mocha and yellow and bright pink.

Men with opulent rolls of fat and hairy chests seemed to be trying to sweat out their age, as though the brutal heat would perform a kind of reduction, and they would emerge closer to their younger, more taut selves.

Men who had harder, younger bodies, like his own, seemed to be performing a kind of distillation, a purification in which all unnecessary fluids were purged to make their bodies more pure and potent.

The women's shapes were varied too, but distinctions of pretty and ugly were obscured in the heat. Such hot bodies in such close proximity seemed, at first, disgusting, but it was comforting and exciting too, because everyone was glaringly human in his or her near nakedness. In a few moments all of Alex's thoughts turned to issues of survival—how to survive the heat, how to survive his duties as a host, how to survive *her*.

Alex and Katrina took a seat on one of the benches. He told himself over and over: This is pleasurable, this is good, I like this.

Faucets poured cold water continually into white buckets, placed around the room, which filled to the brim and then overflowed until one of the heat-struck inhabitants hoisted one over his or her head. Each faucet poured at a different speed, with a different velocity. There was a kind of melody of pouring, of water flowing, that filled the room, punctuated by the frequent loud splashes of someone upending a bucket over themselves.

In the corner two Russian men were beating a woman.

"She's getting a *platza*," said Katrina.

The woman's skin was white. She was plump. Her bathing suit was a bright blue one-piece, and, with the casual ease of someone who knew what they were doing, she pulled it down for them, exposing her breasts. Her pale pink nipples bobbed into view for everyone to see.

Then she lay facedown on a wooden slat. A veteran, Alex thought. But then the men put their fingers under her bathing suit and pulled it farther down. Her ass popped out into the open, and he saw her twitch a little. Once it's out in the open, an ass is just an ass, but the moment of transition between hidden and exposed is always fraught.

Alex remembered the first time he told Katrina that he loved her. Another fraught transition. The announcement caused him pain and grief. Why? It had felt like a surrender, a defeat. It had felt like an awful birth. He was sure she did not love him back, or did not love him enough, or did not have the resources to love him as much as he needed to be loved.

And did he love her? Or was he just talking himself into it? He wasn't sure. At the moment he hated her. He had a primitive and brutal notion of how love worked. He associated love with pain; the pain of *wanting*. He had been loved abundantly but was somewhat apathetic in the face of it. He had a terrible addiction to love as a drop of water that falls into a parched mouth.

He cast a glance at Katrina. Her cheeks were flushed. She blew some hair from her face. Her elegant feet looked pretty against the crude concrete of the Russian bath's floor. She wore a black bikini, wrapped her bottom in a towel, and averted her eyes from the other bodies packed into the sweltering room.

She had told him that her previous visit had been on the all-women day, and that she had stared with utter intoxicated inhibition at the other bodies. But now on co-ed night she was being demure. Her breasts, which normally had such a powerful effect on him, seemed diminished in the heat. It was impossible to have overt sexual feelings in this torture chamber. His penis was in a state of frantic self-protecting retraction. The top of his scalp was burning.

The burly Russian men were beating their subject with oak leaves, creating a sudsy froth on her skin. One man worked her upper body, the other her legs. They beat her and washed her and rinsed her with the buckets of ice water. Her pale skin became pink, then deep red. They turned her over and worked on her front. Bodies entered the room and left it. Alex poured buckets of cold water over his head. Katrina did too.

"It's time to go out," she said. "We're getting too hot."

He compliantly followed her out of the hot dungeon just as he had followed her into Dean & Deluca, where they shopped earlier that day, and into the gallery they had been to. Her assuredness threw him into a heightened uncertainty.

Sitting out by the cold pool, he watched fat men plunge into the water and scamper out, purged of something. It was the cooling section, where people regained their strength before the next episode of self-torture.

"You've got to get a *platza*," she said.

"You think I should do that?" he said. "It's a human car wash." She smiled at this. He loved it when she smiled at things he said.

"I've always been obsessed by car washes," she said. "Maybe that's why I like the *platza* so much."

Making her come and making her laugh had become the two main objectives in his life since he met her. They were both difficult objectives.

"It's the most wonderful thing," she said. "You must have it."

She stood up and walked over to one of the Russian men who had been administering the abuse, a muscular, bald, burly Russian man with a hairy back and a hairy chest but smooth shoulders. He had the vigorous athletic Russian-style body that suggested that his idea of a relaxing winter afternoon was to take a swim in a frozen river and then warm up with some vodka.

She spoke to the Russian, pointed back towards Alex. The Russian man looked at him and nodded.

It was arranged. They went into the scalding room. She took a seat on a bench. They laid him out facedown. The hot air was searing the backs of his legs. As an act of mercy, they threw a towel soaked in ice water over his head. The room went black and he was grateful. The first thing they did was yank down his bathing trunks. His ass was now exposed.

What was she trying to do to him?

The men began to beat him. He gasped for breath in the dark wet airless space under the towel. Every now and then an incredibly strong hand reached down to the muscles of his neck and shoulders and administered a furious and utterly ungentle massage. His legs were burning. The heat was savage and homicidal, and they were beating him. He wanted to call out: Please stop! He wanted to flee. But he made himself go absolutely still. He deactivated the survival mechanism and hoped that he could thusly pass for a man who could take it (whatever "it" was). And then, through the clamor of voices, he heard her call out, in a faintly maternal tone that made the whole situation even worse: "It's his first time!"

How utterly humiliating, as though he were some kind of sacrificial virgin. His ass was in the air being beaten with oak leaves, he was a passive, helpless creature, and his girlfriend and thirty panting strangers were observing the scene, and the worst of it was that he was supposed to rise from this, should he survive it, and pretend to his loved one that it was some wonderful reinvigorating experience.

Afterwards they walked up Tenth Street towards Second Avenue in silence.

"Wasn't that wonderful?" she said. He did not reply. "Oh, come on," she laughed. He walked on, somewhat stiffly, in silence. He was fuming. She had commandeered him in his own city. Nothing was happening the way he'd planned. But that wasn't even true: the most important things, the sex, the intimacy, those were going well. But she refused to admit that there was a connection between the two of them in bed and the two of them in the world. Out in public she kept him at arm's length, at best, or arranged to have his bare ass beaten in a sauna.

He cast a quick glance at her. She looked like what she was: a stylish mom.

They turned left on Second Avenue. It was a cool spring evening. They walked some more.

"Where are we going?" she said.

"It's a surprise."

He didn't know where he was taking her. He just knew he was going to dictate the next move. All his previous thoughts about ways to make her happy no longer applied. He wanted revenge. They walked some more in silence. He turned right on Second Street, and they emerged onto the Bowery right next to CBGB. There was a crowd outside. They were young and most of them had Mohawks or bald heads, or some other in-your-face hairstyle. If her friends were mostly sleek, pleasant, prosperous professionals, then it was safe to say that among this crowd she had no friends. He didn't either, but he felt he knew where he was. The hard-core scene had never made much sense to him even when he went to CBGB to see bands, even when his band had played at CBGB. This was a strange subculture from Queens. But he recognized the pent-up malevolence on their faces, the desire for release.

"This is a famous club," he said. "I used to come here all the time. My band played here a few times."

"I don't want to go to a club," she said. "Can't we just go somewhere for dinner?"

"Just a peek. Come on."

"I'm not in the mood for music," she said.

"Oh, for God sakes, honey. Just trust me."

She rolled her eyes. The place was dark, and the band seemed to have finished setting up. He pushed forward through the crowd until he was past the narrow space abutting the bar and in the open space near the front of the stage. The bassist had just lit a cigarette. He had a Mohawk. They stood together and for the first time he took in the faces around him. It was a smoldering moment.

"Are you ready motherfuckers!" screamed the singer at an excruciating volume. Alex saw Katrina flinch and put her hands to her ears. He felt a small spark of pity for her. A moment later, with the first crunching chords, the crowd would erupt in mayhem. It would be like being caught in a riot. She would hate him. He could already perceive, in the lines creasing her forehead, the beginnings of distress. But he didn't care. He was at last showing her something of New York.

AT THE END of her visit she became ill, and he had to look after her, and take her to the doctor, from whose office she emerged with the news that she had strep throat. She had a prescription, which he got filled, and repeated to him the doctor's one comment: "No oral sex."

"You're kidding," he said, again and again, and no matter how many times she said she wasn't kidding, he didn't fully believe her. He had never heard of that stipulation being made to strep throat patients. But he was a good nurse to her. And when he made her chicken soup and fed it to her with a spoon in bed, and she said, "Can I have some of the chicken bits?" in a soft requesting voice, he nearly melted with affection. "Bits," he thought, was the best word in the British language.

A PLAN WAS made for him to spend two months of the summer with her. He made some inquiries about possible contacts at the BBC, Channel 4, and ITV, and though he couldn't imagine ever working again for a television station, it at least gave him a sense of momentum. Meanwhile, New York had again become a place of fun and possibility. For a while, after he had been fired, every don't-walk signal flashed "You Lose." Now it was almost as if he were visiting his hometown, and he made the rounds of lunches and dinners and drinks like someone with just a little time to do lots of things before he was swept off to other adventures. The principle she had explained to him on their first meeting—people will always like you better if you are just about to leave—now applied to his own hometown.

HE RENTED A car and drove down to visit Aunti B in her nursing home in Pennsylvania. He went every three or four months. They were ghoulish events. He would come into her room and find her in her easy chair, unmoving, unblinking, staring with a horrible kind of absence at the ceiling. Her ankles were swollen, her body gaunt.

"Hi, Aunti B!" he would call out. "I'm here!" It would take a long time for her to focus on him, whole fat ticking seconds of awfulness as her eyes rested uncomprehendingly on his face.

"Look! I brought shrimp!" This was his rallying cry. He held the Zabar's bag aloft. Cooked shrimp with cocktail sauce was her favorite.

At first, she would laugh when she recognized him. The expression of existential horror in which her face had frozen would melt and there would be that same look of incredulity with which she used to regard him when he visited her apartment. And then the laughter. And then the laughter would devolve into tears. Terrible wrenching tears.

"You don't know what they do to me here!" she would scream.

With each visit the Alzheimer's progressed, reducing the metropolis of her personality to rubble, and then dust. Eventually his aunt's speech, always peppered with German, became all German, and then, as far as he could tell, she simply stopped making sense in any language. Every visit began with a long bout of crying at the sight of him.

But there were also moments of happiness on these visits. The nurse would bring dinner, and Aunti B would throw it into the room. This amused her. Once, instead of trying to stop her, he took to throwing food as well, which she enjoyed immensely. For a finale, he smashed a wedge of lemon meringue pie in his own face. This brought down the house.

There was a stereo in her room, and a photograph of Karl as a baby hung on the wall. He was a cute baby but a little distorted. She had ripped the photo to shreds shortly after she moved in, when she still was a little bit herself. The nurses pieced it back together and hung it higher. Alex marveled at her anger. From where did it come? Why Karl?

Karl had left a CD of the Beatles for her. Alex ended every visit with a sing-along to "Yellow Submarine." He jumped around the room clapping and singing while she clapped and waved her arms like a conductor. At the chorus she sang: "La la la la la lala lala lala . . ."

It had been nearly a year since she said anything coherent to him in English. Now whole visits went by with her eyes vacant, her body wasted to almost nothing. He had taken to touching her a lot. Language had lost all meaning. He drove down for the sole purpose of putting his hand on her cheek.

On this last visit he was greeted by an unusually vigorous cry. He leaned over the big easy chair she was slouched in and kept his hand pressed against her cheek while she wept and sputtered hostile sounds. He murmured nice consoling words which he was quite sure meant nothing to her, and thought about going to London.

His habit during these initial cries was to go into a sort of numb state and wait it out. Now he half watched her tears evolve into laughter. Then she put her hand on his and said, in an accent that for a horrifying second captured some essence of her personality that he had thought was forever lost, "I love you."

JUST BEFORE ALEX left for the summer he raced into Nuts and Dry Fruits, a tiny store across the street from him on Amsterdam Avenue. Every afternoon it was overrun with children just let out from the Joan of Arc Middle School up the block, but for the rest of the day it was mostly empty, a tiny cramped space filled with every imaginable kind of candy, glass jars of nuts and dried fruit, and two old men—one bald and one who wore an outrageously bad toupee, both in yellow smocks—who bumped into one another with the absentmindedness of people who have spent years in each other's close proximity and hardly notice each other anymore.

He often bought a quarter pound of Swedish raspberries and made small talk. He liked these two highly particular old men, who, he imagined, had once upon a time been part of some wild gay demimonde, but now were entirely devoted to their nuts and dried fruits. Now he dashed in and bought all kinds of strange things: a Hot Wheels car, a hand buzzer, marzipan, two Pez dispensers and a great deal of Pez to go with them, dipstick, a blue handball, and several rolls of bubble gum tape.

Alex imagined Patrick's face as he stuffed the bubble gum into his mouth. He would put so much in his mouth he would drool while he laughed.

"Patrick!" Katrina would cry out. It would almost be familial.

He paid, got in a cab, and headed for the airport. On the ride out he let this familial fantasy linger.

THE LONG-DISTANCE relationship is a form best suited to the hopeless optimist, or to the man or woman who takes a certain pleasure in disappointment. These categories are more or less the same thing.

How else to explain Alex Fader's presence in the gray halls of Heathrow Airport, walking with a bounce in his step, chin aloft, full of anticipation?

There are certain ground rules in a long-distance relationship, the most important regarding endurance. How long can they endure being apart? A week is fine, two weeks bearable. Once that initial sting of separation is overcome, a month is doable. Five weeks is a serious strain. Beyond five weeks is like swimming in the ocean, past any barrier reef, where the waves are as high as mountains, the creatures are strange and lethal, and the only hope is an oblivious steamer sitting on the horizon.

Their reunion is a splendid thing. It happens in an airport, which lends it an air of almost military formality, as though one of them had been held hostage and was only now being released into the arms of the other. Around them there are other reunions, other cries of pleasure, relief, excitement.

Isn't a long-distance relationship really two relationships in one—the relationship with the person, and with the place? So, like an echo, the thoughts of her skin, her lips, her warm embrace—all these have as a corollary thoughts of black-currant Ribena, Back To Basics, Maison Bertaux, and black taxis.

There is the specific *her* that he is visiting, and the general *them*. He thinks of her accent and then more generally of *accents*. Her tea, the notion of afternoon *tea*. Her somewhat shallow but incredibly stylish and broad erudition, *everyone's somewhat shallow but incredibly stylish and broad erudition*. Her, *England*.

He walks over acres of Heathrow's abysmal carpeting, and at last he sees her.

Now, after they have gotten past those first blushing, giggly seconds of awkwardness, comes the moment they have been waiting for. That first embrace. A thrill like no other. Soon will come the small difficult reacquaintanceships—with her car, her neighborhood, her street, her house, her child. Her. But for now, in these first seconds, they hold on tight, letting their psychic heartbeats synchronize, and begin the delicious process of falling deep into the voluptuous pit of their own private world.

LONDON WAS FULL of blooming flowers and Katrina and Alex were drunk on each other's touch, on the luxury of such physical intimacy. Then things settled down and became a bit more complicated. They had no shared past, and it was difficult if not impossible to look to the future. So they had to exist purely in the present. Sometimes this worked, and sometimes it didn't.

Their fights were like small clouds on a bright windy day; no sooner had they appeared than they were whisked away by the jet stream of sex, to which the fights sometimes seemed a desirable prelude; it was as though they were engaging in a couple's version of autoerotic asphyxiation. This mode of operation, whereby tension is created to an almost unbearable point and then dispelled with lovemaking, was more to his taste than to hers, though she was expert at it simply by virtue of her ability to parry. But their fights were not always petulant tiffs. Black clouds rolled in with sudden force. One minute they would be squabbling about some tiny irrelevant detail of life, and then they would come to a border; you couldn't cross this border and come back in the same condition in which you left. They knew this, and yet they spilled over it again and again. It was much easier to cross this border on the way out than on the way back.

Once, after a huge fight that had its origins in whether they would see a movie at seven or nine, he stormed out of the house. It was raining. He stomped along in the rain for a while until he came to the little green hut a few blocks from her house where the cab drivers congregated for tea. He intended to hail a cab but all the cabs were off duty, and the cars sat in a dormant row while their drivers took refuge. What was he doing in the rain? Where did he think he was going? He had to call her up on a pay phone and, trying to maintain a shred of dignity, ask to come back. She was nice about it, though. When he came through the door she had a tear-streaked look of exhaustion on her face.

"Please let's not fight anymore, sweetie," she whispered into his ear as he held her in his moist arms. "I'm so tired of fighting."

ONE DAY ALEX and Patrick were sitting on the plush carpet of the bathroom floor. Somehow during this long summer visit the strangeness had suddenly left their relations, and Alex ate with him and sometimes even lay in bed with Katrina and read to Patrick from a book. He was amazed at how much he liked doing it.

Now Alex was pulling apart a clementine and throwing the pieces one at a time at Patrick, who sat across from him with his back against the tub. Patrick lunged at each clementine slice like a seal, trying to catch it in his mouth. Most of the time he missed and it bounced off his face and he broke into hysterical laughter. He had bright blue eyes and often when he smiled he shrugged his shoulders, as though he wanted to bury his face in the hollow of his collarbone. His second toe was longer than the big toe, just like his mother's.

Every now and then Alex would toss a piece high in the air and catch it in his own mouth. Somehow, in the presence of Patrick, his success ratio was near a hundred percent. In real life, fifty percent would have been more like it. There is something about being a grown man in the presence of a seven-year-old boy that enhances one's talents for such things as throwing clementine slices in the air and catching them in your mouth.

Patrick squealed with delight when Alex caught a slice in his mouth.

"Alex! You're eating them all!" he said.

"It's a tough world out there, kid," he replied. "It's sink or swim. I'll give you another chance, but if you miss it, you miss it."

Then he began taking aim.

He threw a clementine at Patrick, who had just turned seven and did not possess even the slightest amount of coordination. He lunged spastically in its direction and it bounced off his forehead.

"The problem is that you're closing your eyes," said Alex. "You can't just open your mouth wide and lunge in the general direction. You've got to keep your eye on the ball."

He reached over, picked the clementine slice off the floor, and squinted with one eye, as though he were aiming a dart at a bull's-eye. "Open your mouth," he said.

At such moments Alex sometimes thought of Patrick's father,

who really should be the one sitting here, he felt. He thought of the complex spying apparatus he sometimes was convinced was wired through the whole house, and of Patrick's father watching this scene with the clementines.

Patrick opened his mouth very wide. He really was a cute kid, Alex thought. There was something crushingly kind about him. His vulnerability was terrifying.

When Alex first met him he had been frightened of Patrick. Patrick, at age six, was the master of the house. If Alex was accepted into Katrina's house, he knew it would be at Patrick's discretion.

But they had made friends; at first an uneasy truce, and then gradually something warm and real developed.

Now, however, as Alex held the clementine, he felt those dying embers of resentment towards Patrick flair, as if touched by a gust of wind. As he took aim, he could hear the distant soft thudding of Katrina's footsteps coming up the stairs.

"Open wider," he said.

Patrick complied. His head was tilted back, his mouth a big circle, his thin arms hanging limply at his side, as though his entire being were concentrated on making his mouth as big as possible so he could snare a clementine.

It was a perfect shot. Right down the middle. Its arc was a gentle loop, and it entered that round circle of Patrick's mouth and penetrated all the way to the back of his throat without banging into anything.

And from there it dropped down the wrong pipe.

Patrick's response was slightly delayed. For a second he began to laugh. But then the error became apparent, and his eyes bulged out, and he began to choke. He coughed in long wheezes.

"Cough," said Alex.

"Patrick?" said Katrina from outside, "Is that you?" Her voice

was streaked with a wispy cloud of concern which Alex knew
would darken to storm clouds as soon as she walked in the door.

Alex knelt next to Patrick, slapped his back, and tried to speak
in a calm tone of voice. "Cough it up, just try and *cough it up*."

But Patrick just made a wheezing sound now, the sound of
steam escaping from a radiator.

"Patrick? Patrick? Alex? Are you in here?" Katrina pushed
the bathroom door open and stepped into the small, private,
clementine-scented world that Patrick and Alex had been occupying for the last half hour.

She had been out in the world, which involved cars, and ex-
husbands, and morning breakfasts with divorce lawyers.

"He's all right," said Alex, kneeling over Patrick. "He's just got
something stuck in his throat."

But Patrick was clearly not all right. He sat doubled over, making horrible sounds.

Katrina's response was swift. She slapped him hard on the
back. When this didn't work she took him by the ankles, stood
up, and held him upside down. Even though Patrick was seven, he
was not light, but she did this without any apparent strain. "Slap
his back," she said tersely.

Alex gave him a firm slap between the shoulder blades. He felt
the boy's bones, fragile like a bird's, and cringed.

"Harder," she said.

The clementine popped out, glistening with wet. A moment
later, Patrick started crying. It started with a halting sob. Katrina
pulled Patrick to her and held him as he began to sob in earnest
onto her shoulder.

As Alex watched, he reflected that the two of them were now a
tight family unit of two, and he was merely a stranger, a culprit.
Katrina took a brief moment off from comforting Patrick, just a
split second, to flash a dark glance in his direction, an utterly dis-

gusted enraged glance at the boy who had nearly let her son choke to death.

THEY WERE STRETCHED out on one of her long living-room couches, facing each other, on a balmy Wednesday evening, the light slowly dimming to a summer dusk. Patrick was with Sam; the large house was empty and silent but for their conversation. They had just now showered together. She wore a white cotton bathrobe. He was wrapped in a towel, his chest bare. "There is a great similarity," he said, "between the life of the millionaire and the life of the unemployed."

"Oh really?" she said skeptically.

"Well, it's a weekday. Most of the world is scampering around doing things, and you and I are just lying here as though we were on the beach."

She smiled. How wonderful it was when they didn't seem like strangers to each other.

"Tell me a scene from your childhood I could never have otherwise imagined," he said.

She thought about it for a minute. The light was getting dimmer. They faced each other. Their legs stretched out in each other's direction. His bare foot pressed against her crotch. The terry cloth felt good against her skin.

"One summer we collected wood for the bonfire," she began. "I was about eight or nine. It was a big project. We built it in the middle of a field behind our country house. Every day all summer we dragged these bits of deadwood out of the forest. I was so excited about burning it. I remember thinking a lot about what a enormous fire it would be."

He removed his foot from where it had been resting and slid it beneath her robe, back to its original position, except now it was his skin against hers. The soft arch of his foot against her protruding softness.

"Go ahead," he said.

"Eventually the big day arrived. We all gathered around. There were some neighbors there too, and their children. I remember my father standing there with a pitchfork. I never quite figured out why he had the pitchfork. We lit the fire. It was bigger and brighter than I had imagined it would be. But then a terrible thing happened."

"Go ahead," he said. He nudged her with his foot.

"It went up in flames right away. A sudden burst. And after a minute or so there was this sound, and these little rabbits started darting out from the bottom. They had built an underground warren over the course of the summer and now all these tiny rabbits came darting out of the wood and some of them were on fire. I remember being really confused and upset. People started screaming. There were these little flaming bunnies darting around, and there was a terrible horrible screeching sound coming from inside the bonfire and then I saw my father chasing the rabbits that were on fire and stabbing them with the pitchfork. He was just putting them out their misery, but I didn't understand that. I just saw him stabbing the rabbits to death with the pitchfork, and he was all red and orange, lit up by the bonfire, and everybody was screaming, and there was that terrible screeching sound from inside the fire, and I started to scream too. I never screamed like that before. Or since, for that matter. It was like being in hell."

He pressed his foot against her as if he were accelerating a car. And then his big toe was inside. Neither of them said anything. Their expressions were blank; a slight hint of curiosity on his face, and a slight look of contempt on hers as he moved his toe in and out of her.

―――――――

HIS IDEA OF treating her well usually involved his head disappearing between her legs and then commencing with his tongue. His soft dark hair blended into the darkness between her legs, and she was left alone by herself. He wouldn't stop until he got what he wanted, which was that she get what she wanted, or rather get what he thought she wanted, which she *did* want, but not in this manner, or at least not *exclusively* in this manner.

She was, however, reluctant to complain. She didn't want to discourage whatever small amount of consideration she could get. But when he went down there she was alone, and so her thoughts drifted, often to people and places she would rather have let lie dormant, but which instead were brought by necessity to the surface of her consciousness, and so when at last she got there and pulled her knees together to make him stop (because for some reason he often kept going a little bit beyond that point, as though more were simply better, when if he simply thought about his own feelings on the matter—the way he pulled away, needed to simmer down—it would be perfectly obvious), she suddenly found herself with a grinning wet-chinned man who seemed a perfect stranger.

TEN DAYS AFTER Alex arrived in London he got a message that his Aunti B had died.

That night he and Katrina were going to the theater. It had been a brilliant June day. Their taxi raced towards the West End, around Trafalgar Square, and a ray of sun shot across the black lions and landed on her neck. Her hair was up and her neck looked beautiful.

"My aunt died yesterday. I just got the message."

"I'm sorry," she said, her voice soft. "Are you all right?"

"Yes. But it's not how I expected it to happen."

"One never really expects something like that," she said.

He looked at Katrina and tried to connect the present moment, speeding along in the taxi in London, to his memory of Aunti B.

"She'd been sort of on the verge of dying for a long time" he said. "Long enough to get used to the idea of her still being alive."

"I'm sorry," she said again. She was very decent about it. But for a moment he felt a rage towards her. She could not begin to fathom the person his aunt was, the life she led. For the first and possibly only time he felt a flare of regret that Katrina wasn't Jewish. He didn't know why that would change anything, but he felt it.

HE WOKE UP in the middle of the night. His lip hurt. He sat up. His lip tasted of blood. He had been biting his lip in his sleep.

NINA WAS A tall, nearly ravishing woman with jet black hair and long, highly articulated fingers whose nails were bitten to a nub. Alex felt he knew her for some reason, more than anyone Katrina had introduced him to. What it was about Nina that he recognized was hard to say. She was happily married and lived in impressive style. Nina's husband was a mild, almost self-effacing man whom the various servants referred to as "my lord." At one point Alex had taken one of the butlerish figures aside and asked how long he had known the master of the house.

"Since school days," he said. "We all used to call him Richard."

Nina had been married to Richard long enough to have two young children, but she had also been married previously, and the way that Katrina had spoken of that first marriage made Alex imagine it as a wild, reckless house party that continued until the whole house burst into flames.

Some very important thing had been lost in the fire. Its

absence was something only she could detect and quantify, but it was as though her fulfillment now—her marriage, her children, her houses—was based on a foundation of self that was missing one small but essential piece. He liked that about her.

"NINA WAS BEING very strange on the phone today," Katrina said. They were walking through the still darkness of her street, on their way home from a restaurant.

"Why?" said Alex.

Katrina and Alex had been to dinner at the home of Nina and her husband, John, a few times; they were the subject of regular speculation, if only because the pool on which Alex and Katrina could speculate together was relatively small. "I could tell something was odd and I'm sure that it had to do with John's being out last night at that party without her and talking to me."

"Would she be jealous just because he was out without her? It's not your fault you saw him."

"Yes, but I can just hear him saying, 'Nothing much to report, I just talked to Katrina for a while.' Oh, how that would wind her up."

"But what's the big deal?" said Alex. "They're married. If you're just involved with someone in this nebulous . . ." He stopped himself. "If two people are together in a more informal way, together but not married, I would think they would constantly be looking out for signs that the other person is bored or restless. They would constantly be worried about being left. But somehow if you are married it seems so resolved. It's done. There is no way out. I mean, you can take the one ultimate drastic step of divorce. But otherwise . . ."

"But that's the point!" she flashed. They were at the steps to her house, five high stone steps, and at the top she fumbled for her keys. The brass fist-shaped knocker seemed to be menacing him: leave her alone! For a moment there was an enormous gulf between this small mundane activity of getting the right key to unlock the door and her fury that he couldn't understand the feeling that had once been so much part of her life. "If you are single and you are with somebody, and they don't want to sleep with you, then at a certain point you can just go find someone else to sleep with," she said. "But if you are married, there's nowhere to go. You're stuck. You become desperate. And desperate people do all kinds of irrational things."

She put the key in the lock and turned it.

ONE MONDAY MORNING a bearded man in a trench coat appeared at the front door and handed an envelope to Katrina. She returned to the kitchen and dropped the envelope next to the phone. Alex picked it up.

"What's this?" he said.

"It's this week's money to run the household," she said matter-of-factly. "He sends it over once a week in cash."

"Why in cash?"

She shrugged.

A few minutes later, when she had left the room, he opened the envelope and looked inside. It was bulging with hundred-pound notes.

HIS MONEY WAS getting low. The less money one has, he thought, the greater the apparent velocity of its departure, in the same way that the last inch of water in a draining bath always seems to go down the drain fastest. Yet Alex was stalled when it came to his professional life. His horizon had contracted from the very near future to the extremely near future. Patrick was spending the second two weeks of August with Sam, and Katrina had arranged to rent a house on Long Island. They would have a two-week idyll on neutral territory. Beyond that he couldn't imagine what would happen. He knew he would soon have to move out of his apartment, now that his aunt had died. He knew he had to get some traction with his work. But meanwhile he drifted through London.

There was a stretch of grocery stores and newsstands run by Iranians near Katrina's house. Alex usually avoided them. He felt strangely threatened by the beautiful calligraphy of the Arab newspapers.

One blue-and-white day he ventured inside, tempted by a large sign that said: "Iranian caviar."

The shop was filled with various delicacies, strange moist sweets arranged on metal trays and covered with plastic wrap, an orderly chaos from which Alex could not manage to select any one thing. He stood in front of the pistachio nuts, a whole barrel, peering down at the thin crack in each nut which leered up at him like a smile. In the end he left with a persimmon, its smooth orange skin soft in his hand.

"THAT IS A very good persimmon," Aunti B would have said if she had seen it. "The best!"

HE WANDERED AROUND London and became slowly aware of a tidal pull New York exerted upon him. Curious memories floated up, such as Ellen.

Ellen was not a romantic or even sexual entanglement, though there were weird sexual overtones to his thoughts. She had worked in the cubicle next to his at the network. Whereas Alex did (or didn't do) quirky off-beat "essays on film," Ellen did hard news and had been working on a piece about the inmates of the United States Penitentiary at Marion, Illinois, the biggest and most closely guarded prison in the world, where John Gotti spent twenty-three hours a day in solitary confinement. Her research included a correspondence with some prisoners. The prisoners had a lot of time to write letters. Every day her in box was stuffed with letters, all coming from the Marion Penitentiary, their handwriting full of pathos and squiggly desperation to communicate with someone. Ellen spent her days sitting in her cubicle writing back. At the end of each day, her out box was filled with twenty or thirty envelopes, all bearing the neat impressive-looking corporate logo of the network where they worked.

She developed carpal tunnel syndrome. Yet still she typed. She typed with strange flexible casts over both wrists, her little pink fingers protruding just enough to allow her to keep typing. What was she saying to those prisoners?

He thought of Ellen writing her prison letters. Her pink fingers typing madly. He contrasted Ellen's static life, imprisoned in her cubicle, to the fluid ease of Katrina's existence, her style, her money, her sense of possibility. With whom did he share more? he wondered. This glamorous London mother, or panicked, obsessive Ellen, obsessing in her private and professional New York hell?

THAT EVENING AN old friend of Katrina's, Ernie, was due to visit. Katrina filled him in—Ernie's mother was a star of the London stage, a famous eccentric; his father was a penniless aristocrat who had died young. Ernie had decamped with wife and children from London to Ireland, where he taught and wrote plays.

"God, the English are good at summarizing the big picture," said Alex. "Where the money comes from."

"Everyone wants to know where the money does or doesn't come from, as you may one day discover. And anyway, what's so bad about the big picture? What's so superior about the small picture? You think it's crass to look at anything larger than an eyelash."

"You can make a wish with an eyelash," he said.

"Oh, fuck off," she said.

ALEX WENT BACK to Katrina's house and put the persimmon in the big bowl of fruit that sat on the kitchen table. It was filled with oranges and apples and peaches and nectarines and green grapes. He loved that bowl of fruit!

Not enough attention has been paid to the psychic benefits of having a bowl of fruit on the kitchen table, he thought. In addition to Prozac and Zoloft and whatever else, psychiatrists should dole out prescriptions saying: three bowls of fruit on the kitchen table per week, green and black grapes, peaches, nectarines, mangoes, kiwi. In winter, insurance companies should pick up the cost of imported grapes.

Two days earlier, Katrina had berated Alex viciously for having vanquished a supply of mangoes that, it turned out, had been scheduled to be part of Patrick's breakfast.

"I always try and get some fruit down him in the morning," she had once said, and the passing comment had stuck in his mind, something about the use of the words "down him," as though she was literally plunging something fibrous into one end of his system so something would come out the other. He felt that in this way she was an excellent mother, attached bloodily and bodily, aware of her son's heartbeat and his digestion, ferocious on his behalf. Alex had lessened the odds of her son's having a productive visit to the bathroom by leaving his morning mangoless.

"Do not eat my child's fruit!" she had shouted, as though he was trying to mortally wound her. His thoughts flashed to that weekly envelope of cash—wife support, child support. It was not intended to be boyfriend support.

He took the persimmon out of the fruit bowl and put it on the windowsill, so that it might exist apart from that scene, uncontaminated by the mixed motives of penance. It looked beautiful there, as though the light were emanating within. Then he went up to her bedroom and lay on the bed, shoeless, wiggling his toes and waiting. He was in London to wallow in sex, he thought. Katrina was a sex object. Her son was, for some strange reason he did not fully understand, but nevertheless appreciated, an aphrodisiac. These were cruel thoughts. He let them go. He thought of the tender expression of sadness and remorse that sometimes played around her eyes and mouth, as though she were regretting some long ago event.

He thought of how the first thing she had said when he told her about his dad dying when he was ten was: "That must have been so hard for your mother."

He loved her for saying that.

THE DOORBELL RANG and he went to get it.

"My God," said Ernie, standing in the doorway. "You're enormous. What have you done with Katrina?"

"She's upstairs," said Alex. "Come in."

"Christ, it's a beautiful night," said Ernie. Alex could smell the cold on him; he had traveled by train all the way from Ireland that day.

"I'm Alex," said Alex. He offered his hand.

Ernie's handshake was vigorous but not overly firm. But it wasn't soft either. Alex had been humiliated several times by soft handshakes from English men. These limp handshakes were a physical manifestation of a horribly effective form of psychic kung-fu that English men had apparently perfected over centuries of evolutionary refining, a kind of passive-aggressive martial art built around self-effacement that made the other person stumble over his own forward motion.

The humiliation was not that the limp handshaker wasn't interested in shaking hands, exactly, but rather that it put Alex in the position of being one of those crazed, ridiculous men who are so intent on being masculine that they nearly crush to bits the hand that they're shaking. The handcrushers always seemed to be compensating for something. Alex didn't want to be a compensator.

There was something feisty and childish and faintly apocalyptic about Ernie, something *hearty*, as though as soon as he took off his coat he would begin relating some wild series of events, a near-death experience, perhaps, that had befallen him on that day's journey.

They opened the wine and sat down at the kitchen table. Ernie produced a sack of pistachio nuts and a long slab of halvah. He too had visited the Iranians. Alex felt impressed and slightly jealous. They toasted.

"So do you go crazy in London?" asked Alex.

"Do I go crazy?" said Ernie. His black eyes, with heavy bags under them, widened.

"When you're away from your family, alone in the big city, is it a relief?" said Alex. "I go a little crazy whenever I'm in a new place, wander around, drink too much. And I don't have a family. If I was leaving behind a family . . ."

"You're making it sound like I'm abandoning them!" said Ernie.

"What's going on here?" said Katrina upon entering the kitchen. She was transformed. Her hair was damp and loose around her face, her cheeks were bright, her smile was easy and careless. Her voice no longer had the soft intimate wounded tone with which she whispered to him in bed, but was cheery and assertive, and she was again possessed of the outrageous confidence and sense of prerogative that she carried around with her like a shield.

Ernie stood up from his seat and they embraced. He enveloped her. Alex watched her hands spread out on his back.

"Your friend has asked me if I'm going crazy," he said.

"And what did you say?" said Katrina.

"I denied it vehemently," said Ernie.

"London has different effects on different people," said Alex. "I was asking what effect it has on him."

"I'd like to know what effect it has on *you*," she said.

They sat down to a feast of white wine, halvah, and pistachios, Ernie sitting between them. Ernie's fingernails were bitten down to the nub, and this made his attack on each nut even more frantic and desperate than it otherwise would have seemed. He had long fingers, and they worried the pistachios apart.

Katrina was more delicate in her pistachio approach, inserting a thumbnail, opening the shell, chewing thoughtfully, taking breaks for sips of wine and a nibble of halvah. Alex started at Ernie's pace, but then slowed, drifted to the halvah, its dense sweetness sticking to the roof of his mouth in a pleasant way.

Ernie was talking very animatedly about the Maze, the prison where he taught. He spoke sympathetically of the IRA prisoners, the rituals, the hierarchies, the punishments and isolation meted out, the hardships endured by the inmates, their pride.

"How do your kids feel about the prison?" Alex said.

"They love hearing about it," said Ernie, chewing madly. "Children love prisons."

ALEX HID EVERY Wednesday evening at six o'clock, and also Saturday afternoons at four. He didn't, and this was very important to him, *cower*. He just made himself absent, either leaving the house for some errand or drifting up to one of its upper floors. The transaction he was avoiding, and which occurred every week with great precision and regularity, was between Katrina and Sam. The currency of exchange was Patrick.

His hide-outs were, by definition, externally quiet and unobtrusive events. But they were occasions of regret and anger and weird displaced feelings, as though his life didn't really belong to him.

TWO WEEKS IN the country—high corn, and potato fields, and only the occasional shiny sports car to remind them that somewhere out there in the modern beach house architecture there was a voracious social scene going on. For Alex and Katrina it was two solitary, beautiful, weightless, dreamy, idyllic weeks marked by meals and lovemaking and languor, and marred by one awful weekend when two of Alex's friends, Milo and Jack, came out to visit. Everything went fairly well until the four of them got involved in a game of Scrabble.

C-o-l-o-u-r.

"That's not how you spell 'color,'" said Milo.

"It most certainly is," said Katrina.

"I hate to point this out," said Jack, "but we are in America right now, so . . ."

"They may have a point," said Alex, already laughing at Katrina's exasperation.

What followed was one of those laughter-filled disputes in which somehow everyone fails to notice that one person has stopped laughing. When Katrina threw all her letters down onto the board in disgust and stormed off, the three boys noticed.

"Christ, I'm sorry about that. I was such an idiot," said Alex later. He rearranged various words and phrases around this theme for two whole days before it blew over. He knew she was right. He had been an idiot, siding with his idiotic friends on an idiotic matter.

Other than this interruption, they coasted through a dreamy

green world for two weeks, pausing as they biked home from the beach to watch the horses graze.

At the end he took her to the airport, and to his surprise, she broke down in tears as they hugged goodbye. Not quiet, sad, parting tears, but real sobs.

"I'm sorry our life together isn't more . . ." And, gulping back a sob, she drew a circle with both hands. "Whole," she said.

He cupped her face with his hands. He thought she looked so beautiful, tan and lithe and now her cheeks wet with tears. But she frightened him a little with this comment, pointing out the truth that he had chosen to ignore. He had been wallowing in laughter, sex, and splendor, but it was purely ornamental. They weren't having their cake and eating it too. There was no cake. This was just icing. And she was reminding him that icing is not enough.

"JAY IS GETTING married," she announced. Alex was back in London for October. A frost had developed between them which, even after a week, was refusing to thaw. He could hear the reproach in her voice before she even finished her sentence.

Jay was a good friend of Katrina's, a young man about Alex's age with bright mischievous eyes. The last Alex had heard, Jay was mourning over his breakup with an actress named Rebecca.

"Isn't that a bit quick?" said Alex. He remembered Rebecca; there was a beseeching quality to her eyes he had liked, because their softness coexisted with the burning, nearly mercenary ember of ambition that lit them. She had full, extravagant breasts, and she tended to move around a room as though always aware of where she would be cast in the best light. She had left Jay nine months earlier, just after Alex met them, and it had appeared Jay was in for a hard time. Now he was getting married.

"He met a girl and they fell in love and then six months later they got engaged. That's how it should be," she said. "It's much better than the man spending four years making the woman feel like a piece of shit while he tries to make up his mind."

"Is that what happened to you?"

"No," she said.

"I don't believe you," he said. "That was the authority of experience speaking."

"I spent the four years waffling about it, if you have to know," she said. "And I still felt like . . . I won't repeat the word."

He loved her for not repeating the word.

"I'M A VERY castrating woman," she once said.

"You haven't castrated me," he'd said.

"We're working on it."

PRINCESS DI WAS confessing on television; Katrina and Alex sat cuddled on the couch and watched. When it was over she went upstairs to take a pee. A man named Soams came on the screen and held forth on what a sick, deluded, evil bitch he thought Diana was, though he phrased it more delicately, and how valiant Charles had been to put up with her. He was fat, immaculate in dress, and his accent had a plummy roll to it. Alex closed his eyes and simply listened to the pitch and roll of the man's voice, its *entitlement*. His accent reminded Alex of the way a python slowly devours a live duck (he had seen this on Mutual of Omaha's *Wild Kingdom* as a kid) with a cordial kind of brutality; the man's voice was disgusting but fascinating; Katrina's accent wasn't nearly as farcical and plummy, but she had in her voice a similar kind of cordial brutality, the ability to *dismiss*.

He went upstairs to look for her. His feet were quiet on the

carpet. The room was dark; a slash of light coming from the bathroom lay on the black floor. By the time his eye had her in its
sights it was clear that she had not heard him.

She was propped regally on the toilet, her skirt and panties
down at her ankles, examining her hair for split ends. Every now
and then she brought a strand to her mouth and bit it off. Her full
ass and thighs bulged out a bit on the seat. Something about her
thighs on the toilet was very sweet and childish, as was the way
she was absorbed in looking at her hair. He watched her like this,
and then became aware of just how intrusive he was being, and
how difficult it was therefore going to be to alert her to his presence without scaring her half to death.

He clucked his tongue. A woodpecker's single peck. She didn't
start; her eyes simply moved to where he stood.

"Hi," he said. "You look really cute. You look like a little girl."

She smiled sweetly.

"DON'T SPY ON me," she said when they were rearranged on the
couch. "Sam used to do it all the time and I hated it."

Alex felt the usual pang of curiosity about and hostility toward
Sam. She had told him little about her marriage, and for a while
Alex respected that distance. But now his imagination was filling
in the blanks.

For the first months of their relationship his thoughts about
her marriage organized themselves around a single question: what
had the bastard done to her?

Gradually, though, another competing question began to form:
what had she done to him?

But then he reproached himself for the preoccupation, and for
thinking of her as a little girl. What was his relationship to this little-
girl quality he so liked to see in her? Was he prepared to take respon-

sibility for her? For her son? Was all the vaguely paternal posturing he performed in bed a kind of sick joke on himself, play-acting a grown-up when he should have simply *been* one? There were moments when he felt an outrageously powerful connection to her, and moments when he felt he was just shooting his own home movie which years from now he could fondly consult for the memories.

After a while she went upstairs to get ready for bed and he spent some time flipping the channels, taking in the late-night offerings. At some point he came across a shot of a plain of tall grass over which the sun was setting. Giraffes grazed, other animals were shown lolling about. It was stirring and somewhat familiar. He watched for a few minutes and it got more and more familiar. Then he saw an animal that looked extremely familiar, and the announcer identified it for him. He was watching the Migration of the Wildebeests.

"I COULDN'T MOVE to London," he said.

"Why not?" she said.

"Because New York is where I *live*."

"You seem to be alive right now."

"But it's where my *friends* live."

Her eyes narrowed.

"Do you know what is going to happen to your friends?" she said.

"You're going to kill them all."

"No. They're going to get married. And then they'll have children. They'll be busy with their families, busy *supporting* their families." Her voice was incredibly cold and matter-of-fact, like that of a judge reading a sentence. "And then they won't be your friends anymore, or not in the way you mean when you say that word. Some of them will not be able to afford to stay in the city and they'll move away. And you know what all that is called?"

He didn't answer.

"It's called growing up!"

ASHLEY IN BROOKLYN. Her summertime milk-and-honey skin and soft brown hair. Her almond-shaped eyes with their cunning, quiet perceptiveness. Her deceiving aura of meekness. Her sexual authority over him. The enormous amount of worry and anxiety that was bound up in his love for her. In London, he thought of Brooklyn. They were both places of adventure for him, and sex. They were places of salvation. The network was a bit like high school—he had been expelled from both. In one instance he was rescued by Brooklyn, in the other, London.

He had been such a child with Ashley. And she had been a beautiful, full-grown woman, and a child too. He drifted back to her presence, the clean smell of her skin and hair, his virginal fascination with her.

"Are you a virgin?" she asked him one summery evening as he walked her home.

"Of course not!" he yelped. It was the sound that dogs make when someone has stepped on their paw. And then, "Are you?"

She looked at him with a detached look that suggested that all the information she took in had to travel a long way to the place inside of her that did the perceiving.

"You know I'm not," she said in a calm voice.

It was true. The whole school knew. Ashley was a girl about whom people whispered. That she appeared to be such a sweet, innocent girl made her all the more mythological: "Hurt me."

For all her quietness there was within her something reckless and raging for experience and sensation. He hadn't known what to do with it.

"WHAT'RE YOU DOING?" said a voice behind him.

It was the small, inquiring, fearless voice of a seven-year-old boy. Nine months earlier this voice would have been more frightening to him than the roar of a wild animal. Now he was just startled, and only a tiny bit terrified.

"I'm opening and closing the window," Alex said.

It was, like so many of the statements uttered in this house, a partial truth. What he had been doing was holding the cold brass knobs of the French doors that led onto a small second-floor balcony and opening and then closing them, again and again, while staring out at the changing leaves and rooftops.

Alex was susceptible to autumn. He was finely tuned to endings, and to their beginnings. He was trying to quantify the difference the window made to his experience of the view, and marveling at how clean this boy's mother kept the windows.

Closed: Nostalgic wistful scene of changing leaves, filtered autumn sun, and bright blue sky. Sad and hopeful.

Open: The burst of cold air, the sound of engines revving in the distance carried in on the breeze, raw, bracing, real.

Closed: Silence. The picture has a frame. A sense of closure or possibility makes every changing leaf seem poignant. He is safe.

Open: The sharp air on his face, the grinding gears of the world going about its business, the vicious Darwinistic forces taking their toll on people near and far.

"Have you seen my gun?" said Patrick.

He hesitated. Did Patrick mean had he yet seen the gun? Or had he seen the gun lying around somewhere in the house? For several days Patrick had been running around with his gun, pointing it at various targets and pulling the trigger.

"I haven't seen it," he said, still looking out the window.

"It's got caps," said Patrick.

He turned just in time to see Patrick fire off a few rounds with squinting concentration. There were some duds, but also some very loud pops and good sparks to go with them, and tart wisps of smoke rose into the room, an incredibly evocative smell for Alex. He used to love that smell. Patrick was pointing the gun right at him as he squeezed the trigger.

"That's not nice," he said.

"What's not nice about it?" said Patrick. "It's just a toy gun."

"It's a bad habit," he said rather stiffly, and tried to imagine what he would say if it were his own child.

ASHLEY BABY-SAT FOR a four-year-old girl every afternoon, and sometimes Alex would walk her to the playground as she pushed the stroller, and they would discuss whether or not people thought it was their child. Then one day she let him come up to the girl's apartment. Ashley poured him an iced tea in the kitchen and put the girl in the next room in front of the television. It was a sultry hot day. She walked into the kitchen and he lifted her shirt and began sucking her breasts with an ice cube in his mouth. Something about the child next door inflamed him. In a minute they were on the floor. He went through a kind of cosmic shift upon entering her (life would never again be the same), exploded, and then she pulled her shorts up and remarked, in the same matter-of-fact voice she used for all occasions, "It usually lasts longer than that."

IT WAS NOW early December, nearly a year since they'd met. Alex heard the tumult of Patrick coming home from school with Katrina. He was on the top floor, reading, and he stayed up there, knowing that Sam would be arriving soon. He wondered what Katrina and Sam had been like as a couple and sometimes tried to read it in the eyes of her friends when they looked at her with this American.

"What do your friends think of me?" he once asked.

"They think you're really nice," she said. "Nina says you're very handsome."

"And what do they think nice and handsome mean?"

"I think handsome, coming from Nina, means I should enjoy myself for a while before I go off and find some responsible rich man who can take care of me. Which basically means Sam."

He went to the window and peered down, watching the idling car with its small wisp of exhaust rising in the cold air. He had just returned to London after a very productive stretch of time in New York. He had managed to get a new apartment, and some work opportunities were shaping up. Katrina had responded coolly to both pieces of news. He stared down and waited for the two heads to appear, with their similar coloring, the boy he had come to know so well, and the man he had never met. What must Patrick make of all this? he wondered. Did he talk about his mother's friend with Sam? Alex hoped not.

They appeared, the car rolled off, and Alex went into the bedroom and lay down. The sky was full of low clouds. Soon he heard her footsteps on the carpeted stairs. She entered the room and lay next to him, curled away from him, yet against him. Her socks were thin, brown, feminine, and she pressed the bottoms of her feet against his shins, one then the other, with the gentle padded paw motions of a cat. The afternoon light filtering into the room was dimming quickly. She lay next to him, breathing, and he didn't move and she didn't move except for their breathing. There was a kind of docking going on, two spaceships merging in outer space, securing a passageway, equalizing the atmosphere, making it safe for the inhabitants to commingle. He pulled her against him, pushed his hand under her shirt so he could feel the warmth of her skin.

She resisted.

It was as though they both had to relinquish some resentment harbored against the other; it was connected to the vast distances they had to travel in the course of any minute to arrive on common ground, and also the doubt they each had about how long they could hold this shared space before gravity ripped them apart. She had arrived at this moment having just given her son over to her husband for their midweek visit. He had spent the day wandering, lost, at once exalting in his unbound freedom and vaguely craving something to feel bound to.

And now their intimacy looming. It was such a pressure on intimacy, for it to be the main event, not something stolen but the main attraction. This silent lying next to one another, the exciting mixture of affection and animosity, was their foreplay.

He rested his hand on her hip. He ran his hands up under her shirt, running his fingers along her vertebrae as if they were keys on a piano, squeezing here and there. She remained rigid. Then she turned to him and squirmed against him, her hands balled up into fists; she buried herself in him like an ax in a tree. Finally she embraced him, and their clothes were torn off in an awkward exasperated frenzy. From the beginning the thing they most explicitly shared was an appreciation for urgentness and that trancelike, unreal world to which lovemaking was both the key and the destination. Their connection had to exist *now*, because the past was too ephemeral and the future was too painful to contemplate, one way or another. They had to recuperate from their real lives and find their way back to the small space they shared, as though they had to forgive each other; they had to push so much life away to arrive at these seconds of pleasure within which was so much of what made life worth living.

They began in haste, in a panic almost to retrieve what was good between them. After a while he slowed down and they both softened. They began like possessed strangers, but they finished as lovers.

Then they lay sprawled and entangled across the bed. He pulled the white comforter up over them, and held her. For a moment he thought everything was as it should be. He held her tightly against him. The sky was darker now, blue and dim. They fell asleep in the dusk. It was a mysterious time. When they awoke it was dark.

New Windows

ARNOLD LOVELL STOOD UP TO MAKE HIS SPEECH. HE SUR-
veyed the crowded lobby. It was filled with metal folding chairs, a
sea of them, on which sat an attentive audience waiting for his
words—these were his neighbors.

Arnold's nose was a long and winding road at the end of which
was a kind of cul-de-sac. Several women had, over the course of
his amorous adventures, called his nose sexy. His wife had once
said, "Your nose is fascinatingly disgusting." She had also once
said, "Fuck me with your nose." These remarks were made during
a more auspicious point in their marriage—before it began. It was

a running joke between the two of them that their marriage was best before it actually existed. It was best when it was a concept about which they fantasized, together, like two castaways on a raft, adrift on the ocean, clutching at a map that predicted a piece of land was due to emerge from the mists.

His wife now looked up at him, smiling in a way that inspired in him a complicated mixture of hostility and friendship. She was waiting along with everyone else in the lobby for him to begin his speech. Each second ticked by with the slow and languorously deliberate speed of a giant church bell starting to toll; he thought he could hear his own heart . . . how long would it keep pounding? If he had a heart attack at the board meeting would they change their mind about the windows? Was he willing to have a coronary seizure to make his point?

He peered down at his wife, and she, through her modern glasses frames, those rectangular things that he had, in spite of every effort to restrain himself, criticized as being too modern, looked up at him. The expression on her face was not exactly supportive. She had warned him, two years earlier, against investing in new window frames, a murmured opinion, but still enough to warrant an "I told you so" should she want to inflict that phrase on their already shaky relationship. She did not. But now she seemed amused as she looked up at him. He was not a public speaker, yet here he was, about to speak publicly.

He scanned the faces, making reflexive, impulsive, and weirdly gratifying assessments of the net worth of his neighbors, their fidelity track records, guessing, from a turn of a mouth or the application of eye shadow, at the psychic pain or pleasure these various parents had experienced with the departure of their children for college, and wondering if the consuming rage and anger that had propelled him to this moment was shared by any of the other tenants.

He had written out his speech and he was alarmed to see that the pages were trembling in his hand. His neighbors were silent and watchful. In the back, where it was standing room only, he saw Benny Brown shift his weight from one leg to the other. Benny was a huge hulking man who lived on the C line and wore exquisitely tailored suits. He was black, or light mocha; his hair was always in a kind of semi–jeri curl. His wife was beautiful and voluptuous and kept her sunglasses on indoors. Arnold had always enjoyed Benny's presence in the building. Benny had good karma. Elevator rides with Benny were a pleasure—the smell, the grooming, the gold watch, the Burberry raincoat. But even the encouraging sight of Benny Brown was not enough to stir the words up from within, not enough to fasten his eyes to the piece of paper and make him begin his speech. Other speeches drifted through his mind: "Give me liberty or give me death . . ."; "I have a dream . . ."; "Ask not what your country can do for you, ask what you can do for . . ."

At the front of the room, behind a table set up on sawhorses, sat the co-op board. Nine of them, like the Supreme Court. In their midst, like some fierce animal, sat Ms. Ganesh, the president, the proverbial chief justice.

Arnold cast a long apprehensive glance at Ms. Ganesh. Her nails were painted a fiery red. All the better to claw you, he thought. And from her ears sprouted bulbous little earrings that were a glaring bright gold; they were shaped like tortellini and had the effect of lights strung up around road construction: slow down, stay in lane, *proceed with caution*. Her hair was cut in a short brown helmet of curls that had been laminated into position. He had never seen her with a hair out of place. And the red lipstick on her mouth was applied with the precision of diamond cutter. For a fleeting moment Arnold Lovell found Ms. Ganesh attractive, or rather he had something akin to a sexual feeling for her, but then that subsided and was replaced by the customary hate.

This was the woman who was making his life miserable, if only because she was sopping up so much of it.

"I'm Arnold Lovell," he began. "A resident of the building for twenty-four years." He paused to let this sink in. It was as though he were talking about military service, not a co-op on the Upper West Side. But he was in a battle frame of mind. Twenty-four years!

"I've lived here without any incident or cause for complaint all this time. I've been a good citizen, if that is a word one could use in this context, for all my time here. Ever since I moved in I've enjoyed the building, and my life . . ."

He hadn't written "and my life." It was an ad lib. He paused to chastise himself for this outburst. It sounded ridiculous. This isn't group therapy, he told himself. This is a board meeting. And yet his hands shook and he felt his own words in his chest vibrate with emotion. He scanned the room briefly to see if people were listening. They seemed to be listening. His eyes caught Ann Melrose's, and she gave him a tiny nod of affirmation. Ann was one of the small group of schemers who had put him up to this.

"In short, I've had no serious complaint with the way the building is run," he went on. "Until now. Now I stand before you with a complaint. The complaint is twofold. One, as we all know, there has been a mandate, an edict, a command, issued from on high, that we must all replace our windows with a very specific kind of window, at great expense to ourselves. That is the major issue. The windows. The other issue, more abstract but equally important, is the appalling manner in which this edict has been handled, the bullying, uncivil behavior of the board and particularly its president, Ms. Ganesh, and . . . and that is what I am here today to say. That this windows issue must be discussed and also that I am nominating myself for a seat on the board, as a write-in candidate for this evening's vote. I am the anti-windows candidate."

He sat down.

"We already discussed the windows issue last meeting," someone called out in complaint.

"Well, let's discuss it some more!" came a cry from another part of the room. A mood of insurrection was slowly taking hold. A murmur swept the room. It was a strange unnatural sound, as though a secret tunnel existed deep below the building through which a trainload of troops and weapons was rumbling along in the dark, far beneath the slippers and loafers and sneakers and spit-polished shoes that sat on the cool marble floor of the lobby of this august civilized building on Riverside Drive that, like many stately old buildings, had a name emblazoned on its awning. The building was named after its most famous tenant, with the peculiar article "the" placed before his name, as though to accentuate the fact that this wasn't a man, it was a building.

Thus: "The Babe Ruth."

ELAINE GANESH WAS president of the board of directors of The Babe Ruth co-op. She was halfway through her current two-year term as board member. It was the fifth consecutive two-year term she had held. Every two years a piece of paper was circulated to all the apartments in the building naming various candidates for the board of directors. These names had brief but intense biographies attached to them. You didn't move into the building without credentials and money, and in the few sentences available the candidates spelled out, in varying degrees of discretion, what their credentials were and how they had made their money. Usually they were lawyers or investment bankers.

Ms. Ganesh, as it happens, was neither. She had run, along with other members of her family, a stationery store on Broadway,

Ganesh Stationery, that her father had started. For most of her adult life she had been employed full-time at the store, along with her brother. The store had put her brother and her through college. It had been her father's entire life. It was prosperous at a time when Broadway was practically a slum. It was a tightly run ship, which her father captained; she and her brother were the lieutenants. She had grown up a few blocks away, at Seventy-eighth Street and West End, and when she and her husband, Jarell, moved into The Babe Ruth after they were married, in 1970, it gave her an intense satisfaction to think that there was now a neat triangle formed by her store, her home, and her parents' home.

Then her father died, and if that wasn't bad enough, her brother immediately began the heresy that had split them ever since. He wanted to expand Ganesh Stationery—not just increase the size of the home store, which her father had been slowly expanding for years, but expand into other locations. And in order to do this he would have to borrow against the store, to mortgage the main store so he could open a shop on Seventh Avenue and Thirty-fifth Street.

Seventh Avenue and Thirty-fifth Street was not a Ganesh neighborhood! Hordes of people from everywhere swarmed across the avenue. A stationery store thrived on a combination of regular customers and people who were so flummoxed by the idea of buying a gift that they resorted, with great relief, to buying a pen. A pen could be fancy, opulent, and interesting and was, by definition, useful, since absolutely everyone had to use it once in a while, if only to sign a check. Her father had understood this and, on several occasions, been presented with a plaque by the Montblanc corporation naming him as one of its most productive sales outlets in the United States.

Her brother's idea was to set up a shop devoted exclusively to pens. And the horror of it was that in his will, her father had left her and her brother an exactly equal amount of shares, but they were joined, also as an equal partner, by their Aunt Flo, her father's sister, who lived in New Jersey and had a perverse and infuriating love affair going on with Elaine's younger brother, whom she had attacked with pinches and gifts and little baby sounds since the day he was born. Of course she would side with him! And did. And in her fury at this turn of events—that the course of the steady moneymaking ship of Ganesh Stationery should change so abruptly, and so soon after their father's death!—she had, in protest, sold out to her brother. She had washed her hands of the whole mess. She had walked.

And once she realized, like someone jerking awake from a bad dream, the enormity of what she had done, of the break she had made with her routine and her past (but her father was dead! And at the hands of horrible careless doctors and forgetful nurses! So what was there to break from anyway!), she threw herself—with the same energy with which she used to patrol the store's floor, scoping out potential shoplifters and keeping an ever-vigilant eye out for bashful and slightly ashamed gift-shoppers who needed a kind but firm hand to guide them to the pen section and a nice $125 Montblanc—into the process of steering the groaning, tottering, leaking ship of The Babe Ruth.

By sheer force of will she got herself elected to the board on her first try, and she became its president—which meant that she received more votes than any other candidate—on her second. She radiated competency as the sun radiates light. People were blinded by it, burned by it, basked in it, hid from it, rued its force, but on the whole were resigned to its presence. For the last ten years she had been preoccupied with the fate and well-being of this building, and now a small group of residents were showing their ingratitude with this display of churlish, childish whining. She knew what was good for the building. These complainers just lived in it.

Her long, red, perfectly manicured fingernails tapped gently against the table as Arnold Lovell spoke, making a barely audible clicking sound, like the feet of a cantering horse. She used to stand behind the pen counter, with its glass case perfectly polished, not a smudge on it, the various pens sitting in their velvet cases like precious jewels, and gently let her fingernails rap against the glass. She had a superstitious idea that this sound, this brittle yet gentle clicking sound, was like a mating call to pen buyers, who would hear it subliminally, and drift, without knowing why, to the pen counter, where she would greet them with a dazzling smile and a list of reasons why this day might be the day they stepped up to quality, to the top of the line, to the best that money can buy: Montblanc.

EVE FADER SCANNED the room one more time looking for her son. She was part of the small band of renegade tenants who had convened to discus how to combat this horrible windows problem. Everyone had his or her own particular motivations. For some it was the expense, and for others it was the intrusion of workers smashing around in their house, and for yet others (though the minority) it was aesthetic, a protest against the cold modern windows and dead metal frames replacing that which was wooden and old and had character and a certain warmth. For Eve Fader it was all these things plus the sheer bullying audacity, the uniformity of it, the centralized authority handing down an edict that could not be questioned. It touched a still-raw nerve related to the intractable rules of the kibbutz where she had grown up. These were her windows and no one was going to unilaterally tell her what to do with them! The old windows had nice wooden French panes, civilized if a little disheveled, and the new ones were cold brown metal that created one big pane of glass, a dumb slab of cold modernity through which the outside world could pour unmitigated. Alex had promised to come as a show of support as soon as he got off work. They saw each other for brunch every two weeks or so, but she let him float freely in the world and waited for him to come to her. This was a rare request. Her eyes sifted through the crowded lobby—more crowed than she had ever seen it—but she didn't see him.

ALEX SAW HER, though. He stood way in the back, almost at the elevator, watching Arnold Lovell speak, while a single thought palpitated over and over in his mind: "I saw his daughter's vagina."

Normally the word "vagina" was one he tried to avoid, because it seemed medical, and he didn't like his sex to be medical. But now that phrase flashed like a blinking neon sign in his mind. "That man who stands before you has a daughter whose vagina was the first I ever saw!"

The assembled throng—normally a group who could be called people, or civilians, or citizens, but on this occasion, shmushed into tightly packed metal folding chairs, amidst the strange no-man's-land of the lobby, wore the peculiar mantle of "shareholders"—elicited from Alex all sort of confused feelings. This windows thing had completely engrossed them; he had never seen so many people at a board meeting. It seemed preposterous and also somehow wondrous that he was standing in the building where he had grown up. He had left the place of his childhood, but the place of his childhood hadn't left. It was still here, as were many of the people.

He saw his mother's neck craning with concern, looking for

him. Her face wore that serious expression she got when she felt a serious injustice had been done and needed to be combated.

It was a cold November night, and the lobby was steamy with so many people. He took off his coat and dropped it over his bag. This bag, though not a proper briefcase, had a distinctly professional air to it.

He had just arrived from Panda Productions, where he had for the last year been working. He had signed on with the idea that he might get to travel the world helping produce and shoot the nature documentaries the company specialized in. But instead he had spent the last six months working as associate producer on a documentary called *The Suicide Seed*, about the effects of a special genetically engineered seed that produced one bountiful harvest and then promptly died, requiring the farmer to buy a whole new batch the next year. It was generally known as "the Terminator Seed."

The Suicide Seed was the idea of the documentary's director and driving force, and, therefore, his boss—a committed ecologist turned filmmaker named Claire Marshall. She was a sleek, beautiful woman in her thirties with murderous bedouin eyes, the eyes of someone who has lived through war and witnessed horrible things. That was his first impression of her, at least. The war she had lived through, it turned out, was a marriage. The war/marriage was now over.

Claire was a serious woman. She laughed rarely, but when she did laugh it was almost frightening. She became convulsed, her face scrunched up as though she were weeping, and the whole thing took place in utter silence, with occasional little trills escaping. It was as though some demon had possessed her. Alex had seen her weep with laughter about the most ridiculous things, but mostly she spent her days being furious with the world and whichever of its inhabitants happened to be in her immediate vicinity.

If all this wasn't enough to keep Alex at an utterly respectful and self-preserving distance, she happened to be English. Her accent was deliciously imperious, clipped, and regal. Mary, the receptionist, referred to her as "her majesty," but only behind her back.

The Suicide Seed. He thought it was catchy. But mostly he had proceeded with a sense of ironic detachment. The work was interesting, though. He had traveled to Idaho to interview farmers, there was a shoot in India scheduled, and he had corresponded extensively with all sorts of activists from Peru to Seattle. Gradually his ironic detachment slowly evolved into something else. He had decided Claire was really onto something.

Alex had taken one look at her, heard her accent, felt the delicious causticity of her gaze, observed her madly energized proficiency, her competence, her zeal for making the world a better place even if it meant working absolutely all the time, and promised himself that he would not get involved with this woman.

Almost immediately, he got a crush on her. But the next line of defense was to simply ignore the crush and maintain a professional relationship. That line had held. Whenever his eyes fell upon her he thought: Don't do it! But just the other day he turned around to find Claire behind her desk, phone held idly in hand, staring at him with those panther eyes while she absently stroked the space just above her upper lip with her index finger. Her shapely, cruel mouth, to which he had begun paying a great deal of attention, seemed especially full and carnivorous. There was so much sexuality in that absent-minded stroking of the ridge above her upper lip that he had nearly broken out in a sweat.

He had managed to divert his growing interest in the woman into a growing interest in her cause. Now, standing in the lobby of The Babe Ruth, he though about how the suicide rate among farmers in India was apparently at an all-time high because they were being forced to deviate from centuries of farming tradition by American multinational corporations. He was in the midst of planning the three-week shoot, setting up interviews, helping Claire script the general architecture of this segment of the movie. Faced with such concerns, who cared about new windows!

ARNOLD LOVELL DRONED on. To Alex's not very responsible thirteen-year-old self this man had entrusted his two-year-old daughter, Amy, and her older brother, Robert, age five. It was Alex's one and only foray into the entrepreneurial world of baby-sitting. Amy had lain in her diapers on her back, in her crib, nearly as white and pale as the sheet beneath her, but for the wild blue-ness of her eyes and the puckered gurgling pink of her mouth.

Was it his fault that her diaper had somehow become unfas-tened? Some technically faulty Pampers product was responsible for the sudden and unexpected visitation upon his thirteen-year-old consciousness of a part of the female anatomy that he had been speculating about, with skin-abrading intensity, for months. But he had not been speculating about it in its two-year-old incar-nation! But there it was. Who was he to complain?

Alex had thought it would be Robert Lovell, the skinny-necked, wide-eyed maniac whose eyebrows kept shooting up into the vast expanse of his oversmart forehead, who was going to provide the real baby-sitting challenge. But at nine-fifteen in the evening, a mere forty-five minutes after his bedtime, Robert the lunatic had been board-gamed to sleep, and it was pretty little gurgling Amy who lay awake and ready for action in the bright white lights of her pantrylike room.

In the lobby, seventeen years later, it occurred to him that he was supposed to turn off the lights. Idiot! No wonder the kid was awake!

But then he remembered that he had done so; he had flicked the switch and taken perhaps half a step towards the door in darkness, when suddenly the pudgy living breathing and until that moment utterly docile baby let out an outrageous earsplitting near-death series of cries and yelps. So he had flicked the switch back on, peered into the crib—the very act of which calmed her—and then left to watch *Charlie's Angels*. At ten, the Lovells were still not home, and he had sauntered back in to discover the baby just where he had left her, on her back, smiling in the bright light, except she had somehow disrobed herself, shed her Pampers, and was in the nude.

Baby nudity had never before meant anything to Alex. But the illicit thrill of being alone with another human being who was substantially less powerful than himself, and of being alone in someone else's apartment, and of being in charge of everything when he was so obviously and manifestly incapable of being in charge of anything, including himself, all this had conspired to suddenly fixate Alex's attention and energy on the small smiling slit of this two-year-old sex goddess. He looked for a few moments until a wave of disgust mixed with silliness came over him and he went back to the TV. Now he stood in the lobby and thought, can you damage someone just by looking?

"I have recently, and at great personal expense, installed a set of steel windows in all eight of the windows in my apartment," Mr. Lovell said.

Alex scanned the audience for signs of the conspiratorial group that had put Lovell up to this. They had scattered throughout the crowd as though in precaution against attack. The Meyers, Ann Melrose and her husband, Mel, the Siegenthalls, and his own mother, who watched with a mixture of pride and real concern as Mr. Lovell spoke. He saw in her face a lovely kind of nobility. Her sense of justice was an anchor which was secured firmly in the ocean floor of his soul; knowing it was there allowed him to range freely on the high seas of immorality.

She had a fantastically good ear for corruption, and not just your local-politician-with-hand-in-till variety. She had perfect pitch for the small corruptions of the soul. She sincerely believed that this whole windows episode was an outrage against that which made life livable.

Alex himself wavered on the matter.

It was true that the board had always seemed unnecessarily unpleasant. Since it was a co-op, his mother was a shareholder, not a renter. This was not a situation where there was an evil landlord versus innocent tenants. The tenants were, in a sense, the landlord, so the evil landlord was an evil within. And Evil's personification for the last ten years had been the horrific Ms. Ganesh, a figure both unique in her Mephistophelian countenance and also incredibly familiar; nearly all of these old buildings that lined Riverside Drive and West End Avenue, and onward to points east, had volunteers whose life revolved around running them, volunteers whose altruism had somehow become perverted into a crazed power hunger, who saw their buildings as ships of which they were captain. There was something about co-ops that was like a fertile swamp from which such larvae always sprang.

It seemed as if there had always been a feud between his mother and the co-op board, a feud that began over Alex's incessant throwing of things out the window, his drum-playing, and his endless throwing of a tennis ball against the front of the building. The latter had provoked a sign, installed when he was eleven, that read "No ball playing." Sad as he was not to be able to play ball, it nevertheless instilled feelings of pride in him every single time he passed it, knowing he was solely responsible for the fact The Babe Ruth had a sign that read "No ball playing" right next to its entrance.

Long after all of this drama had subsided to a low hum of animosity, he had nevertheless jumped with gleeful joy when he came upon, deep in the Metro section of the *New York Times*, a strange photograph in which six portly men in bad suits marched towards the entrance of a building all handcuffed to each other. Each of these men held a newspaper up to his face. It was a lyrical image, this parade of men with newspapers for heads. But the caption below the photo identified the men as having been convicted of taking bribes from contractors. People were always thirsty for culprits for why New York apartments were so expensive, and here were six of them in handcuffs, with newspapers over their faces. In an amazingly spiteful gesture to those obscuring newspapers, the newspaper of record named the indicted chain gang pictured above and the company they worked for. There in black and white was the name of Mr. Fred Tuba, the very man whose name had appeared on the bottom of all those surly letters that had always so upset his mother.

He had called his mother up excitedly. She had seen the picture too! They laughed about it, he with glee, she in a different way. She was not so vengeful or possessed. She laughed as though she was reassured about her judgment, her instrument of discernment, and sense of justice. But he knew that she could, when she wanted to, hate.

HIS EYES BORED into Arnold Lovell's profile. Lovell turned slightly on his hips, swaying a little and alternating his gaze between the piece of paper and the crowd before him, looking less and less at the scripted speech and speaking with more and more passion. As if Arnold Lovell didn't have enough troubles in the world, he was now volunteering himself for a meat grinder of a task: to be on the board of directors of The Babe Ruth. To attend all those meetings, to sit in breathing distance of vituperative, sinister Ms. Ganesh, Evil itself. Alex could think of no worse fate.

Yet the forces of Good had to somehow mobilize against the forces of Evil, and they (the forces of Good) had descended on Lewinger and made him their man. Could he not rise to the call? How long had it been since anyone called? Maybe he was flattered? Two days later a piece of paper was posted in the lobby listing the newly elected board of directors. Elaine Ganesh had a seat, but was no longer president. And there was one new name: Arnold Lovell.

WHEN THE MEETING was over, and the shareholders had all cast their votes in the ballot box, Alex and his mother went up to the apartment.

"Do you want some tea?" his mother said. "Or are you hungry? We could order Chinese food."

"Let's order Chinese food."

He dialed. She paused to consider what she wanted, as she always did, and then got beef with snow peas, as she always did. They sat at the kitchen table and ate. In the study, and in his old room, and even in her bedroom, there was a terrifying accumulation of debris. His mother was getting worse and worse at throwing things out, and he had, in the past, erupted in outbursts of exasperation on the matter.

The sight of his mother pausing over a piece of junk mail to give it, if only briefly, her full attention sent him into near hysterics which he struggled to contain. Couldn't she tell right away it was junk mail? On his last visit he had found stacked in his room about twenty empty shopping bags. What did she need all these bags for? Against what natural disaster was she hoarding shopping bags?

Whenever he allowed these thoughts to escape into the articulated world they had a terse, almost nasty exchange. She was at work on another book, and it required all her attention, and when she had time, she said, she would deal with the disorder. So now he bit his lip. He didn't want to fight with her about it. She put the Chinese food in bowls and they ate in silence. At one point he looked up at her, and for a moment, as he saw her chewing, he was struck by a terrible flash of grief on her behalf. She had been widowed with a ten-year-old boy. Who could prepare for that? This grief was as sudden and blinding as lightning, and like lightning it disappeared an instant after it arrived, and was followed a few moments later by a low dull thunder that rumbled plaintively through his chest.

"What's the matter?" she said instinctively, looking up at him.

"Nothing," he said. He ate a little more.

"It's too bad about the windows," he said. "I always liked the way that they got frosted on the inside on really cold days." He glanced at her to see how she would respond to the pragmatic nugget lodged in the comment; the whole point of the new windows was they saved on heating. They were theoretically going to cut down on waste.

"It's awful," she said, sighing, and putting down her chopsticks. "They are so *ugly*. But there is a special attachment you can put on them that makes them look like French windows. I'm going to get it."

"What's a French window?" he said.

"These," she said, and gestured to the old windows behind her. The windows did not look particularly French. They were divided into panes of glass, six rectangular panes of glass on the bottom part and six on the top. This was, as far as he was concerned, what a window normally looked like. The new windows wouldn't have the wooden slats dividing the panes. It would be one big piece of glass.

"Mom," he said. "Part of me thinks this is absurd, the whole deal about the windows. And part of me is incredibly sympa-thetic. I'm sort of torn on the matter."

"What is absurd? They're very unpleasant, the whole way they have gone about it. And the windows are just . . ."

"Ugly. I agree. But it's also like, people are . . . so resistant to change!"

"Well," she said. "Some changes are worth resisting."

"Really," he said. "Which ones?"

She didn't answer, just looked down at her food for a moment and then back at him. She gave him a knowing smile. "You'll have to find that out yourself," she said.

Acknowledgments

The author would like to thank the following individuals and institutions for their assistance, in one way or another, in the writing of this book: Jerome Badanes, Jill Bialosky, Mary Evans, Elizabeth Grove, St. Ann's School, Yaddo, Kip Kotzen, Daniel Pinchbeck, Scott Smith, Rob Bingham, Robert Towers, Randall Poster, Jan de Jong, Sam Green and his excellent documentary *Rainbow Man/John* 3:16, Alba Branca, Paul Beller, the Writer's Room, Liselotte Bendix Stern, Hava Beller.

Thomas Beller's fiction has appeared in *The New Yorker, Elle,* and *Best American Short Stories.* He is a founding editor of *Open City* magazine and edited *Personals: Dreams and Nightmares from the Lives of 20 Young Writers.* He has worked as a staff writer for *The New Yorker* and the *Cambodia Daily.* He is the author of a collection of stories, *Seduction Theory,* and a Web site, mrbellersneighborhood.com.